Praise for *By the Mountain Bound*

"Numerous fantasy authors adopt the tropes of Norse mythology, but Bear actively pursues them, channeling those myths directly rather than overlaying them on more familiar ones. The result demands much from readers but repays it in vivid, sensual imagery of a wholly different world." —*Publishers Weekly*

Praise for *All the Windwracked Stars*

"You should read this book; you should read it because the entire thing—from beginning to end—pushes sense-of-wonder buttons so hard you almost want to hit the pause button, forget about the plot, and *look*. Bear holds nothing back, and everything that she pulls into her story just gleams with that special wonder of discovery. I could not put this down." —*The Magazine of Fantasy and Science Fiction*

"Hugo winner Bear perfectly captures the essence of faded hopes and exhausted melancholy in this postapocalyptic melodrama based loosely upon Norse mythology. . . . Readers will be captivated by Bear's incredibly complex, broken characters; multilayered themes of redemption; and haunting, world-breaking decisions. . . . Its finale is both rewarding and compelling." —*Publishers Weekly* (starred review)

Tor Books by Elizabeth Bear

A Companion to Wolves (with Sarah Monette)
All the Windwracked Stars
By the Mountain Bound

By the Mountain Bound

Elizabeth Bear

A Tom Doherty Associates Book
New York

BY THE MOUNTAIN BOUND

Copyright © 2009 by Elizabeth Bear

All rights reserved.

A Tor Book
Published by Tom Doherty Associates, LLC
175 Fifth Avenue
New York, NY 10010

www.tor-forge.com

Tor® is a registered trademark of Tom Doherty Associates, LLC.

ISBN 978-0-7653-5852-3

First Edition: November 2009
First Mass Market Edition: September 2010

Printed in the United States of America

0 9 8 7 6 5 4 3 2 1

To Ken Woods and Chelsea Polk,
who midwifed it,
and to Marissa Lingen,
just because

Acknowledgments

This book would never have become a finished manuscript, nevermind an actual printed object, without the support of my friends, colleagues, and critique partners, on and off the On-line Writing Workshop for Science Fiction and Fantasy. I wish I could single them all out by name, but it would be a very long list indeed. However, in particular I'd like to thank Kyri Freeman, Ken Woods, and Chelsea Polk, each of whom went above and beyond the call of duty.

I'd also like to thank my editor, Beth Meacham; my agent, Jennifer Jackson; and all of the amazing and hardworking production staff at Tor who helped to make this book a reality.

I'd also like to thank everyone who reads it. Because a story doesn't really exist until it's heard.

1

In bondage now bides
The Wolf, 'til world's end
—Lokasenna

The Wolf

Fear. I know the scent of old.

Einherjar sleep not if we are unwounded, but I have spent the afternoon in the smooth fork of a copper beech in a sort of daydream, contemplating the curve of a crimson sun settling behind the wooded Ulfenfell. A chill gilds air raw with hanging winter, the nearby sea, the musk of leaves. And a woman's terror.

The scent lifts my hackles. A silken collar—an old fetter half-broken—galls my throat when I stretch too far, breathe too deep. I am accustomed. There is more news on the wind. Mortal woman. And a mortal man. They prey on their own.

I run the length of a horizontal branch broad as a horse's back and drop to the leaf litter, steadying Svanvitr's hilt with one hand. The pack wakes, rolling from crackling leaves like wood-red and smoke-gray and tarnished-silver shadows. They shake earth and dry grass from coats already silkening against frost, motes sparkling in slanting light. Milling around my legs, they grin.

Alas. Not my brothers, these, though I live among them in preference to the mead-hall, and the einherjar.

My gloves are in the hand I offer a bitch. She sniffs, allows the touch. Fingertips burrow through slick guard hairs and dense undercoat to brush skin beneath. When I touch her flesh, I can speak to her, she can speak to me. *You need not come. I take the shadowed road.*

She laughs at me. I draw on my gloves. Bound for where men are. Humans, I touch not.

Words for them.

Blood-scent soaks the air. There is a thing—an einherjar thing, not of wolves nor men—the *swanning*. Knowledge granted, and a task to complete.

If I were another einherjar, it might swan me now: *East—and quickly.* I am not as they. I am unique, older, not exiled but not accepted among them as I am among the pack. I became as they are, starlight made flesh, when I swallowed a sun.

They have the words of the Light to guide them. *I* have the scent. Blood on the wind, and fear.

I step into the shadow of the ponderous beech. And out the other side.

The place between one shadow and the next is cold and silent, wrought of firefly lights and dancing beliefs. A breath of ice. A stink of char. A dead world left behind.

I cross quickly.

Even here, the fear-scent lingers. Or perhaps it hangs only in my mind, as if borne on unworldish wings.

The shadow of an oak is my gate back to Valdyrgard. I hold my step and watch. A flaxen-haired maiden in a cloak dyed with bloodroot twists away from a sour-smelling man of middling size and age. She has spilled her basket, bread and weedy late wildflowers. Her lip is split. He has blacked her eye.

I see no need to draw Svanvitr. Furling my cloak over my shoulder, I clutch. One gloved hand catches the man's wrist, snaps. He releases the girl. She staggers. A knife into the other hand, and I take it, cast it to the cool waiting forest. It rings on stone, rustles through leaves.

I force him to his knees.

Now comes the Light. It streams from my eyes, my fingertips. Fills my mouth. The cord under my gray woolen collar clenches like a hand, but the Light is stronger than broken chains, and I was stronger than them too, when it mattered. The girl scrambles back, twig-crunch and rustle, too foolish in her fine wove cloak to run.

"I mark thee." I touch my gloved thumb to my tongue and draw the letter *thorn* on his forehead in silver-blue starlight. "With *Thurisaz*, which is the mark of strife. Do thou no more harm to innocents, or I shall know of it."

He whimpers. I squeeze. My dark braid falling forward strikes him across the face. "Is all plain between us?"

Frozen until he remembers to nod. Then I loose him. He falls back, scrabbling like a cat, pissing himself before he flees. The girl hunches between oak-roots.

"Fear not."

She draws away, though I offer a smile.

Her mouth shapes words. "Who are you?"

"Mingan. Called the Grey Wolf. I am einherjar, a child of Light." The name soothes her not. But I am not my warrior brothers: I am slight where they are broad, dark where they are fair, old where they are young.

I am not meant for comfort. I should have stayed a wolf in more than name.

I close the space between us, drop my hand upon her head. "This is my wood. I dwell here."

She draws herself closer and smaller. I turn and step back into the shadows that are my home. She does not hear me sigh.

I'd stay and see her home through the twilight, but she would thank me not. I have other business to attend in the morning, and work before. With my scent on her, the maiden will come to no harm in the wood.

The night is used in the hunt; when the sun rises the deer on my shoulder is a buck, three points—young and tender, caught with my own hands. I bring him to the wolves in apology: the next night, I will not run with them across the moon-soaked mountains. I am summoned.

They dine on well-bled meat while I take myself to Strifbjorn's mead-hall where the einherjar gather. I do not count the days among the wolves, but I attend when my brothers call. I walk the valley road, not the shadowed one, passing under trees in the short cold morn. Patches of frost linger in the shadows, but the mist coils off the land, burned by the sun overhead. I glance upward, some memory I cannot quite reconstruct raised by the tug of the cord about my throat.

Mountain-clutching trees break above a hillocked green meadow, which sweeps down a gentler slope south and east until the flank of the mountain plunges into the sea. Close to the lip stands the mead-hall. It is built as long as two ancient pines grow tall, solid of seasoned logs and shingled bark. The sea lies at my right hand and before, the mountain at my back; the meadow gives way to birch and poplar to the left.

A pale form arrows across the sky, plunging furled by the turf-roofed mead-hall. A thing like a two-headed stallion stands in the midmorning light, tossing his horns and mantling those giant wings. A slender figure, clad in white, slides down his shoulder; she acknowledges my approach—but barely—with a raised hand, turns and strides into the hall.

My brethren arrive for the feast and the council. For me, it is no homecoming.

Not until I enter the door of the mead-hall, and an elk-shouldered shape steps over the fire trench to meet me. My braid is silver-black where his is like winter butter, but his eyes are gray as mine and as full of starlight.

"Mingan!" Strifbjorn embraces me. His clasp is iron bands, fingers that would break mortal bones clenching on my forearm, his other arm falling around my back.

I return the clasp, looking up to see his smile. A bear-fur cloak broadens him that needs no broadening, the pelt grizzled silver over rich brown. It contrasts with the swan-white shirt and trews. At his hip, Alvitr's bronze hilt matches Svanvitr's.

Pine-scent rises from the strewn branches, mingled with the smell of cold fires and hot honeyed ale. Strifbjorn does not flinch from the heat of my hand through the glove.

"Strifbjorn, my brother. You are well?" I smile to see the light in his eyes flash, and *he* does not turn from it.

His voice drops. "Very." He leads me to a seat near his, at the south end of one of the long tables. On the left, below him along the bench. We will share our trencher. The great gilt chair on the north wall sits empty. Our Cynge is not with us.

He never has been, but I taught them to keep his chair ready, and the Lady's at the south end of the mead-hall.

The waelcyrge cluster at one end of the hall, around the bride. Menglad, who wears a red far more pure in shade than the muddy carrot-color of the blond girl's cloak.

One of them leaves her sisters and brings us mead in horns, bowing her head when Strifbjorn's fingers brush her hand. She is the little one, Muire, with the darkest hair, golden-brown as buckwheat honey. Her eyes also slide from mine, but it is not modesty that drives her to turn away. Strifbjorn is fair and handsome, his prowess unmatched in renown. As long as he remains unmarried, the Daughters of the Light vie for his regard.

Mine they avoid—for I am Mingan the Grey Wolf, who walks alone, who acts alone, who does not hear the voice of the Light in his ear. The children—except Strifbjorn and perhaps Yrenbend—fear me.

It is not their weird to seek understanding of things that shake the pattern of their days. Except perhaps Muire, who is a blacksmith and a poet, which are not such separated things as might seem. She writes history. I would she did not fear me. I would she might ask what I know.

I remember things—some shadowy, some crisp—that took place before the children, einherjar and waelcyrge, were sung out of the starlight on the ocean and in turn sang the mortal creatures from the stones. I know of only three old enough to remember another world, and of those I am the one who walks among the children of the Light.

I drain my nectar-scented mead, and the smell brings remembrance. A fetter, a sword, a scorching heat, the taste of blood. Pain, inside and without. The scent of a man I trusted as I have trusted none other, save Strifbjorn. The scent of a man who betrayed. I remember these things, but not with a man's understanding.

I recall them as a wolf might. But so my brothers name me.

"You are distant, my brother." It is not Strifbjorn speaking—he has turned to the side, listening to an einherjar who has come up on his right. It is the waelcyrge Muire, the chooser of the slain, who has returned with more mead.

She meets my eyes for a long, quiet moment before she glances away, still not gazing at Strifbjorn. I witness the longing in how she refuses to look at him, and I see his denial of it in the stiffness of his shoulders as he bends closer to his welcome distraction. He is trapped, my brother, in the expectations of his role—and the mistakes we both have made.

"I sorrow, my sister," I say to her at last, continuing to examine her clear gray irises at an angle.

She is, I have said, an odd one, not so unlike the other waelcyrge as I am unlike my chosen brothers, but unlike enough. There is a thoughtfulness in her small nose and pointed chin that I am unused to seeing in the children of the Light. She collects herself, and I am reminded that she fears me. But she speaks out around the fear. "Why do you sorrow?"

This softest and most exact among us—a sparrow hawk. "You're the skald," I say. "You tell me."

Her face muddles. She stammers and flees to the crossbench with her sisters, those who have so far arrived.

The hour is early still.

The Historian

(M)englad was married on a day late in fall in the five hundred and seventy-first year of my immortality, the five hundred and seventy-first year of the world. And the Grey Wolf joined us for the wedding. He was not a stranger in our midst, but neither was he a commonplace. Instead, he came like a raven on the storm, to festival, to weddings, to council of war when war came upon us.

I remember it well. I remember the night because I was the one who served him—him, and Strifbjorn, whom I loved. The other waelcyrge did not wish to wait upon the Wolf, so I walked the length of the shield-hung hall, a horn of mead in each hand.

I remember the night very well, for it was the beginning of the end.

Strifbjorn, disdainful as always of his sisters, barely turned when I brought his mead. The Wolf . . . after draining the mead horn, he studied me with that disconcerting gaze, a frown on a face one might more expect to see hewn from a mountainside. I could not make my eyes meet his. A mortal thrall, captive of war, brought me new horns of drink, and Mingan's gloved hand lingered on mine for a moment more than propriety demanded when I handed him the new one. His flesh burned hot as forged metal through the gray leather. I thought of sunlight on dark fabric.

There were stories, of why he burned. I stammered in answer to his question, the hot blush rising. He released my hand; I fled back to the cross-bench, the trestle table and my sisters at the north end of the hall.

It was a long walk beside the fire trench, under banner-hung roof beams lost in the dark high ceiling. It seemed every eye in the hall watched my flight, although I knew from the murmurs that my brethren were engrossed in their gossip, renewing acquaintances. Nonetheless, I caught my skirts about me like the shreds of my composure and hurried to my place among the women.

Menglad, called the Brightwing, reached from under her crimson wedding veils and caught my mousy-colored braid. "Herfjotur says her steed says the Wolf desires you, Muire." She giggled, gesturing to the proud-nosed waelcyrge on her left.

They all were *watching*. I raised an eyebrow at the bride, amber-haired and fairer-skinned than I, her sword slung properly at her hip rather than across the shoulders as mine must be to keep from dragging. Skeold slid down the bench to the right that I might sit beside Menglad. I gathered my wide skirts, lifting them clear of my boots as I ascended from the scented pine branches littering the floor, onto the step where the women's bench rested. Turning, I allowed the silk to flare, the snow-pale surcote contrasting with the spangled midnight-blue kirtle.

My clothing matched that of my sisters, though they were taller and more golden. Gathered around Menglad in her crimson and gold, we resembled jays mobbing a cardinal.

The groom had not yet arrived, nor had most of the einherjar. Perhaps four hundred of my brethren. Half the number that would fill this, our largest hall. They sat along the benches or walked, chattering. Two extra trestles, running the length of the hall, held the overflow.

I leaned close to Menglad. "The Wolf could have his pick. He has no need of such as I."

I saw by the gleam in her eye that she was teasing me. "He's never offered for anyone," she said. "Perhaps he's waiting for someone to notice him back."

I chuckled. "If he fancied me, he would speak to Yrenbend. Or Strifbjorn—they're close as shield-mates."

The mocking Light was still flickering behind the storm-blue of her eyes. "Are you insinuating that all those waelcyrge who sigh over Strifbjorn must compete with the Wolf for his passions?"

"Strifbjorn is waiting for something. And the Wolf—either he prefers to be alone, or the one he wants is bound to another." I grew uncomfortable, shifting in my seat. "And strong as they are, they can do as they like. Who would dare censure them?" I wanted the subject changed. It was too close to mockery.

But Menglad always was rash, sharp and bright as a chipped glass blade. She shivered, her eyes on the Wolf, and kept talking. "Aye. But his prowess and courage aside, who could be truly glad to go to that wild bed, and share him with his mistress, Darkness?"

There was no answer to that. I watched the one black-brindled head among the golden as it bent close to Strifbjorn's. We dined only for pleasure; we slept only when hurt. We came together, my brothers and sisters and I, in the face of war or the cause of celebration: not as we used to, for the sheer joy of singing the world into being. Back before men were made, and creation was complete.

But that night was a wedding, and there would be a feast in the hall. And after the feast, there would be fighting.

Oh, it would be fine.

"Are you nervous?"

Menglad gave me a sidelong look behind her veils. "Nervous?"

"About the wedding night." Her eyes behind the veil were more blue than gray. The starlight that suddenly filled them was tinted silver.

She leaned aside and dropped her voice. "Shall I tell you a secret, Muire? Of all of us, I believe you can keep one."

"I am a historian, after all. The only secrets I whisper are those of the dead."

She pursed her lips; it smoothed her brow. "You are not like the rest of us, Muire. I do not envy you. But I do not know what we would be without your voice."

I brushed her strangeness away with my left hand. "You were about to give me a secret."

She took a breath, licking her lips moist. "I've been to Arngeir's bench," she whispered, leaning so her veil hid the shape of her words against my hair.

"In the mead-hall?" I couldn't imagine how she kept that secret. Despite the dark of night and the averted eyes of politeness, one notices such things as a shared niche. Especially when the benches are not often used for sleeping.

Tonight they would be, however. Used for sleeping, and for other things. I might spend the night in the field, or on the mountainside.

She shook her head. "We've met in secret. I'm sure Strifbjorn knows, but as Arngeir offered for me, there has been no scandal. He can be kinder than he seems—Strifbjorn, I mean."

I leaned closer, speaking so softly she must have strained to hear. "What's it like? And have you . . . have you shared the kiss yet?"

"We decided to wait. It seemed safer: what if something happened? Before we were wedded, I mean. We'd both be . . ."

. . . *unmarriageable*. Yes. It was one thing to marry a widow, knowing you would be taking on a bit of another as well. Different entirely to join with someone, expecting to find oneself half of a whole, and discover the taint of a third already woven into the bonding.

She picked up her thread after a moment of silence. "As for the other . . . Well, it hurts. At first. But it's a . . . good sort of hurt. Not to be feared. Much less than a sword-cut."

I shook my head. "I am content with your reports." Over her shoulder, I caught a sneering glance from tall, fair Sigrdrifa, who I knew also coveted Strifbjorn's hand.

I stood and excused myself with fortuitous timing, for as I took horns of mead from the thralls, more of the einherjar began to arrive—Arngeir's party, but not yet the groom himself. We seated them across the fire trench from Strifbjorn.

My sisters scurried to assist me, leaving Menglad stranded on the cross-bench in her trappings of crimson and gold, with a wide divided skirt. She seemed small and alone when I glanced back; I wondered at her courage in the face of the great unknown—her marriage, her bonding, her future as half of a larger thing than herself.

I shook my head, and turned my attention to the task of carrying the honey wine.

Some time later, when the drinking and the revelry were underway, Arngeir arrived. I was still on my feet, distracting myself from the Wolf's stare and Menglad's attempts at merriment before the crude jests of our brothers. I met Arngeir with a horn of mead before he was well into the room.

My sister's husband-to-be was tall as any of my brothers, and more handsome than most. Clad in red like the bride, he strode in as if claiming the hall, his golden braid bobbing down his back. As I raised the horn, I heard the scrape of a bench. On the far side of the fire trench Strifbjorn stood.

"Will you drink a guest-cup, traveler?" I asked.

"I will, maiden." Arngeir took the horn, drained it and gave it back.

As warm horn slid into my curled fingers, Strifbjorn called out.

"Who comes to my hall?"

Arngeir winked at me. Out of the corner of my eye, I glimpsed the Grey Wolf rising, coming forward at Strifbjorn's left flank. On his right was Yrenbend, my favorite brother, lean and ascetic in his shirt and trousers of immaculate white.

"One who seeks a wife," Arngeir responded.

"There is a waelcyrge here who awaits a husband." Strifbjorn glanced down the hall at Menglad, who had risen from the cross-bench and stood surrounded by our sisters, a last red berry on a snow-covered bush. She swept the length of the hall, the train of her divided skirts and her veil rustling across the pine branches. "Sister," Strifbjorn said, his voice the essence of courtesy. "Will you have this man to husband?"

She drew herself up straight and proud, examining Arngeir with the critical eye of a shrewd farmwife about to purchase a stud horse. She looked along her nose at him, and I could see her fighting both a smile and a shiver. Strifbjorn stepped closer to me. I smelled the clean woodsmoke scent of his skin . . . and then the rank animal musk that seemed to hang around the Wolf like his gray cloak, that self-colored dark charcoal wool no other wore.

I held my gaze away from Strifbjorn, although his sleeve brushed my wrist and the heat of his body warmed my skin. I knew why Menglad shivered.

"How will you prove your worth?" Menglad's voice dripped hauteur.

"Rich gifts I will give, my sister, my intended," he said. "To each waelcyrge of your household and to all the children of Light here gathered."

"Gifts are well, but they do not prove a man's wit or might. Which of those do you offer?"

"Might," he answered.

Strifbjorn stepped forward again, blocking my view. "You will strive with us for the privilege?"

"I will."

"With words or swords, my brother?"

"With swords."

Menglad must have smiled; her voice lifted. "Let us feast, and then let this one who thinks to claim me stand and fight."

Strifbjorn and Arngeir clasped wrists. A delighted laugh broke out throughout the hall, and then each einherjar turned and walked to his respective place. Strifbjorn let his hand fall on my shoulder in passing and leaned to murmur, "Well done, little sister." He nodded once, not catching my eye, and walked away, the Wolf following as if at heel.

The shiver became a shudder as I watched him leave, and along his path I caught the look Sigrdrifa shot me—naked as a venomed blade. She stepped forward, but Yrenbend insinuated himself exactly as if he did not notice her. He caught me around both upper arms and spun me into the air. "Tonight, Muire, you must fight at our side." He set me in my footsteps as if I weighed nothing.

I sent a longing glance to Menglad and the others returning to the cross-bench. "I will, Yrenbend. I'll stand by your side."

I pulled him down to me and kissed his cheek. "And I'll serve your ale tonight. If you expect Brynhilde to be busy."

Yrenbend cast about the hall, but did not find his wife. "She'll be attending Menglad during dinner," he sighed, "and then, of course, she fights with the valraven during the tournament." Brynhilde, like Herfjotur, was partnered with a warsteed.

And how like Yrenbend to make an offered escape seem like a favor tendered him. "Then I shall be pleased to assist."

The Warrior

Strifbjorn let his lips quirk as Mingan glanced sidelong, folded his gloves, and tucked them into his belt, fastidious creature. He drew a small knife and sliced meat from the haunch on the trestle. The pieces he laid on the plate he and Strifbjorn shared. "You are troubled."

As the Wolf looked at Strifbjorn, Strifbjorn nodded. If all went well, they'd solemnize a marriage tonight. It would only be a formality: Strifbjorn saw how Menglad's eye followed Arngeir while he drank and feasted in preparation for the coming battle. A love-struck girl doesn't watch that way, all knowledge and amusement. If she thinks she's watched, she flirts. She preens coyly, and glances and giggles. Adults, confident in another's desire . . . preen differently.

So there was that to worry him. And, really, the least of his problems.

Strifbjorn watched his brothers and sisters eating and wrestling and laughing, trading ribaldry, and was watched in turn by two or three hopeful waelcyrge. At his left hand, Mingan tore his bread mannerly and dipped a morsel at a time in the juice on the trencher. Strifbjorn thought, *He knows me well, to follow my thoughts with the line of my gaze.*

"You must choose one eventually," Mingan said, leaning in. His breath stirred the hair that escaped Strifbjorn's braid. Strifbjorn turned enough to glimpse his profile. To say he was hatchet-faced would be a kindness; his nose sloped and broke, and his cheekbones made his eyes seem to sit glittering in caverns.

A quip died aborning. "You know I can't."

He'd cut the meat. Strifbjorn pushed a morsel across the platter with the tip of his knife. A waelcyrge brought mead and Strifbjorn drained it, returning her the horn with gratitude. *A married woman, thank the Light.* As if reading his mind again, Mingan chuckled.

"I'd rather you laughed with me."

His hand fell on Strifbjorn's forearm. On the strength of the excuse, Strifbjorn turned to regard him fully, but he watched something the length of the hall away. Mingan's voice came like a tickle inside Strifbjorn's ear, like light caught on cleaved shale. *Then choose one who will protect you.*

Should I saddle some innocent girl with my secrets? The children of the Light could not speak untruth.

Silence is no lie. Some would count their luck to be asked.

Brother of my heart— But he stared at Strifbjorn, and Strifbjorn faltered and turned away. *I cannot. A physical liaison would be one thing. I won't pollute a marriage bed.*

Then all your conquests are in vain. You will lose them one way or the other. He took his hand from Strifbjorn's arm, leaving coolness where heat had been.

"Then I'll lose with what honor is left to me," Strifbjorn replied, ignoring the hurt he felt in the shifting of Mingan's frame. They knew each other well, truth be told.

But it often isn't.

If Strifbjorn could make Mingan laugh, he thought the Wolf would forgive him. He tried through the afternoon, with about as much success as he expected. At least making the effort alone might buy a little pity, later.

After what seemed a long time, Menglad stood in a column of crimson cloth, and accepted a horn from a thrall. The hall fell silent as she paced its length from north to south, walking alongside the seething fire trench, her gown much the color of the flames.

She strode up the line of Arngeir's party and they stared ahead, silent, and dared no jest. Her reputation with the crystal blade at her belt, bronze hilt sparking, was unmatched. Even by such as Strifbjorn.

She'd stop before Arngeir and turn to him with the drinking

horn. *Her lover.* Strifbjorn wondered if they had been foolish enough to share the vow and the kiss in anticipation.

It'd been a long time since such a scandal had haunted his hall. In any case, it'd be over by midnight. *Let it end well for them, whatever risks they've taken. Oh, let it end well.*

Strifbjorn's shield-mate still stared into the middle distance. Strifbjorn said, "It's a time of celebration. Eat."

Mingan turned haunted silver eyes. "For some." He quirked a smile. "Observe, brother. The drama begins."

Menglad paused and turned, raising the horn. Strifbjorn bit his lip; it was all very silly, but it wouldn't do to ruin the ritual with mirth. From the curve of her mouth, Menglad wasn't having it any easier maintaining a solemn veneer. "Arngeir, my brother says to me that you would have me to wife."

Arngeir deliberately turned from his quiet conversation with the einherjar next to him, placed both hands on the edge of the table and levered himself to his feet. "Your brother speaks the truth."

Where she declaimed, he answered in a calm carrying tone, sounding less like he was about to fall over himself.

"If you wish to drink from my cup this night, O Arngeir, you must best my sisters and my brothers. Stand you ready?"

Arngeir was her brother, too, inasmuch as any of them were. They were all born together, of the starlight and the sea. But that mattered not, to how the game was played.

Silly.

He laughed. "Bring them against me." He turned, stepped over the bench behind him and strode from the hall. His warriors followed.

Strifbjorn stood, and didn't look at Mingan. "Ready?"

He nodded. Silent as a padded footfall, he was already on his feet, one hand resting on his pommel. He shot Strifbjorn a wolfish, sidelong grin, starlight pooling in the gray part of his eyes. "By all means, my dear Strifbjorn. Let us find us a war."

Except for Menglad, the waelcyrge had retired to their niches at the women's end of the hall. They emerged re-garbed, clad still in white, rectangular indigo capes swirled and pinned at the right shoulder with a brooch like a four-pointed star. For fighting, they wore split skirts or trousers, and tunics with bloused sleeves and open seams. Herfjotur and Skeold led them among the einherjar, their swordhilts and hair shining in the firelight. It gladdened Strifbjorn's heart to see.

The einherjar retrieved shields from where they hung among the rafters, iron-banded wood painted with brave colors and devices. In winter, the thrall-children used them for sleds.

One of the waelcyrge stalking Strifbjorn, Sigrdrifa, shot a look down the length of the line of einherjar—but chose another warrior to stand beside. Strifbjorn was relieved to see the little historian, Muire, stand with Yrenbend—laying her hand on his forearm and looking up at him with a brief, troubled smile. Herfjotur it was who came toward him, the blue silk of the hall's pennant laid over her shoulder, the pole in her right hand—Herfjotur, widowed, was a valraven's rider, and seemed content with that partnership over seeking a new husband.

She lifted the indigo banner, showing the silver stars embroidered across its surface: the banner of their hall. The Raven Banner of the children of the Light hung behind the Lady's chair, a stark white sweep of cloth from hoist to fringe, no black bird marring its surface to portend war.

"Won't you ride your steed?" Only she knew his name.

She pouted a *no*. "He does not approve of ritual combat."

"Ah. I didn't know the valraven disapproved of things."

That made her laugh, which made Strifbjorn glad. He must be so careful, with so many of them, but Herfjotur . . . she was all right. She didn't require an armored and impervious war-leader, just one with a will and a plan.

She checked the hang of the banner one last time. Then she came and took Strifbjorn's arm, leading him forward into battle.

They arrayed on the greensward, in the light of the setting sun, pair and pair. The Grey Wolf stood lean and solitary in his gray wool and leathers. No one had come to fight beside him. He went shieldless also. Arrogance: it worried Strifbjorn.

Mingan caught him watching. Thin red lips parted in a deadly smile. "Do not worry so, Strifbjorn," he called over the jesting and taunts traveling back and forth between the lines. "It will make you old."

Herfjotur braced the banner-stave at her belt and through the loops over her shoulder, drawing her sword Solbiort into her right hand.

Strifbjorn hefted his shield. "It's my nature. I'll try to stop. But by the Serpent that bears all Burdens, get yourself killed and I'll come across the river after you and drag you back by your hair."

Mingan thought and then he said, "Agreed. I shall hold you to that."

Menglad Brightwing came out of the mead-hall and lifted a silver-chased horn in her hand, light sliding like oil along the filigree. The banter silenced. The sun slid down the sky, the cold north sea hissed against the flank of the mountain far below, and silence reigned.

The crimson-clad bride raised the horn to her lips and sounded it, deep and long.

Like ocean falling into ocean, the battle was joined.

Of course Strifbjorn and his hall let them win. Several brothers and two sisters had to be carried inside, bandaged and laid to bed, but there weren't any deaths. A . . . fortuitous . . . omen, supposedly.

Strifbjorn would have had to think back many years to the last time one of the children died in a game, though they still died when they rode to war. Rest would heal the wounded within days, but they would miss the party.

The waelcyrge carried mead around again while the einherjar found their seats. Strifbjorn crossed the hall diagonally. His place was on the step before the Cynge's empty chair, and Arngeir and Menglad came to stand before him.

He looked over his brothers and sisters, einherjar and waelcyrge, chosen and choosers. They were a brave array, even wearied and bloodied from the fight—Sigrdrifa, with all her wounded pride and the swiftness of her blade; Ulfgar, smooth-voiced and sharp-tempered; Herewys, who thought no one knew when he slipped injured birds inside his shirt.

Mine. Strifbjorn swallowed too much pride.

Arngeir had healed the wound across his breast that Herfjotur had delivered him, but the bloody rent in the red of his shirt remained. Menglad looked cool and dignified, but the war-leader read excitement and perhaps a little fear in the toss of her head. He wanted to reassure her, tell her that what was coming would complete and not constrain her.

But Strifbjorn wasn't supposed to know that.

"Menglad," he said, when the murmur of voices dropped away, "take your husband's hand."

2

A seat of status, a post at table?
The gods shall never grant you.
                        —*Lokasenna*

The Wolf

Something stirs in my breast. An old hurt, an old heat. The bride and groom walk the hall in parallel, separated by the fire trench. They stink of dread, hope, joy.

They stop before Strifbjorn, who stands where the Cynge would stand. If we had a Cynge. I lean forward on my bench, the better to see, queue falling over my shoulder again. At the foot of the hall, the waelcyrge rise, their swords naked in their hands. Flickers of starlight run the dark edges of their blades. Little Muire fidgets out among them, nervy as if she can feel her own difference. I glance away, back at Strifbjorn.

And the couple he will bind into one.

He is laughing silently, as he does. He flicks a glance toward me, then down before I catch his eye. So be it, but the searing in my chest flares, fades, although it never quite all vanishes.

Strifbjorn speaks quietly and Menglad reaches through the fire and places her hand on Arngeir's. The flames trace around them. Fire cannot harm us. Strifbjorn smiles now without guile.

"Arngeir." A louder voice, one that carries throughout the hall: "What say you to Menglad, sister of my heart?"

"That I will have her to wife," Arngeir replies, and turns to her through the flames. "Menglad, wilt marry me?"

"I will."

A cheer rocks the high, smoke-scarred beams of the hall, beams hung with the tattered banners of enemies who trouble us no longer.

"Menglad," Strifbjorn says, "what say you to Arngeir, brother in the Light?"

"That I will name him husband." Her voice breaks. "Arngeir, wilt marry me?"

He hesitates a moment, stretching our nervous chuckles. And then, "I will; I will," he cries, and another cheer greets them.

"Then you must kiss," Strifbjorn tells them, "and seal the bargain." He laughs; I know he laughs, though only I can see.

The pyre in my chest flares hotter, more terrible. Strifbjorn's gaze could be a weight, but I train my eyes on the couple about to be joined. I stand and draw Svanvitr as all around me my brothers rise.

Arngeir and Menglad turn face-to-face. He leans forward, steps into the flames that cannot burn us, draws her into his embrace. Coals glimmer dark at the edges of their boots, doused by the pressure of their feet. I see him whisper something to her, and I see her close her eyes. Tears of silver Light leak down her cheeks, staining her ember-colored gown. Arngeir lifts her veil with hands that can be seen to tremble, even at such a distance.

He takes a breath, drops her veil among the coals—where it sparks and is consumed—and draws her into his arms for the ritual kiss.

Their lips touch, mouths open. We all know by instinct how it is done. She seems to swell as he breathes into her open mouth. I hear him moan, see the white-knuckled grip of his fingers on her shoulders. Her arms link around his neck. I cannot smell them.

I smell only the fire.

The pain beneath my breastbone is impossible, sharp as the thrust of a sword. Light—pure, simple, white as the feathers of a swan—flares in my eyes, shudders the length of my upraised blade. A third cheer rises from hundreds of throats; a Light blazes from eyes and swords and open mouths, filling the mead-hall with starlight until the flames seem like shadows.

I would throw back my head and howl, but instead—blood filling my mouth, the sweet white Light flaring about me, surrounded by the company of those I cannot touch—I cheer with the rest of them as Menglad's fingers knot in Arngeir's hair, and a blue flare rises about them, eye-blinding. The Light of the bond taking hold, of two souls forged into one, left hand and right, will and action. The band at my throat is tight, tight, tight.

A marriage.

Forbidden me by fate and my own mistakes, forever.

They fall to their knees amid the embers, flames rising over their heads almost invisible in the starlight that fills up the hall, our blades, our bodies.

At last, they part. Arngeir stands amid the scattered coals, extends a hand to Menglad Brightwing, leads her from the hall

and to his waiting mount—a mortal horse, a dapple gelding—
as the cheers renew.

I walk from the darkened mead-hall. Strifbjorn finds me above
the border of the forest. Even here, the wind brings sounds of
laughter, and softer sounds occasionally, too.

I turn to him as he comes up, towering over me—a kind,
dangerous bulk like a well-mannered stallion. "Herfjotur," I say.
"She would understand. Or the little one, the clever one. Muire.
She will shatter into wisdom."

"I'll not marry," he says—the old argument.

And I am supposed to answer, *But thou must.*

Not tonight. Tonight I cannot bear it. Tonight there was
the girl flinching from my voice, and the waelcyrge's hand re-
treating from my touch, her longing for the einherjar beside
me so powerful I felt it clean as a blade. Despite the gloves.

Tonight there is the Light, and the shadowed darkness, and
the stricture of my collar, and the sting beneath my breastbone
of a gulped sun.

I take Strifbjorn by the sleeve, draw him into the shadows
of the ancient trees.

He does not struggle. The need in him tingles my fingertips
as I lure him on. Soon we reach the bower of a scholar-tree old
as the mountain we stand on, old as this young world we made.
His body is a bow: strung tight, yet it twists to my touch. I take
his face between my hands and, drawing him down in the shadow
of the tree, I kiss his mouth.

This is wrong.

The wrong is done, I answer.

He pulls me close. At first he teases. We kiss like mortals, tongues and lips and groping hands. His cool mouth, wet, tastes of hops and honey. I press him to the trunk, hauling on his plait like a rein. No decent rider would manage a horse so. He goes willing, opens the smoke-smelling bearskin to enfold me. I cast my cloak over our heads. My hands on his back, broad with knotting muscle. His hands are gentle where mine pinch and maul.

I bring him to the earth, tangled in cloaks, pull him over me like a shelter. He rests his elbows on the ground and cups my shoulders on his palms. I scratch his neck, his shoulders, bite his mouth when he kisses me softly again.

We take each other always in my domain, under the cold staring sky, never under roofs, in beds. Another night, I might shed my garb, strip his. We might take our pleasure skin to skin, lingering over moans and murmurs. The overture, only, for the kiss.

Tonight, I bloody him. His hands pin mine, but I still clutch his braid. It hauls his head down, twists his neck, holds his mouth where I can reach. I strain up, elbows planted, and lick red from his lips. His weight on my wrists creaks the bone.

We move in rut. He presses between my thighs; I hook my heels and thrust against him. Sharp things in the hard earth stab. He binds me. I trap him. Rocking, sliding, hard prick against hardness, separated by cloth and leather. He is cold to my touch.

Naught but fire and sunlight feel warm to me.

He bites my mouth this time. Hard, on a diagonal, tenderness fled. I take his mark, reply with a tongue sharped between his teeth. He welcomes.

I release his plait, break his grip, leave shreds of skin under his nails. And then *my* nails drive hard behind his ears, down his nape. I lift my shoulders from the earth, hang from his sweating strength. He says my name into my mouth. My name. A breath. An offering.

I take it. Hard and fast. Arched to his stone strength, not the slow sharing he thought to offer but driving, sucking, taking, rough and deep and without reserve. Alvitr jabs my ribs, and I pull the sword from his harness, push it blindly aside, unbuckle my own belt so he can slither it and my blade out of the way.

He breathes out and I pull him in. His substance, his core. Light flares, dazzling, muffled by our cloaks, showing his bones through the flesh. Sharp. Sweet. Perfect agony, except it is savor. My name becomes a moan; the moan becomes a growl. He sucks, bites, panting, and every breath I breathe in and give back. His hands on my waist. His weight is an anchor. He fumbles my trousers open and jams his hand inside.

My own breath tangled in his, saying his name into his mouth as his hand works between us. He nurses my tongue, stopping my breath when I would push it into his lungs again. I'd cry out, but his mouth seals mine, tongue and palate pulsing, cruel deferral until he breathes me in again and all starlight blossoms. Him. Me.

Us. Elbows and knees and rough palms in the shattered darkness, mouths locked as I arch against him, a tiny irritating pleasure lost in the sea of the kiss. Blinding. It hurts. It's splendid. He wrenches my mouth to his, fingers sticky in my hair, still kneeling between my feet. I squirm and kick my trousers down until they catch on my boots. The cloaks suffocate, trap the blazing against our skin. I pull them tighter, pin the edge under my shoulder. They cannot slip.

The kiss broken, rejoined as we fumble his fly. He tries to make it easy and I won't wait. Teeth, nails, blunt striving as he presses my legs up and then together and I drag his mouth open with my hands and breathe into him, hard, matching his rhythm, giving back everything I get as he bucks. Making him feel it, take it. Owning him owning me.

I dress and don my cloak and gloves again. I mean to leave directly after, back to the wolves and the mountain, but there's a voice. A woman's voice, and weeping. So softly, and I know her grief is private, but I am drawn. Perhaps the flayed ache under my heart cries for proof that it is not the only pain in the world.

It is Muire. I pause, ferns about my knees, and watch: she is lost in her grief. She must have taken her hair down to brush it, for it falls about her shoulders in ripples from the braids. Darker and smaller than her sisters—as if distilled. She's stuffed her fist into her mouth to smother sound, leaned her forehead against the rough bark of an ash. Moonlight reveals the marks of teeth on the knuckles.

She still wears white, though she has left her cloak behind. She is barefoot. Something sent her running from the mead-hall half-undone. I watch, voyeur as always, consider going to her. Her grief is private, though, and I suspect her rivals as the source. And she flinched from me.

But then I step back into the darkness and scent her back trail. She came from the direction of the scholar-tree.

The Warrior

This is a story that begins and ends with a kiss, Strifbjorn thought, watching Mingan vanish through shadows cast by tree boughs in a waning moon. He sighed, tasting the Wolf on the outflow. Strifbjorn felt rawness inside. A fragment of what had been lost to their embrace, or given to it. The unbearable, forbidden kiss.

Mingan'd returned a splinter of his own soul, paid the debt in the secrets of his heart. His fierceness and craft fluttered in Strifbjorn like a banked flame, spreading warmth and will. All his wild old strength was there, and all the love he bore. Shadows of his temptations and truths and the choking sorrow he rarely spoke. Strifbjorn would not share him.

Strifbjorn would not be shared.

They'd find a way. Strifbjorn had half a plan, though it all strung on Yrenbend. He could stand in Strifbjorn's place.

If he would.

But for now, Mingan had evaporated in that way of his. And Strifbjorn? Strifbjorn turned and walked away. Not to the mead-hall. He must wash off the Wolf's scent, rinse his taste from his mouth before he went back, and he wanted those a little longer. So he picked his way down the cliff path overlooking the sea.

Mingan had wrapped Strifbjorn in his cloak to hide the Light that flared around them, cocooned them in thick woolen folds. The Wolf was in Strifbjorn still. He held that trace like an ember in cupped hands, blew across it, studied the resultant glow.

Strifbjorn thought Mingan didn't know himself if he only

argued Strifbjorn toward marriage to save face, when he knew
that it was futile, or if he really thought he intended to protect
Strifbjorn. Or if Mingan's own longings—Strifbjorn knew; he
knew he wasn't enough for Mingan; he knew the Wolf *wondered* about others—drove what he said about Herfjotur, about
Muire, all the women he pressed on Strifbjorn. If you want
something you think you can't have, the next best thing is to
talk a friend into it.

In truth, to stay war-leader Strifbjorn needed to marry. In
truth also, he couldn't, for the kiss would reveal their tryst to
a wife. And what waelcyrge, even if she didn't repudiate Strifbjorn in the wake of such a betrayal, would care to be linked
to the Grey Wolf? It'd be . . . basest treachery, unworthy . . . to
so deceive someone.

They feared him. Strifbjorn knew what that fear cost him.
Better to risk his own place in the Light than inflict that on
two he cared for.

The greensward lay wet with dew under his boots; the moonlight turned each drop to cold pewter. Below, the ocean rolled in,
stately. He scrubbed his fingers on his thighs, his bruised mouth
swollen. He couldn't bear to heal it yet.

Strifbjorn was sore everywhere Mingan touched him, and
glorying in it. He savored the thought for a minute, then ruined the mood laughing at his own melodrama.

It was foolishness. He knew the price the first time he kissed
the Wolf, and had decided even then that no one would ever
make him regret it. The assignations could be forgiven: A small
enough transgression. Something that would not be spoken of.
No one would insult two warriors, so long as they showed no
other weakness. Even if their brethren suspected.

The rest—the kiss—was anathema.

They were expected to marry, Mingan and Strifbjorn. Expected to bond a wife with whom they might get a child and replenish the children of the Light. Even long marriages proved fertile only rarely, and the ones that did were notable in the strength of the bond between the pair.

The bond of their kiss.

Strifbjorn owed his brethren children, if he could get them. As did Mingan. *Damn us all.*

Strifbjorn slid down the path as much as walked. Rocks and scree skittered from his boots. It was all broken shale, and tricky, edging on a sheer drop, strewn with boulders and bits of rock. The moon was falling and the strand glimmered pale, littered with seaweed and shells that crushed under his steps. He skipped a stone, counted bounds. Seven. With the sea so smooth, he should be able to do better.

As he stooped for a flat rock, a glitter of crimson and violet caught his eye—foreign colors in the moonlight monochrome.

Her skin was white as the strand, the long wet gown that draped her more beige or golden, her hair pale and matted with salt and sand. She lay still as a ridge on the beach: Strifbjorn never would have seen her if not for the moonlight caught on the collar of jewels and golden wires that cinched her throat.

He stared at the shadows and outline for seconds before he realized what they meant.

A woman. On the beach like so much flotsam, dead or unconscious, her pale hair twisted with seaweed.

Hand on Alvitr's hilt, Strifbjorn sprinted across the wet sand to where she lay, her fine pleated gown waterlogged and drifting about her ankles as the tide rolled down her body.

She could not possibly be alive.

He dropped beside her, knees digging furrows. As gently, as swiftly as he could, he turned her. His hand under her nape, he straightened her neck and arched it. She was not breathing. Something littered the sand beneath and around her—a tangle of sodden falcon's feathers, stripped and broken by the tide.

Strifbjorn pressed his fingertips under the line of her jaw and held his breath. Her skin was clammy and gray, but a moment's patience rewarded Strifbjorn with the slow, staggering thread of a heartbeat.

Oh, Light.

He did not know her: a mortal woman, not one of the waelcyrge. He could breathe for her without fear.

He drew her mouth open and bent over her, probing down her throat with his fingers, straightening her tongue, remembering Mingan's rough fingers prizing his own jaw open. But his mouth was hot; hers tasted briny and cold when Strifbjorn pressed his lips down, pinching her nose shut. Salt in the toothmarks reminded Strifbjorn to will them healed, so only the first breath stung.

The force to fill her lungs surprised him. There was muscle under that silken gown. Lapping waves wet his calves and knees, round stones buried in the sand bruising as he breathed for her, out and gasp and out again. He had no hope of saving her, this mortal woman with her body battered by the sea, but the thread of her pulse grew stronger under his hand cupping her jaw, and at last she gagged around his breath.

He turned her on her side and let the water trickle from her mouth as she convulsed. She retched and purged, and when she was done she lay quiet, breathing on her own, moonlight threading the jewels of her necklace.

He had torn the skin of his right hand on the wires. He healed it with a thought, all the remaining bruises and scrapes and the hard marks of Mingan's loving hands. And he scooped her into his arms.

Leftover blood smeared the sand-colored cloth of her ruined gown. Her eyelids didn't even flutter as he carried her back up the treacherous cliffside path to the hall.

The Wolf

I hurry from the mead-hall in the meadow, the mortal town below it. From whence I found the waelcyrge weeping. Away from my sisters, my brothers, and into the dark. I run into the night's embrace. Already I draw my gloves off, loping up the mountain amid the leaf-lorn oaks and beeches. They give way to conifers, and above that meadow and above that finally bare gray rock and ice. I will not run so far. The wind floats a wolf-howl to my ear. That ear feels as if could almost perk and swivel.

It is not yet time to return to the pack. While the hurt is fresh and sweet, while my body still aches with unwise passion and wiser pain, I climb to a high knoll screened by pine and spruce. There, the wind is colder. It carries a scent of woodsmoke and the sea, the scent as well of wolves, of the distant human town, of bucks in their autumn rut. I turn to the ridge of Ulfenfell, flickering in the moonlight with a cool blue gleam. There is a sharp wind from its peak, and another scent on that.

"Imogen," I whisper into the wind, "come to me."

She is swift and all but invisible. Even to me. Her wings are feathered soft as an owl's. Her eyes are paper lanterns. She settles before me, furling her pinions close as a cloak about her naked form.

"My Lord," she whispers.

His mistress, Darkness. Oh, I hear what they say.

But she is my sister. Half sister. As old as I am, in a world too young. She is my sister, and she obeys me.

Hunger would not kill her. Nothing can kill her. Starvation is her plate, and famine her knife.

But how can I leave her to suffer?

She steps closer, velvet black fur slicked with gleams. The moon is setting: some of that light shines from me. She comes like a gnat into a candleflame, her red mouth an open gash in her face, showing teeth pointed as thorns. She mews, hungry. Always hungry.

I open the collar of my shirt, the heat in my center cresting, flaring, burning under my heart. My fingers brush the too-tight silken ribbon clinching my throat. Droplets of pale light leak. I touch the knot that cannot be loosened, brush tender bruises where I strained against the fetter when I lay down for Strifbjorn.

I bare my breast to the demoness.

"Feed, then. I shall be a feast for thee tonight."

Her nostrils flare as she leans forward, ducking her head to taste my skin. Her tongue rasps a little, softer and wetter than the tongue of a cat. Her wings fold around us, a shelter or a cage: I pinion her wrists gently, protecting my shirt and my flesh from her small, sharp claws.

She finds a place over my heart and leans into me, breath

and feathers tickling as she nurses like a babe, straining for a moment against my grip, claws flexing.

Relief. All the grief, the sorrow of the night and all the nights before, flows into her, drawn from my body like a stain. I straighten, will and strength returning, release her right hand from my left and stroke her head. Copper sweetness—my own blood—fills my mouth; the scabs have broken. I raise my eyes to the sky, bask in the light of the stars. False dawn glows on the horizon. Her claws scratch as she lays the hand against my chest, but—settled now and feeding—she restrains herself, dainty as a sparrow, and does no harm.

When I can bear the grief again, and I am staggering with tiredness, I whisper, "Enough." The Imogen raises her head with a faint high whine.

Still hungry.

Always hungry, but if I permit it she will eat me to a husk, and then fill me up with sorrow again. She is a weapon—born and bred for nothing else.

She is my sister, after all.

After the Imogen leaves me on the mountainside, I find my way back to the wolf-lair at the copper beech. They have not returned from their run. But though the carcass of the foolish young buck is much gnawed, there will be enough for tomorrow. They are not hunting, merely running for the sheer joy of it. I am about to climb into my favored perch when I notice something odd at the margin of the clearing: straggly wildflowers, tied with a red ribbon, set beside a checked cloth bundle.

I crouch and touch the bundle haltingly with a fingertip. A scent of spices arises. I unwrap it.

Gingerbread, with cloves and cinnamon laced through it, redolent of molasses and brown wheat flour. A rich gift.

There is a trace on the red ribbon other than the flowers— the girl in the russet cloak.

An offering? Or simply thanks? And who tracked the wolves to our lair? The girl? Perhaps.

Unlikely.

The pack returns, surrounding me, snarling at the reek of woodsmoke and ambergris clinging to my cloak. The red bitch rubs against me, at last, coating me with her scent; her mate, dark as old bronze and dusted with silver across the hackles, soon follows. I laugh as they take my forearms in wolf-gentle mouths, press me down, wrestling and yipping and marking me their subject, their pack, theirs.

Later, I try to share the spice cake with them, but only the red bitch and a ghost-pale two-year-old will touch it.

The Historian

The mead-hall blazed with torches when I returned from weeping in the wood, picking my way barefoot across the turf. Herfjotur's steed raised one of his heads to watch me. He half-unfurled snow-white wings in greeting, and then lowered the antlered head again to crop the summer's last long grass.

The great doors stood open, and I stepped inside, dirt and leaves staining the hems of my trousers, pine needles tangled in my hair. I braced for attention and whispers: I had expected to return to a quiet hall.

No one noticed me.

My brothers and sisters were clustered in the southeast corner. Worried murmurs reached me as I walked beside the rekindled fire trench. I drew even with them, crossed before the Lady's empty chair and came up beside Yrenbend.

"What has transpired?" I stood on tiptoe to reach his ear until he hunched to accommodate me.

"Strifbjorn has rescued a drowned mortal girl on the beach," he said. "We're annoying him." He raised a wry eyebrow and smiled at me from the corners of silver eyes laced with a cast of green. His queue was a dark golden-red. I wanted to reach out and yank it.

"Will she live?"

He turned away from the crowd and laid a companionable hand on my shoulder. "She is breathing on her own. Come. There's still mead to be had." He led me back down the hall and served us both from the cask near the Cynge's chair—in round-bottomed bowls that could be sipped and set aside, not the horns that must be drained at a draft. "She has not awakened."

We sat together at the end of the trestle table, and he watched me drink. I pulled a knife from the sheath on my thigh to cut some scraps of the cold roast that still lingered on the table, and gave him my best attempt at a smile.

He reached out and touched a lock of my unbound hair, pulling a swag of pine needles from it. He smelled of leather oil and salt sea-spray. A silver flute hung in a case at his belt: a flute I had made for him. "You look unwell, sister."

I sighed and glanced around the hall, leaning across the table closer to Yrenbend once I saw that no one was near us. There was no privacy, in a mead-hall. "I'm troubled, Yrenbend." I poked at the venison again, cutting a hatchwork of lines in the side of the roast with the point of my knife.

"Strifbjorn?"

Something as dark and ravenous as the Suneater raved in my breast. *Hope.* And a terrible thing hope can be. "What else? I had myself all but convinced that there was no chance. I'm not the bravest or the best of us, by any means . . . and plain as a sparrow, I know that, too. But I went walking to-night, after Sigrdrifa teased me. . . ." Yrenbend would know the details. Word passed quickly from the women's end of the hall to the men's. Yrenbend's wife would have told him what Sigrdrifa said, regarding Strifbjorn and whatever feelings I might have for him. And the likelihood of those feelings being returned.

I realized that my voice had trailed off only when Yrenbend prodded me. "And . . . ?" He sipped his mead, both eyebrows rising in an expression that never managed to make him look surprised.

I stuck my knife into the mutilated roast, tip grating on the bone. "I heard something I shouldn't have. The Wolf and Strifbjorn, speaking in the shadow of a tree."

He retrieved my knife and carved a bit of meat, which he pleated meticulously before tucking it into his mouth. He watched my face while he chewed.

"Mingan—the Wolf—was counseling Strifbjorn to marry. And quickly." I took the knife away from Yrenbend, attacking the roast so that I would not have to meet his eyes. "And me."

Not the whole truth. But not a lie, either. And whatever else I'd overheard . . . was not mine for the sharing.

"Really." Yrenbend did not sound astonished, but then he never did. "Naught else?"

I risked a glance. He seemed thoughtful. "I walked away. It seemed indecent to eavesdrop." *Not a lie, not a lie, not a lie.* But as close as I had ever come.

"Your honor does you credit." He finished his mead. "Let me see what I can learn." Standing, he dropped his hand on my shoulder again and turned away, back toward the dispersing knot of our brethren at the far end of the hall.

The next morning, I left walking southward, to make myself useful in the world.

The Warrior

The waelcyrge and thralls laid the woman on the bench in Strifbjorn's cubby and tucked blankets about her, trickled brandy under her tongue, brought braziers of coals to warm the space.

She shivered in her sleep, and when she woke, a long time later, she woke up screaming.

Skeold, who sat by her, shouted. Ulfgar and Strifbjorn were closest. They came at a run before the crash, snapping wood and the thump of falling bodies. An instant later, two people plunged through the arras, and the blacksmith and the war-leader checked hard.

The blond stranger knelt over Skeold, one fist in the waelcyrge's hair, the other pinning her wrists. She was nude, the bed-clothes discarded. Her chest heaved, her eyes and mouth wide open. Skeold strained against the grip, and could not shift it.

No mortal girl, this, then.

Strifbjorn had no blade in his hand. He spread his arms wide, showing open palms. Ulfgar, with a sideways glance, did the same. "Peace," Strifbjorn said.

"You're not giants," the woman said. "You're not Aesir."

"There are no Aesir anymore. No giants. You're safe. All dead, and on another world." She still stared, disbelieving. His hands fell to his sides. "You've come across the water to the next world. I'm Strifbjorn. Release my warrior, please."

She blinked, glanced down at her hand—white-knuckled in Skeold's hair—and then at Strifbjorn. Meticulously, as if it pained her, she unclenched one finger at a time. She knelt back, stood, offered a hand to Skeold, quite as innocent in her naked-ness as any babe. Ulfgar stared, and Strifbjorn did not blame him.

Skeold, after a moment of shock, took the hand and al-lowed the stranger to pull her to her feet.

"The giants pursue me," the stranger said, and tossed her hair over her shoulder, her breast rising with the sweep of her arm. "By the all-Father, I pray I've come in time."

3

Fenrir the Wolf-son of Loki, caged from a cub, grew so fierce that none would approach to feed him save Tyr, bravest of the gods; it was decided that the Wolf must be chained away from the realm of gods and the world of men.

The advice of dwarves, clever craftsman, was claimed. They wrought a binding-cord from the six improbable things: the footfalls of cats; the beards of women; the sinews of bears; the breath of fish; the spittle of birds; and the roots of a mountain. The cord was flat and smooth as a silken ribbon—barely wider than a thread—feather-soft to the touch.

Unbreakable by god or man. Or Wolf.

The Wolf

I expect the girl in the russet cloak. But it is Herfjotur who finds me a few sunrises later. She leans against an oak and waits for me within the pack's range. I find her by her scent.

The pack comes, yellow-green eyes unholy in the light of the dawn. I stalk toward her, drawing on my gloves. "Sister."

She smiles more calmly than most. "Wolf." She crouches, slim and strong in her white leather, and extends the back of her hand to the boldest wolf, the ghost-gray adolescent. One gold braid falls over her shoulder as she bends. She shoves it back. My gaze slides down the arch of her neck, the delicate ear. I feel . . . *disloyal*.

She looks up. "Lovely." And stands. "I bear a message, Master Wolf."

"Mingan."

She arches an eyebrow. "Indeed." At least the smell of concern on her isn't fear. "Strifbjorn requests your company. And counsel. This afternoon—he cannot get away now."

It is not love or even lust I feel. It's melancholy for something I can never be. Yes, I am powerful, and yes, I could win a wife by strength of arm—but I can never be a part of their family.

I should be grateful for what I do have. Strifbjorn, and the pack.

She leaves me with a bow.

I watch her glide down the trail. If Strifbjorn would not court Muire, perhaps I'd pursue her myself. Perhaps—

Whatever she overheard on the mountainside, she has kept it to herself. Or I would have learned of it by now.

When I descend the mountain later that day, Strifbjorn waits for me—unobtrusively, by the trail he knows I favor. He finds me always, in darkness or in daylight. He carries a splinter of my soul lodged in his heart.

From the shard of him I bear, I can read worry in the pretend-calm of his face.

"Trouble," I say. He nods tightly. Fine lines mark out the

corners of his eyes. He glances around and then reaches out, palm of his hand flat to my face. His flesh lies chill on my burning. "What sort of trouble?"

"A new sort," he says, and I ease an inch.

His hand is on my face. *Not us.*

Nay. But, Mingan, I think the Lady has returned.

"The Lady?"

He nods, letting the arm fall. "I found a woman on the beach three nights ago, all but drowned. She—well, Mingan, come and see for yourself."

I stare, turn, stalk before him down the trail. We walk without talking. His boots crunch gravel, twigs. The mead-hall smells emptier, even before it comes in sight. Less smoke, fewer brethren.

A great white drake—one of the valraven—slumbers along the length of the cliff overlooking the sea. Many of my brethren will have gone on errantry following the bonding of Menglad to Arngeir, and others have returned to their scattered halls. All told, there are less than a thousand of us.

So few, for a task so great. "You found her the night of the wedding?"

His voice over my shoulder. "She gives her name as Heythe."

"And yet . . . our brothers and sisters have dispersed?"

"She didn't wake for two days. And we thought her merely a mortal lass, washed from a ship, perhaps."

"And then?"

"Well," Strifbjorn repeats, catching me up, striding past me, "come and see for yourself."

The Warrior

When Strifbjorn and Mingan returned to the mead-hall, Heythe, the drowned girl, stood within the south end, at the center of a ring of einherjar and waelcyrge. She wore an open-collared white shirt and leggings borrowed from somebody larger. Skeold faced Heythe down, her crystal blade balanced lightly in her right hand. A thin rill of Light ran its edge, as if dark transparent stone caught the reflection of a fire, except the fire trench was cold and the radiance silver.

Skeold's expression of soft concentration would have warned *Strifbjorn* not to cross her.

Heythe smiled.

She carried no weapons. She turned in her footprints, scuffing the withered pine branches out of the way as she followed the deliberate, wolflike circling of the waelcyrge. Her eyes, open at last, were a bright enough blue that Strifbjorn noticed it from a distance, even in the dimness of the hall, and her necklace sparkled with a light of its own under her open collar.

Mingan tensed beside him, drawing a breath. His hand rose in a gesture that might seem feminine to one who didn't know about his double collar.

"Watch this," Strifbjorn whispered in Mingan's ear, leaning into the animal scent hanging around him.

Skeold lunged for the girl in the borrowed clothing. Sharp feint, perfect recovery, followed by a sweeping sidestroke that, had it been delivered with the edge and not the flat, should have driven into Heythe's side. Except Heythe stepped back, stepped in and caught Skeold's wrist in her right hand. A jerk upward disarmed the waelcyrge and brought her to her knees.

They struggled, thrashed. Heythe laughed, kept laughing as she pushed Skeold down, face-first into the earthen floor. Branches crackled.

Skeold raised her other arm in surrender.

Mingan leaned into Strifbjorn, shoulder brushing shoulder as he spoke into the war-leader's ear. "No mortal lass, that, brother mine. Shall I challenge her and see?"

"See?"

"If she is the Lady, she may be back just in time."

Strifbjorn followed the fluid gesture of Mingan's arm and spat an oath. The swan-white sweep of fringed Banner hung behind the Lady's chair was stainless no longer. Upon it had appeared the image of its namesake—a Raven displayed, wings spread wide, mouth open and talons grasping, moving or seeming to move in the dimness of the light cast by the torches and trickling in the high, narrow windows. A portent of war. And of victory.

If its wings were folded and its head were bowed, it meant their brethren would fail in the coming battle. They had fought many wars, and Strifbjorn had never seen it so blazoned.

Tall, ice-pale Sigrdrifa ambled toward the waiting einherjar, resplendent in white and silver furs and linen. She nodded to Mingan and smiled warmly as her gaze brushed Strifbjorn's. Despite the curve of her lips, her hard gray eyes narrowed. So transparent. *No, sister. Not if you were the last angel on earth.*

She laid a long-fingered hand on Strifbjorn's forearm. "War-leader."

A bare nod was his best politeness.

"Will you challenge the . . . newcomer?" She hesitated before that last word. *Lady?* Some of the brethren had already decided. Mingan stepped on Strifbjorn's foot.

Strifbjorn's shrug knocked her hand away, as if incidentally. He looked back at the ring. Heythe was helping Skeold to her feet. "Perhaps later."

Skeold retrieved her sword and left the bear-pit. Heythe straightened and surveyed them all. "Will any challenge my right to sit in this chair?" she asked, quite mildly.

Ulfgar, the blacksmith and a valraven's rider, stepped forward. Strifbjorn expected Heythe would deal with him quickly.

Sigrdrifa nodded. "She is . . . impressive. If I were warleader—which, of course, I am not—and if I did not intend to hand over the reins of power quietly, I would be courting allies."

Ever-subtle. Her arm brushed Strifbjorn's.

Ulfgar grunted as Heythe twisted him into a submission hold, and raised his fist. Strifbjorn pretended ignorance and turned toward the Wolf. "What do you think?"

As if in answer, Mingan unclasped his soot-gray cloak and passed it to the war-leader. Strifbjorn draped it over his arm and accepted Svanvitr, too. "Is this wise?"

His grin was wolfish. He unlaced the cuffs of his shirt.

His silent motions attracted attention—Heythe's, and that of the brethren. Yrenbend left his place in the circle, next to Brynhilde, his wife, and crossed to them. "No sword?" Low and concerned.

"Hands will suffice," said the Wolf, strongest and strangest among the children of the Light, tugging his fingers free of his gloves one at a time. Strifbjorn's lover. The keeper of half of his soul. And a wild thing he barely understood, even when he could look within and see him blinking back. "If they do not, then she is as she says. Another survivor of the world before."

Like the Grey Wolf, Strifbjorn's brother. And the demoness bound to his will.

It wasn't a battle Strifbjorn could fight for him. It was one he had to fight for Strifbjorn.

Mingan tugged his shirt open. Beads of light from his collar spilled across his chest. Yrenbend jerked his head, drawing Strifbjorn's eye to Heythe. She stood at the foot of the dais; her eyes widened at that glimmer, and she took a half step back.

"She fears you." Yrenbend, murmuring.

Mingan stripped his shirt over his head and gave it to their brother. Yrenbend folded the charcoal cloth, ducked his chin and hid a smile.

"They always do."

His body was hard and white as stone—lean with running, the muscles laced beneath his skin in tight relief like twisted yarn. Strifbjorn slapped Mingan's back, his heartbeat slow, passionless under the palm of his hand; the skin hot, familiar. "Light with you."

He didn't acknowledge the war-leader. He took one step up.

"I will challenge you, Heythe." His voice, however soft, always carried.

Chin lifted, she examined him. "Your name?"

"Mingan." He scuffed his boot among the boughs. "Some call me the Wolf."

"Ah," she said. "Yes. I accept."

He went forward, and the ring widened to enfold him and then closed to hem him in.

The Wolf

Heythe draws up as I sidle forward. Strewn dry boughs crackle under her steps, but I move silently. Her eyebrow rises; the edge of her lip curls in a smile.

She is lovely. Her hair is of a color with the mellow, age-worn brass of Svanvitr's hilt, and her angled cheekbones tilt the corners of eyes blue as the winter-bright sky above. Her gaze drifts to my boots and then back. To my collar, spilling light. She pitches her voice low, raising a shiver along my neck. "I remember you. You were not prophesied to live."

I do not understand her. I do not know her.

I will not tell her that. "Things happen as they are intended. Until they do not."

She steps closer. I smell ale and mint on her breath. "If I defeat you, will you take service?"

"My blade is sworn. But if you are the one we wait to serve, we will serve you indeed. For the Bearer of Burdens, and the future of the world."

"Your form was not so fair when last we met." She lays a bare hand on my shoulder, and my skin contracts as if she stroked my fur against the grain. She does not draw away from the heat, but lets the coolness of her palm soak into me.

"I do not recall," I tell her.

And then I know her, for half an instant, through the contact of flesh on flesh: the drive, the power of her will. Ruthlessness and strength and a fine-edged humor: *What would it be like to kiss him?*

Her face shows nothing of the thought. I step back, startled, and lick my lips. She smiles, and I know I just proved something to her. "Shall we begin?"

She steps away and drops a curtsey, which should seem clumsy in leggings. She manages with grace. I bow, and then she is swaying to the side like a serpent.

I do not strike. Rather I watch, waiting, turning on my heel so that she cannot flank me as she circles, stately and fluid at once. I widen my awareness, my ears bringing the rustle of her boots through the boughs, my nostrils the scent of her sweat, of pine, of ale. I watch her eyes and her center and I am ready when she moves.

It helps me not at all. Fast, fast as an adder, she comes under my guard and slides around behind me before I can finish my turn. Her boot strikes the small of my back, and the breath leaves my body. I turn the stumble into a roll. My brethren dodge away, and I rise, pine needles clinging to my skin.

"Yield?" she offers.

"Not, I think, so soon."

She grins at my defiance, comes after me again. I sidestep and thrust out my boot. She trips. I dive after, knee at the small of her back, left hand on her neck and right hand twisting her wrist behind her. My brethren's excited shouts. Branches crackle under my weight and hers.

Her left hand is pinned across her chest.

"Your question back to you, Heythe." She goes slack, but

I am not duped. Her body twists, cool and slick and strong as a sea creature. No surrender in her. I tighten my hands.

Her left arm jerks straight. She thrusts herself over, landing on me, shoulder into my chest. A snapping sound is not the branches breaking; her right arm fractures in my grip. She rips it free with a shout. I drag at her hair with the hand that slips off her neck, sharp sticks tearing my shoulder. She kicks back and down, catching the side of my knee. Shattering heat takes my breath away.

It hurts to take it back. I shout a word—"*Isa*"—and draw the straight line on her shoulder blade with my thumb. Her skin glows blue, the tang of winter. She laughs, drives her left elbow into my midsection and flexes, rolling to her feet in an evolving motion.

"Better than your brothers, little Wolf." The arm I broke straightens. She curls her fingers, testing, balls a fist.

I push myself to a crouch on the good leg. The other one complains until I heal it, begrudging the tiredness. Spring forward without warning, uncoiling, striking her midriff with the crown of my head. She falls. Voices, shouts, wagers.

She's stronger, faster. I must hurt her badly, and fast.

I land on top. She grunts. I strike her across the face with my closed fist, an unpulled blow.

I've never hit one of my brothers so hard. She takes it, reaches up, clutches of my braid, swallowing the blood on her lips. "Lovely!"

She hauls herself up my queue, hand over hand up a rope. I hit elbow to forehead, and she rocks back, keeps her grip and kisses me hard on the mouth.

I've never been kissed by a *woman* before.

Shock, recoil. I try to yank my head away. She's strong, though, and with one hand clenched in my hair and the other gouging into my neck I cannot break her hold. I strike again, elbow into her sternum, and she gets a foot on the ground and rolls me, knee into my belly and then, again, into my groin.

Nauseating, hot pain. Mint on her mouth. I hold my breath, even when her blows make me gag. She shoves me down on my back, one knee on my chest, blood smeared on her torn white shirt. She gives me an inch, hand tight on my throat—"Yield!"—as both my own clench over her necklace and squeeze. Cut stones rip my hands, pain I am willing to endure—must endure—to choke her into unconsciousness.

"Hah!" she gasps, and shoves her fingers hard between my neck and my collar, twisting.

She slips from my hands. I scrabble at her face, her fingers. Need to get her hands off that bit of cord. Shove, twist, shouting, and she tightens her grip, thumb pressed hard under my ear, and the light from the collar flares *bright*. The hall in stark flare and shadow until the brilliance splinters, shatters, and I fall through it, tumbling into darkness.

The Warrior

Mouth full of the metallic taste of fury, Strifbjorn came into the circle of his brothers and held out one hand. He could not look at Mingan on the floor among the pine boughs. Heythe stood slowly, wiped her hands on her shirtfront—smearing it with his blood—and glanced up.

Strifbjorn bent over the hand she offered.

"Is that all it takes to prove myself to you?" She smiled, and then she squatted and slid her arms around Mingan's shoulders and under his knees. He was breathing, Strifbjorn saw with relief. She stood easily, as if his weight were nothing.

"Perhaps not *all*," Strifbjorn answered.

"Which is his bench?" she asked as if she had not heard.

He shook his head. "He does not stay here."

"Then which is yours?" She glanced up at him impatiently. He pointed to a niche near the head of the hall, and she bore Mingan into it.

He turned away and walked toward the door, and Yrenbend. "Bring the others back," Strifbjorn told him quietly.

He nodded. "I'll start with the Historian, and I'll ask Brynhilde to see to the Wolf," he said, his chin indicating Heythe, visible bending over Strifbjorn's bench through the disarrayed arras. She pulled furs and the eiderdown over the Wolf's still form. "Shall all the halls be notified?"

"Aye," Strifbjorn told him, and clapped his shoulder before he turned to go, too wary to let him see welling gratitude.

Menglad would not be getting much of a honeymoon.

The Historian

Not sleeping presents its own unique difficulties: keeping occupied, for one thing. Which is why, in the darkness of a late autumn morning a week or so after Menglad's wedding, I came to be pacing a muddy street in the coastal town of Sanura.

There seems to be some rule that the worst and best areas in any city will run alongside the waterside, almost as if wealth and poverty are both cast up by the sea. At that, I suppose they are.

The scent of blood caught my attention as I rounded a corner into a narrow side street—the scent of blood, and the *swanning*, the received knowledge, of a death hanging on the air, about to descend. They led me to a doorway.

In the doorway was a girl.

A girl who had been slit open ear to ear, and slumped against the stones, blood still seeping between the fingers clenched tight around her throat and bubbling from her lips with every faint, weakening breath.

"Fear not," I whispered, crouching beside her on the blood-sticky ground. "I will comfort your passing, and you shall not cross the river alone."

Her eyes were wide, and her lips moved to shape a word. I shook my head. "Yes, I am waelcyrge. And I will claim your vengeance for what has been done to you. Are you ready?"

She blinked once, and I bent to touch her blood-slick lips with my own, holding her torn throat together. The breath had almost left her, but there was enough, just enough—one gasp.

The other purpose of our kiss, besides the bonding: the taking of vengeance, and the choosing of the slain.

Her life flowed into me, brutal and brutally cut short. Fifteen, orphaned and alone: Ute found whoring paid better than washing, and serving ale was just whoring with sore feet thrown in. I saw her life and her loves and her ragged little dreams—*ah, candle-flicker, what a sad brave little light you were*—and last and most important, I saw the faces of the two men who had cut her throat for the pennies in her purse.

Some would say, *At least they didn't rape her*. As if it were worse to be raped and alive than unmolested and dead. The girl in my belly wouldn't have thought so, and as she breathed her last into my mouth and fell slack against the wall, her soul squirmed inside of me and called out, *Vengeance!* Strength— the strength of the slain girl—ran through me, heady as wine.

I wiped her blood from my mouth. Then I stood, and faced the hunt.

Their trail was fresh through the muddy streets, a footstep here, a hand on a stone wall there. The cutthroat lads had gone in search of other prey, drunken sailors or desperate girls out too late on a night that promised rain. I found them lounging in an alley not far from where Ute the whore had died. The mud of the streets had worn the blood off my boots by then. *Vengeance*, Ute's voice demanded.

One of them straightened as I came forward. "Far from home, mistress," he said to me in a voice like silk.

I smiled at the implicit threat and slid Nathr into my hand. "Farther than you know," I said, and killed them both where they stood, starlight flashing blue-hot along the crystal length of my blade.

Candle-flickers. A brief tide of sorrow washed me as the girl's shade fled into her rest. I flicked blood off my blade. Freezing rain began to fall.

Choosing comfort over usefulness, I slipped into a tavern a few blocks from the southernmost of the town's two greens. It wasn't likely that press-gangs, drunks or further cutthroats would brave the rain, anyway.

Eyes came up when I walked into the tavern. Two guardsmen, off duty but not out of uniform, diced at the blackened table in the corner, and a tired woman wiped a spill off the bar with a brown-stained rag. Several other patrons seemed deep in their cups, and the scent of stew from the kitchen was cold.

The barmaid straightened at the sight of my white blouse, worked in silver thread around the collar, and the indigo swordsman's cape that left my right arm free for fighting. Her hazel eyes rested longest on Nathr's hilt over my shoulder.

"Bright one," she said, hurriedly tidying hair streaked with swirls of gray, as if she had brushed a paint-stained wrist across it. "We are honored by your presence."

A tinge of concern colored her voice, showed in her hurry to do me honor. Some of the humans do fear us. Some of my brethren stand on ceremony far more than do I.

Some of them, also, are more than merely bemused by the mortals, creatures so like and unlike us. If we were more different, perhaps we could understand each other better. But I suppose we are like siblings, the children and the men—jealousies are inevitable. Though the Bearer of Burdens dwells within us all.

"Honored enough to let me buy a mulled wine and sit out of the rain?" She didn't expect the informality; I saw it in the quirk of her eyebrow.

"Of course," she said. "Sit where you will be most comfortable. I will bring your drink. Red wine?"

"With honey if you have it." I found a table against the wall and seated myself, resting my pack beside me and unlimbering Nathr so I could lean comfortably into the paneling and rest my eyes on the inside of the shutters. There was a draft, which was why the table was unoccupied, but the cold didn't trouble me.

The barmaid heated my wine with a poker drawn from the fire and brought it. She tried to wave away the bit of silver I passed her, and I thrust my braid behind my shoulder. "You need the money more than I do."

I tossed the coin. She caught it reflexively and grinned. "As you wish it, Bright one. I can warm you some supper."

"Just the wine please, and a quiet place to sit."

She nodded, withdrew, and I thought I saw a spring in her step. I had overpaid.

The wine was good: hot and sweet, and she'd served it in a wooden goblet so it didn't taste of metal. I sipped slowly and called for more. The warmth relaxed my shoulders and neck.

I leaned my head against the window ledge and let the air flow over my tongue as I breathed in and out. The looks Mingan had given me before the wedding hadn't seemed the sort a man gave a woman when he was matchmaking for a friend. But then, they were more than friends, weren't they?

Lanternlight cast a soft sheen over the oiled wood of my goblet as I twirled it. The warmth of the wine soaked through slowly. After a little, the noises of the tavern resumed: the rattle of dice, the murmur of quiet conversation.

No one had left or entered. Through the shutters, I glimpsed grayness. The sound of the rain had ceased. I left a coin on the table to pay for the second wine and slung Nathr back over my shoulder as I stood.

"Thank you for your kindness," I said to the barmaid as I passed. She nodded and wrung her towel between her hands.

I stepped out into the gray light of morning, boots slipping in the ice-crusted mud of the street. "Shadows," I swore half-heartedly. The ruts were not so deep at the edge of the road. I walked toward the docks.

Silence, except for an early ale-wagon lumbering past. Closer to the sea, I heard the shouts of men unloading fish. No one else seemed awake yet, and the whores and drunks had gone to bed.

So a white-garbed figure strolling toward me along the same street was remarkable. I raised my hand in salute, and Yrenbend returned the gesture. When he was a little closer, I called out. "Looking for me?"

He glanced around, as if seeking someone else, and closed the rest of the distance while I laughed. I tilted my head at him. "What brings you to lovely Sanura-on-the-Elder-Sea?"

"You do." He turned to fall into step. He dropped his hood down his back, revealing sunrise-colored hair. The town awakened around us, groaning and cursing as it stretched into the day. Yrenbend reached down and slid his flute out of its oiled leather case and raised it to his lips to play a trill. "Where's your violin?"

"Fiddle. I've rented a room. We are summoned home already?" Apprehension rose up my throat, and I swallowed it. "Is everyone well?"

"The Wolf was injured in a challenge"—I blinked at that news—"but he will recover. No, more important"—fingers rippled along the length of his flute, chasing gold and copper vines I wrought there—"the Lady has returned, and the Banner shows a Raven."

I stopped and turned to him. "You're not joking."

Light flickered, swirled from the holes in his flute like mist around a hurrying messenger. He dropped it from his lips. "I am not."

"To my room. Then we will speed our footsteps home."

We returned to the seedy rooming house where I had stowed my belongings and retrieved my fiddle and a long white cloak lined in fox fur.

"How bad is it?" I asked as we walked to the edge of the ice-rimed green and found a place screened from view. My fiddle was out of tune: even the lower four resonating strings had slipped in the cold. I tightened them while he took a breath.

"It's . . . confused. Mingan was hurt, she won, and then she left—on whatever errands concern a goddess, I suppose. I've been organizing a council, and Brynhilde was caring for the Wolf. Strifbjorn expects to lose his place at the head of the table. I suspect he's not unhappy."

"And the Lady? Where did she come from?" I rosined my bow and set my fiddle under my chin.

"That's the odd part." He blew across the flute, and a liquid silver note floated forth. "It was that girl that Strifbjorn found nearly drowned and brought back to the hall. None could stand before her."

"Does she have a name?"

"Heythe. Some are already calling her Lady, though."

"I see. Are you ready, brother mine?" I laid the rosined bow across the top four strings of the fiddle—the melody strings— and took a long, slow breath of the salt sea air. We would be traveling fast.

In answer, he shaped his fingers along the barrel of his flute and blew.

The music fell from our instruments cheery and light, a swirl of brightness that lifted us on a breeze so we stood some inches above the earth. Seven-league boots, but better. I took a step forward in time to the music, Yrenbend beside me. Sanura retreated to the horizon. Another step and it vanished, replaced by rolling hills.

Before noon, we saw the ragged peak of Ulfenfell on the horizon ahead. Yrenbend dropped his flute away from his lips. "Almost home," he said. "A deep breath. And who knows what we will find? Perhaps Heythe comes to bring harmony among us."

"Perhaps," I answered, and drew the bow down one last time.

4

Witch nor woman womb of hatred
Man-mother of monsters three
> —**Baldur's Dreams**

The Wolf

Char and cold mist.

Burning.

I burn. Burning inside, and the world is cold, and I am still alone.

I taste blood and hair and fragments of bone. I smell hard winter over the reek of a fire. Something strangles me. But something has been strangling me for a long time. Half-awake, I paw at it, whining, and stop.

I open my eyes and tilt my head to look down at my hand.

A perfectly formed—human—hand.

I nose the paw—the hand—and snarl. It smells like the hand of a man. I could crunch it in my teeth, turn my head and tear—

I lunge up, as if to scramble away from the treacherous man-scent, but it follows. I cannot stand: it hurts my hindlimbs and back to move, and I sit back on my haunches in the snow to consider the strangeness and my legs bend wrong. The snow melts away from my naked flesh. My knee and elbow joints are in the wrong places along my forelimbs.

I have no tail. I put my head down and choke, clearing clogging foulness from my mouth. My tongue scrapes hair from blunt teeth, will not loll. I rub my face in snow. It melts and runs.

I remember chaos. Retching, the taste of oiled steel and my own blood. Choking. Rearing up, rearing back, pulling against the fetter that chokes me a thousand years. A sword-blade crunching between my jaws. Searing light. Sudden darkness. Hot blood and fury.

I was a wolf.

And now I seem to be . . . a man.

Dark as Hel, cold as Niflheim. No moon, no sun above, but the cold radiance of the stars reflected on drifts of snow. I breathe deeply, grateful that my sense of smell seems not much worse. I smell char under the rawness of ice like the ice at the top of the world. On the horizon is a dark, tall shape that reaches to the sky: the silhouette of a Tree. Stars sparkle among its branches, and it is the only thing in the world besides myself, and the ice.

I stand, unsteady on two bare feet. I walk. I fall, but the snow cushions the fall. And when I stand again, I move once more toward the Tree. Until, once more, I fall.

I turn, see my trail behind me, straggling through snowdrifts that, in places, reach my thighs. The snow still melts away from my touch.

Even once I am close enough to look up and make out the outline of the boughs against the starfield, the Tree seems no closer. I have been walking for days, months, years. I do not know. I fall; I stand. I go forward.

Toward the Tree.

Mortal lifetimes later, I lay one hand on the rough gray surface of a trunk so vast I can barely see the curve. The skin of my palm is . . . soft. I feel a pulse.

The sap is rising.

And within, the awareness of the Tree. It remembers battle, ice, frozen spears of winter as long as mountains are tall dripping from its branches. A ship clinker-built of the nails of dead men.

The howling of a sea of wolves.

I am alone a long time. Around the Tree, around the Tree, until I find shelter among its wildly twisted roots. I kill a snake here, in this hollow, and rip its flesh from narrow bones with my blunt and useless teeth. Its blood is pale and insipid, cold with winter. I sleep and grow stronger, leaner. But I do not hunger.

I have always hungered.

Now, the burning in my belly precludes thirst, assuages hunger.

The snow piles higher, and my hair grows long, like a human warrior's, and matted, like the coat of an arctic beast. The sun never rises, and neither does the moon. Thinking of them, a flicker of memory. My fetter chokes me, and I cease to think. It is less painful not to think.

From the Tree, or from the snow, I come to understand something is pending.

The snow falls and falls and melts never. It piles higher than my head, up the trunk of the mighty ash. I tunnel out, wanting the stars, the wind.

When the stars have turned and turned again, she comes to me. On black wings, her eyes shining stiff gold, she settles on heaped snow. "My Lord."

I rise from my hollow and go to her. The black wings come around, folding me away from the cold that never chills me. She *pulls me close, her new name flickering against my knowing when her skin touches mine. She is my sister. Father renamed her. Or she would have died. "Imogen."*

She presses her lips to my throat where the big vein pulses like the sap up the Tree. She closes long lashes over lightsome eyes, and drinks my pain like wine.

Light flares, silver and blue as the starlight that has fallen on me these days, these months, these years that I have waited by the Tree. My collar strangles, but I throw my head back and call to the pack.

What I howl is no wolf-call. But a song.

And we fall, Imogen and me—fall between the stars, into darkness more than darkness, and I must sing, and keep singing.

The Imogen bears me up, soft-black owl-soft wings slapping air with textured silence. Below, a dark ocean ripples with starlight.

Darkness, starlight and song. . . .

A form unwinds from the water, a smooth convoluted camber like a root of the Tree. Translucent and radiant, it uncoils in an impossible, endless curve. Scales ripples along its side, and then— rising—the blunt head, broad lidless eye calm as a whale's.

The colossal Serpent regards me momentarily. The Imogen backbeats furiously, steadies us in the tossing air.

MINGAN, it says, and though the name is not a name I have known, I understand that it is to be my name, that Father re-named me as well. TELL THEM TO REMEMBER THE LADY AND THE CYNGE. TEACH THEM TO AVENGE THE MURDERED.

It is like me. Like the Imogen. A survivor of the world before. But where we are renamed and saved, it has no name at all. The forked tongue flickers twice, long as a shaft of lightning; it brushes my face and the Imogen's, and is gone with a parting benediction: SING.

I sing. And the Imogen makes her sound, a high soughing warble, and sometimes a keen. It's hard for her.

She does her best.

Another voice joins mine, and then a third, and all around I see them—clad in white, singing as if they were born to sing, their hair pale and gleaming and the Light blazing around each. Below us, the ocean foams like breakers against a cliff face.

Something rises from it.

A land.

Vast and green, revealed in the sudden moonlight as a scarred silver orb rises above the ocean to the east. The Imogen sets me on the shore, her wingtips hardly brushing the earth before she speeds away toward a new and waiting mountain. Ice gleams moonlit on its heights, but its shoulders are lush.

A wolf howls from its reaches. I step forward, over sand that sticks and slides under my feet.

A hand falls on my shoulder.

"Hold," he says. I remember the word for what he is. Einherjar.

Except not. Not as they were. They are the opposite of me; they have kept the old name, and become a new thing.

He is taller, his platinum hair drawn back in a severe braid that makes his forehead seem prouder. My nose wrinkles at his scent, the intimacy of his touch.

"Strifbjorn." I know his name to give it to him. My fingers itch where I touched the Tree. My back itches where the sap of its gnawed roots fell on me.

He draws back his hand and stoops. He rakes his fingers through *the sand. Something long and dark glitters in his hand when he stands. "This is yours. Her name is Svanvitr."*

He thrusts the sword at me. I grasp her hilt by reflex and she flares into hurting Light. Along the beach, other swords spark, kindle—one, ten, five hundred. Some brethren glance at me and then glance down, as if recollecting something unpleasant. I hold my sword and have nothing to say.

He is our war-leader.

He will name the blades, and I will name the einherjar and waelcyrge. And I will tell them to wait for the Lady and the Cynge.

Strifbjorn lifts another blade from the strand. He stands, places his hand on my elbow.

"This is Alvitr." And then, looking at me calmly, though the others flinch away: "Come, brother Wolf. Let me braid your hair."

The Warrior

Heythe, seeming to Strifbjorn contented, had assured Brynhilde that the Wolf would not die. Then she had called up a red mare from somewhere and been on her way, promising—or threatening—to return. Strifbjorn couldn't show his concern for Mingan, who didn't awaken quickly from his healing slumber. He thrashed and tore and cried out in his sleep, and by the next morning Brynhilde was plainly worried.

A day later, the Wolf awoke with a shout, clutching at the pale glowing cord about his throat. Brynhilde cried out for help and pushed him back on the pillow, but he fought her. Strifbjorn was at her side before it occurred to him that it was not seemly for a warrior to interfere at a sickbed.

When he saw the green tinge and the haunted expression on Mingan's face, his repute ceased to matter. *I've lost my place here anyway*, he thought. *Heythe leads them now.*

He went to Mingan and held his shoulders while Yrenbend's wife pinned his wrists. Mingan writhed and clawed at first, but the tenor of Strifbjorn's voice must have soothed him. At last, he lay still except his trembling.

"Hush, Wolf," Strifbjorn whispered. Good, quiet Brynhilde stood and withdrew, and the war-leader spared her not a glance. He pulled Mingan into his arms as one might comfort a child. "What's come upon you?"

Mingan pushed Strifbjorn back. "A dream. A memory."

"A memory?"

He shook his head. His hair was out of its queue—Brynhilde had unbound and combed it. It fell across his lean, pale shoulders in a curtain of silver and black. Strifbjorn hooked his thumbs in his belt and stepped back as Mingan swung his legs down from the bench, speaking. "I . . . dreamed of thee, and the Imogen and how I came here. Of a time of ice." He didn't seem to notice that he'd thee'd Strifbjorn, which was a measure of his distress.

Otherwise, he only used the familiar to Strifbjorn when they were intimate. The thought brought a fresh clenching of pain. "You were screaming in your . . ." He hesitated to call it sleep.

"I am bound." He drew his knees up, distance an echo in his voice. "Bound and tormented. The vision is unclear, as if through layers of gauze. The chain parts, and I run free. Something flees me, and I pursue it. Something threatens me, and I slay it. And then . . . darkness. I awaken afire, surrounded by ice. This part is clearer. There is a Tree, and the Imogen, and . . . then I fall into darkness. And you know the rest."

"I do?" Strifbjorn didn't even remotely understand him, but as he spoke his hands relaxed on the furs.

"Raising the world from the waters. Our song."

"Ah. Indeed." Strifbjorn brushed Mingan's hair back from his face, hiding the gesture with his shoulders. They shared a moment's regard.

"I'm leaving," Mingan said quietly. He stood, casting about for his clothes. His blade leaned against the wall by the narrow head of the bench.

He was already pulling on his leathers when Strifbjorn stopped him with a touch. "Leaving?"

"Back to the mountain. I cannot stay. I cannot breathe this air." He gave Strifbjorn a look of feral desperation. Strifbjorn backed away.

"As you wish, brother of my heart." The war-leader pitched his voice low, but Mingan reacted to it. He fumbled his shirt off a hook in the turfed log wall.

Lacing the collar, he turned back. "Come and find me," he whispered. "Soon."

He caught up his cloak and his blade and was gone out the door. Not running, still he appeared as if he fled.

The Wolf

At the edge of the wood, the pack greets me. I have been gone too long, and they are fearful at the strange stinks that cling. The odor of my own blood that hangs on me. They like not my unbound hair, nor the scent of a woman on my skin.

We run. After, they pace me to our denning-place. No flowers wait this time, and I am sad. The roughly cleaned corpse of the buck begins to stink despite the chill. I plait my hair. Then take the carcass by the antlers and drag it where scavengers cannot get it and it will not foul the den.

When I return, the wolves quiver on tiptoe, hackles raised. Each faces west, inland, across the shoulder of the Ulfenfell and down into the valley, where a village called Dale lies. I swing into the wind and I, too, catch the scent.

Strifbjorn. Already.

I did say "soon." I leave my not-brothers and go to meet him on the trail, smelling the trouble on him before I come close. The veering wind brings me another scent—the flower-gathering maiden. But distant still. She must wait, if it is me she has come for. I step from shadows, into the presence of my brother. He smiles when he sees me, his eyes tired. "Are you well?"

"Well enough." I close the distance. He reaches out roughly and pulls me into his arms. The embrace should be suffocating, but it comforts and enfolds. I lean my head on the soft, smoky bear fur around his shoulders and sigh.

"You frightened me," he says into my ear.

I look up. "The terms of the combat were not death."

"But you would not yield."

"No. I will not yield." It is good to stand in his arms. Rarely may I touch him thus. "You should not be here."

He steps back, takes my elbow and leads me to the arching

root of a gnarled oak. He straddles the root, leans against the trunk. He pats the bark between his legs. "Where should I be?"

I swing a leg over the root and sit. He pulls me back until my head rests on his shoulder. "Bringing the brethren together. Finding a high point, a place of power that they will serve you even in the face of this Lady. What does the Light say of her?"

"I'm granted no *swanning*," he admits. "The Light is silent." His chest shifts against my shoulders. He passes a drinking skin. It sloshes when I take it, and I raise it to my mouth and jet expected wine or mead down my throat.

I cough ferociously on what I get. Eyes streaming, I complain. "Brandywine? You could have warned me."

He reclaims the skin, drinks. "I thought the occasion demanded hard liquor."

Another laden silence follows, during which I drink again. More than I should. "Thee," he says against my ear, changing tone. "I have had enough of leadership, Wolf. There is another to take my place now. Let me come with thee."

Temptation. I taste it on a tongue numb from the liquor he is taking out of my hands. Could he roam here, with the pack, with me?

No.

"Thou art what thou wert made for, Strifbjorn."

"If I were not . . . what I am." He stops, drinks, wipes his mouth on the back of his hand. I retrieve the skin and copy him. Liquor sharpness stings my sinuses, thickening my sense of smell.

"If I didn't need to maintain face. We wouldn't have to hide this. In the face of thee, I do not care for my fame."

I drop the wineskin into my lap. He glides sideways and

slips his fingers and then the palms of his hands up the sides of my neck, outlining the edges of my ears. His hands are callused and rough from the hilt of his sword. He tilts my head aside and bends down, bear fur tickling the back of my neck. I shiver at his breath, moreso as his mouth slides down the side of my throat to the high collar of my shirt.

"It's thee I want," he whispers.

Thou wouldst tire of my world quickly, my love.

He ignores me, pulling my shirt collar open, letting me feel his teeth lightly just below the circumference of the ribbon around my neck, right where my shoulder begins. The wolf in me shivers from the submission implied by accepting the caress. Something else exults. I turn away, press my cheek into his shoulder, baring my throat to him.

"Yes?" he murmurs against my skin, his mouth cool and gentling. I nod, unwilling to break the moment with speech, breath catching in my throat. His hand grazes my neck. He unfastens my cloak and lets it slither between us. Then he's standing, a hand on my shoulder to steady me, leaning down to nuzzle my ear while he fumbles his bearskin loose with the other hand. It falls.

Among tangled roots, bare branches spread high, the earth almost frozen, I recall a hollow beneath another Tree entirely.

The Warrior

Strifbjorn kissed Mingan, and at first his mouth was stubbornly tight. But he knew how to coax until it softened— Strifbjorn made a sharp noise and stroked Mingan's hair—and he relented and kissed back. He nibbled Strifbjorn's mouth open and probed with his tongue, cupped his cheeks in knobby hands and pushed thick, broken nails into his hair. His own was but crudely plaited, three uneven strands and not the four or five Strifbjorn used to take up the length when he did it for him. He found the end and worried the bit of rawhide from it, wishing he could pick the knot in his collar apart as easily.

"Do you have a comb?" Mingan asked.

Words against Strifbjorn's mouth. He inhaled them and licked his lips, the air chill after his heat. The creases at the corners of his eyes folded together, eyelashes meshing at the corners of his squint.

Strifbjorn pulled a wooden comb from his pouch and gave it to him. He ran a ragged thumbnail along the teeth and cocked his head at the sound. Mingan made Strifbjorn kneel on the bearskin, back against his knees. Laid alongside, Alvitr was unhooked from his belt; Mingan ran his hand along Strifbjorn's queue. The leather tie was swollen. He unknotted it with his teeth. Then, with deft motions, he broke the plait, smoothed kinked sections over Strifbjorn's shoulders and began to comb each one bottom to top with short strokes. He held the comb in his left hand and supported Strifbjorn's head with his right, and Strifbjorn eased at his touch, feeling as if breath filled his lungs completely for the first time in days.

Even when Strifbjorn's hair fell smooth, rippled from the queue over his shoulders and down to the small of his back, Mingan ran the comb through it again and again, like a mortal lover combing out the lice that never troubled einherjar.

No, it wasn't fair.

Strifbjorn reached up and took the comb from Mingan's

hand. Mingan parted the mane over Strifbjorn's nape and pressed lips and teeth to his spine. Strifbjorn shuddered. Strifbjorn covered Mingan's hand with his own and made him change places.

Mingan's hair was vital, wiry, the silver coarser than the black, so it sprang out among the dark strands like spray leaping from a hard-running river. It was longer than Strifbjorn's, and thicker. Strifbjorn had to make him stand again and kneel behind him to comb the ends, which brushed the tops of his boots when unbound.

When Strifbjorn had it all combed to his satisfaction, the bits of twig and leaf picked out, the strands covered Mingan like his discarded cloak. Strifbjorn tossed the comb to one side and put his hands on his hips, the gray leather trousers as warm as living hide. Strifbjorn turned him. He tucked straying locks behind Strifbjorn's ears.

It's harder to work someone else's belt, but Strifbjorn fumbled Mingan's open, pushed his trousers down and held him steady while he balanced against his shoulder to toe out of his boots. "Shirt," Strifbjorn said, and Mingan stripped it off. His hair showered over Strifbjorn in disorder, mingling, brushing shoulders and arms. His scent enfolded Strifbjorn with it, pungent as musk.

Mingan threaded his fingers through his gray locks and Strifbjorn's light ones, knotted his hands, holding his head between his fists. Mingan tried to hurry Strifbjorn, to make it rough and sharp and quickly over. That was always his trick, his way of keeping his distance and keeping control. But sometimes Strifbjorn could coax him into being softer, and he needed more just then.

Strifbjorn didn't let Mingan control him this time. He tasted of salt and sex, and after a moment he stopped trying to manage Strifbjorn and let him do his will, though the grip of his hands didn't ease. He shuddered and grunted through his teeth and Strifbjorn sucked him, though he gulped slippery bitterness. He kept at it while Mingan rocked against him, still hard, until he finally hauled Strifbjorn's hair and his savagely enough that Strifbjorn let him pull away. "Lie down for me," he whispered, harshly. Strifbjorn rubbed his face against his belly behind the coarse rasping veil of hair.

Strifbjorn let go of Mingan's hips and unlaced his own cuffs, shook Mingan's hands from his head and pulled off the shirt. He stood and tossed boots and trousers atop Mingan's, then kicked the bearskin cloak out flat for a bed. And as he had asked, Strifbjorn lay down and helped Mingan fuck him, naked under the cold mountain sky, the light from his eyes and the light dripping from his collar beading on their skin like a dew of sweat.

The Wolf

Some time later, Strifbjorn lifts his head from my shoulder, grins at me. "Thou'rt the one who insisted we keep her chair on the dais."

My lip curls slightly. "It's thee they'll follow."

"I know." Anger creeps into his voice. "This hiding demeans us."

"And they need thee."

Slowly, he nods. "When this is settled. When the Lady has her hands on the reins and we see that she's fit to rule . . . I'm done. Six hundred years is enough to play war-leader."

"If thou dost admit to me, thou wilt be outcast."

"I don't care."

I do.

He reaches for the comb. "Come here. I'll do a better job on your hair."

He does, a ladder plait in five strands that hangs only to the small of my back. My heart is troubled, but my step is lighter when I return to the pack, at dusk. I know before I reach the clearing under the boughs of the copper beech that something's wrong.

The scent of the girl in the russet cloak hangs on still air. I skip a stride, stumbling into a run, but halt amid the big tree's curtain of autumn-crisped leaves before I venture into the clearing. Cautious of ambush.

She is backed up to the bole, the pale cub crouched laughing at her feet. The rest of the pack—farther away—sit, lie or pace about her. The red bitch sidles up to me and thrusts her cold nose against the palm of my hand. Strifbjorn's scent does not make her snarl. She is accustomed to it.

I tousle her ears and focus on the girl.

She stands on the tips of her toes although the pale cub is not close. His plume wavers in amusement. Her eyes are shut. Except when she steals a glance at the cub, then closes them again.

I walk into the clearing. The adolescent cub stands as I come up, laughs once more and strolls away. He vanishes into the darkening wood. The girl's eyes are closed.

"Thou art safe now, lass," I say.

She jumps, clutching her small bundle to her chest, and opens her eyes. "M-Master Wolf!" she stammers, glancing around as if seeking the cub. Then her eyes come back to me and widen.

I chuckle, wander a step closer. "Fear not. Thank thee for the flowers and the cake, but thou shouldst not be here. Darkness comes."

"Oh, aye," she says. "I came . . . to thank you in person. And to ask, are you . . . a woods-spirit? Must we honor you some way?"

I crouch amid the leaves. She comes a step away from the tree, feeling safer as I make myself smaller. It works with most animals, and humans are no different. "I need not be propitiated."

"Hagrim the Baker has told my father that you are an evil spirit, and that he saved me from you."

"Thy father has not heard of the children of the Light?"

It takes her a long while to decide what she will say. "My father is . . . he is a good man, Master Wolf. But he is angry."

"Angry thou wert saved?"

Her eyes tell me that there is more, but she will not say it. At last, she shakes her head. "He wishes me to marry Hagrim, who is a widower. And Father says the einherjar do nothing to earn what they take from us."

Interesting. "And what does thy mother say, lass?"

Her pale face grows whiter. "My mother died when I was but little."

"Should I be concerned by thy father's anger? Does he threaten thee, lass?"

She lifts her chin. Young, just barely old enough to be thinking of marriage and babies. She still has the pride of youth on her. Hard work and birthing will strip that quickly enough. The human fate—and no matter how we strive to better it, they are at the core doomed to suffering and a quick death.

Better to be a beast in the wood.

"I thought to tell you that he might threaten you, Master Wolf. And my name is Rannveig, if you do not mind. The woodcutter's daughter."

"Rannveig," I say softly. She steps toward me. "Return to thy village; look to thy safety. I thank thee for the warning."

She seems to want to say more, but it takes her time to shape the words. "And there is nothing more I can do to thank you, Master Wolf?"

I stand and mince a step toward her. She startles back against the tree with a gasp. *Braver than many, even to make the offer, to come here alone.*

"Thy thanks are understood, lass. Hie thee home."

I step aside. She bolts past me, down the narrow trail west toward her village. *Candle-flicker*, I think. *Such a brief, bright life.* I walk into the embrace of the tree, crouch against it where she stood, shake my plait over my shoulder so I can tug it with my hands.

In moments, my pack is around me.

The Historian

I recalled her the instant I saw her, with a shock of identification when a friend unseen for decades heaves into silhouette at a ridgetop, and one knows him by stride and stance long before his face is visible. Of course, I had never met her. Of course, I knew her not.

But I recognized her.

She stood at the clifftop, the light slanting around her, yellowing grass stirring about her knees and the blue-green skirts of her gown. She stared at the horizon, her fingers moving restlessly on a stiff cord. As I came up to her, I saw she plaited stems, and when she lifted her chin jewels in seven colors flashed against the cloud-white of her throat.

"You must be the skald," she said, and dropped her braid before her feet. "I am Heythe."

"Muire," I said, and curtseyed, feeling as if I wore her stern and sober expression about my shoulders like a yoke. I waved past her to the empty sea beyond. "Were you waiting for someone?"

"The pursuit," she said. "I fear I've brought enemies among you, waelcyrge. It will not be long now. Their teeth scored my heels when I fled; they have pursued me from dead Midgard across all the worlds that hang like fruit upon the tree; and having come to you"—she shrugged, her braid-tip flicking from hip to hip with the shake of her head—"I can flee no longer."

"Enemies?"

"Giants. Giants of frost and fire, armed with axe and hammer. They will come in my wake, and lay waste to what they find, for they care only for destruction. They are the last remnants of the armies of chaos, as you are the last remnants of the armies of the Light."

The silence dragged, the cry of gulls, the hiss of the sea far below. I was surprised to hear myself answer, "We were made to stand with you. We were sent ahead for that purpose, to await your coming. We remember that; the Wolf remembered, and Strifbjorn."

Even in profile, I saw the corner of her smile. "And will you stand with me?"

I knew she didn't mean *me*. Frail Muire, the least of the brethren. "I do not speak for the children, Lady."

Lady. And whence *that* conviction?

She turned in place to face me, her train a puddle at her feet. "Strifbjorn speaks for the children."

"Yes," I said, and watched her shoulders settle under the gown like waves rolling back down the sand. "We have always followed Strifbjorn."

5

Threshold-crossing   full foe-heedful
Unsounded doorways   lead to dark doings
Lurkers loiter   and lancing strike
                                   —*Hávámál*

The Wolf

Days later, Yrenbend smiles and reaches out as I approach the mead-hall door. I clasp his wrist. "Another day, another mystery," he says.

Muire stands beside him, all startled eyes and dark blond braids. She ducks when I share my smile, but flicks a small one back. She's not pretty, but has an interesting face.

And I'm so pretty myself, to judge.

Whatso'er she overheard in the wood, she's kept quiet. When she might have used it for blackmail. Or revenge.

Muire and Yrenbend follow me inside. The hall is crowded—more brethren than our own attend. Menglad and Arngeir hold hands near the unlit fire trench. Yrenbend falls into step behind me, Muire silent beyond him. "Has our new Lady returned yet from her errands?" I ask.

"Briefly," Muire says.

I glance over, surprised that she deigned to speak. She adds, "She spoke with Sigrdrifa and some of the other waelcyrge who favor her, and with Strifbjorn for a little; then she rode off again."

"I do not like this coming and going," Yrenbend adds, with slow consideration.

"You do not trust her?"

"Brother Wolf, I do not trust anyone."

We pass the length of the hall. The dry pine boughs from the floor have been swept out and replaced with rushes and sweet hay. At the top of the hall, Strifbjorn sits on a bench, ringed by einherjar and waelcyrge. His attention is on Sigrdrifa, with her narrow shoulders and bright hair.

I enter in the midst of the conversation.

". . . the Lady proposes sense," says Sigrdrifa. "We toil on behalf of the mortals, protect them at risk of our lives, end their wars. Why should they not pay us just tribute?"

"Other than the thralls they send to serve us?" Strifbjorn leans back, seeming at ease. But I can translate his furrowed brow. "Food we do not need, gold we have no use for . . . and not all of them are pleased with arrangements as they stand. What could they pay us in, then?"

"Souls."

Beyond Yrenbend, Muire gasps.

"Not in my hall." Strifbjorn stands, commanding the room. He looms over Sigrdrifa, though she squares her shoulders and stands tall. "Not while I live."

Silence follows.

And Sigrdrifa speaks through it, gesturing to the banner on the wall. The grasping Raven floats bold in black on its white weave. "The Lady comes on the wings of crows. The war that follows her we can win only if we obey her without question."

Strifbjorn steps forward, sharp-scented in his fury. His hand is not on Alvitr's hilt, but his fingers curl toward it. "The Lady," he mocks, "who must be followed without discussion or recourse? Is that what I taught you?" He glances at me. "Is that what the Grey Wolf taught you?"

I step to his side, and Yrenbend and Muire are behind me. Four to one.

"We see the Banner. We saw her perform the seithr." Sigrdrifa draws herself up. "You saw her perform the seithr. Do you deny the truth of it?"

Four to two: Skeold comes to stand behind Sigrdrifa, frowning.

"It's radical," Skeold says, before Sigrdrifa can answer. "But the Lady has come, as promised, to lead us. Is it not as the Grey Wolf said? Has she not proved herself by might of arms?"

Strifbjorn shrugs massive shoulders, shifting his fur cloak enough to show that his hand rests now lightly on Alvitr's hilt.

But surely he will not draw his blade in threat? Not against a child of the Light.

"But she hasn't challenged me directly, has she? And we haven't had a flyting yet." Strifbjorn smiles a slow, arrogant smile. "You seem to have chosen your mistress, Sigrdrifa. Extend to her my challenge, if you please."

The Warrior

Sigrdrifa would've stared Strifbjorn down if she could, but she hadn't the will. She stepped aside, implicitly accepting his order and authority, and when she went Skeold didn't follow. Instead, Skeold ducked Strifbjorn's gaze and backed away, her midnight-blue cloak furling from her shoulders with the haste of her gesture when she finally turned.

With Mingan, Yrenbend, and Muire, Strifbjorn held the center of the floor. And around them, the children pretended with great business that they hadn't seen a thing.

When enough time had elapsed, Strifbjorn turned to his allies. Muire gave him a quiet smile when his gaze came to rest on her, then glanced away, ostentatiously distracted by some movement across the hall. With a mumbled excuse, she fled.

Yrenbend followed Strifbjorn's regard as it followed Muire. "I don't have to tell you her feelings. She's worthy of any einherjar in your hall. Don't spurn her because she isn't tall and fair."

Strifbjorn glanced up at the Banner hanging behind the Lady's chair. The breath of wind that had flicked Skeold's cloak stirred the restless Raven. "It's a bad time for marrying, Yrenbend," he answered. "But if I were about to, I would certainly heed your counsel and Mingan's above all else."

Mingan's eyes met Strifbjorn's. He gave a mocking half-smile. "I cannot fault her courtesy, her courage," Mingan said, glancing at Yrenbend, who was looking at Strifbjorn, "or her discretion."

Something in his always-layered tone implied a deeper

meaning. The shard of the Wolf Strifbjorn carried within supplied an explanation.

Muire the Historian was keeping their secrets.

She stood before the Lady's chair, facing the Raven Banner. Her back was slim and straight, despite her small stature and her shyness. Strifbjorn frowned at Mingan. "After the war, perhaps. Whatever war may come."

He snorted. "What Sigrdrifa said about souls. Explain, please?"

Strifbjorn couldn't. He shook his head and concentrated on peeling his clenched fist from Alvitr's hilt.

Yrenbend cleared his throat. "Heythe has said that we will not be strong enough to defeat the giants—"

"Giants." Mingan's disbelief couldn't have been more polite, or more archly evident. Strifbjorn loved him with all his heart.

"We must, she says, use our kiss to draw the strength from mortals."

"As we do," Mingan said. "When we avenge them."

"No," Yrenbend replied. Strifbjorn watched the Wolf's eyes narrow. "She would have us take every breath but the last. Take their strength."

"Slay them," Mingan said, stating flatly what Yrenbend couldn't quite force himself to give voice to. "Steal their lives."

"Yes," Strifbjorn said. "Is that your Lady, Wolf?"

He placed his gloved hand on Strifbjorn's arm and gave him an odd smile. This one Strifbjorn didn't understand at all. "Oh," he said. "Yes. I dare suggest it could be. Do we expect Heythe soon?"

A fey half-answer. Chilling. "She seems to move at her own whim, like the wind . . . and fast, as if she travels on music. She's contacted several of the brethren who then returned here—Sigrdrifa, for example."

"Obviously," Yrenbend said. "She's always been hot-tempered. But something moves her to fury with you personally. Forgive me for speaking bluntly, but I wonder"—his voice dropped—"about her promise that she is pursued by giants. What if the war the Banner predicts is one between us and Heythe?"

"She is the Lady," Strifbjorn answered.

Mingan's cold little smile continued, twisting on his lips. "She is indeed. But is she . . . our Lady? Or another one?"

"*Another* one?"

He shrugged. "Many things are possible. She is stronger than any of us, yes. But so is the Bearer of Burdens, whom we serve. And the Imogen, who serves us. Strength is not all, my brother."

"It is to her. That she'd have us fattening on the mortals, poor candle-flickers, as if they were cattle. That smacks to me of a worship of strength."

"It's exactly that," Yrenbend concurred, and Mingan, though motionless, seemed to take a half step away.

"What troubles you?"

He shook his head once, tossing his streaked black braid over his shoulder. "A worship of strength," he said, and would speak no more.

In the morning, Heythe returned to the mead-hall.

The Wolf

The drink is drunk. The dice and draughts are set aside at the waning edge of a long night of testing conversations and edgy murmurs. I watch as Strifbjorn leans back on the bench, stretching. The first sunlight slides through high, narrow windows, painting the ceiling. I wish I had spent the night with my pack, running in the wood.

The great doors swing open and Heythe comes into the hall. Sigrdrifa follows, chastened and uncomfortable. Heythe hesitates, scans the hall and strides directly toward Strifbjorn.

She has found better clothes somewhere. Green and gold, the colors of spring. The dark moss tint of her cloak makes her hair shine all the brighter, and the green contrasts with the brilliant blue of her eyes.

Sigrdrifa takes two steps to follow the Lady. But Heythe brushes her aside. The waelcyrge stops, her mouth downturned and sulky.

"Strifbjorn," Heythe says as he and I rise to greet her.

She dimples at him and chooses not to notice that he does not offer her his hand. Turns her smile on me. I do accept her hand, bow over it clumsily. "Well?" she asks.

"Lady," I say. "Hale, thank you."

"I should be most displeased to learn that I had done you lasting harm." She squeezes my hand through the glove, not flinching away, surprising me. "We'll need to stand together, all of us, when the time comes."

"Yes," Strifbjorn interjects. "That's something we need to speak on, Lady. I'm . . . uncomfortable . . . with what I hear."

"Yes," she says. "We must talk. May I sit with you?"

As if I had ceased, again, to exist.

He cannot in good conscience refuse her, so we three sit along the bench and speak quietly, Heythe in the middle. Sigrdrifa stands off to right, just within earshot. The rest of the brethren avoid us except for Herfjotur, who rises from the cross-bench where she has been attending her armor, and brings us drink.

"I flee a terror," Heythe begins. She sips her mead, then balances the horn between her hands so that she need not drain it at a draft. "I fled a land much destroyed by war—a war of the gods against the gods."

She glances at me for confirmation. Dizzy coldness swells at the base of my skull. I must remember not to gasp for air, remember I am not being strangled. My collar binds tight as a noose, and I force myself to breathe only lightly.

Fighting the snare only deepens the wound. One must lie in wait, hoarding strength until the hunter returns.

I shake the vision from my head. Less than a memory, more than a fancy. Only a moment has passed.

Heythe speaks still. "The battle was fierce, and I thought"—she glances at me again—"that only I escaped. But the Wolf here, he is also from my world."

Strifbjorn gives me a narrow-eyed look. "Keeping secrets, Wolf?"

"I recall it not. . . . No. Not precisely true. I recall snow, and hunger and falling. And then the song, and the land. That is all."

Heythe seems to study me. "And you recall nothing of the time before the ice? It was a hard journey getting here, and I would not have survived it without this einherjar's help. In fact, the cloak of falcon's feathers I used to fly here did not survive the journey." She nods to Strifbjorn. The war-leader regards her much as a bird regards a snake too near its eggs.

"Not . . . clearly," I say, and stammer, because she places her left hand on my right thigh, above the knee. She smells of moss and fallen leaves. She turns quite indifferently to pin Strifbjorn on a look.

She slides her hand the length of my thigh and lets it slip into her lap again. I am stiff in my seat for a long moment after she no longer touches me.

She might have forgotten I was there. "You're troubled by what, Strifbjorn?"

"Ugly rumors I would like you to dismiss."

His words hang. She waits, leaning in. I draw slow breath, willing myself to sense anything—some shift in the wind bearing scent or sound—to say where the danger lies.

He does not fill her silence. I applaud him his control. Eventually, she leans a little more toward him and murmurs, "Rumors?"

"You mean to fat your army on the souls of innocents."

She does not laugh, though for a moment I would expect it of her, like the villain in a saga. She sighs, and says tiredly, "Innocents? No. Criminals and captives. Waste not, want not."

"Lady"—Strifbjorn, his own horn drained, folds his arms over the table—"although I owe you service only after the Bearer of Burdens, I will not stand silent."

She stands and quaffs her drink as well, and lays down the horn. She places one hand on his shoulder and one on mine. Her nails graze my neck. A shiver follows.

She leans close to him, not me, and speaks into his ear. "Strifbjorn. You'll understand, I promise. We'll need that strength—your strength—when the giants come."

Then she pats him on the shoulder, lets her other hand brush down my arm and turns and strolls away.

Strifbjorn turns to watch her go. He lifts her horn and

stares into the dip until it cracks in his white-knuckled fist. The pieces he places on the table with a long and eloquent sigh. "Wish she'd keep her hand off my thigh."

I sigh as if in agreement. But know not if I agree, or if I crave the touch again.

The Historian

Of the mead-halls, Strifbjorn's was oldest, largest, and of the most primitive construction. The outer walls were turf-chinked log, and within, against them, we had each an alcove for our tools and clothing and whatever things we did not hold in common. The alcove walls only stretched a little above head-height—for Strifbjorn, that is; they were quite taller than me—and each niche was closed by a curtain.

My own niche was thick-walled with the old texts, and my bench laid over slabs of rune-etched stone, and my books filled the next alcove as well, which had been ceded to me by an amused Yrenbend when he joined his fate to Brynhilde's.

I needed the soporific of work, and I needed to be away from Strifbjorn—and the Grey Wolf as well. I had drawn a table and a sand-tray outside into the meadow, to write under the clean, pale light of the wintering sun. The book roll I was working on lay pinned flat with lead-stuffed leather weights as I bent over it with my pens and colors. No gold leaf out here where the breeze would tatter it in instants, but with my finest brush and a clamshell of crimson tempera I was succeeding in bringing light into the heart of a page of verse.

The letters were designed for scratching in wood or stone,

and we still did so when carving a spell in a stick or a ring. But they paint as neatly on vellum, and it makes for tidier storage.

I loved the work.

I was not the only one distracting myself with mundanities. The rhythmic belling of steel on steel rose from the seaward side of the mead-hall: Ulfgar the blacksmith at work on the forge I also used for my instruments and sculptures and bits of jewelry. A comforting, domestic sound after recent turmoil.

Herfjotur emerged from the hall perhaps a quarter hour after Heythe entered it. She waved as she passed; we shared a worried glance. This was not how it should have been—the brethren divided by one who should have unified. But as we looked at one another, Heythe followed Herfjotur from the mead-hall, and so nothing was said.

I did not watch the Lady. But, tempera thick on my brush, I turned on my bench and watched Herfjotur pick across the crisping grass. She stopped a few dozen yards past me and casually held out her arms. A shimmer raced through the air, weft of silver across the warp of daylight, and her valraven stood before her.

The great steed was horselike in general form, two-headed, enormous wings translucent as quartz half-spread as he stepped out of thin air. Herfjotur took the last two steps to him and threw her arms around one of his necks while he bobbed his heads—one horned and one antlered—over her back.

I didn't know his name, of course: the valraven were few, and gave their names only to their riders. Each was different; Yrenbend's Brynhilde partnered a steed like a miniature dragon, all pale wing-leather and blinking gold eyes.

Not for such as me.

I looked away, to give them privacy, and saw Heythe staring as I had been. As if she felt my notice, she shook off the seeming trance and stepped forward, whistling jauntily, veering slightly to pass near my table. I did not look down. And she returned the stare.

When someone's eyes are said to be sky-blue, how rarely is the true color meant, in all its implications. Hue and darkness, and a certain transparent depth. It is not just blue; it is a blue you could pierce, sound, sail up into.

Heythe's eyes were colored like sky. And something in the reaches of them brought a vibrant flash, the vivid memory of a foundry pour.

I tilt the crucible, metal flooding out in a silken river. It had always been difficult to resist letting it splash across my hands like icy water—so fluid and so bright. I was waelcyrge; fire could not burn me. And this fire is so close and so real that the heat warms my skin and the stink of hot metal and char fills my nostrils.

The mold tops too quickly, metal bulging at the rim. Some spatters the floor, catching a piece of planking alight. I stamp out the flames, the metal sprays from beneath my boot, falling, freezing in the shape of a splash, red cooled to silver, still too hot for human touch.

I blink. Blinked.

And Heythe's gaze slid from mine, her expression haunted by unspoken terror or wrath, and the seething metal receded from my awareness.

But the disturbance roiling my stomach remained. Heythe walked toward the cliff over the sea, and I turned away to see that a drop of tempera had fallen from my brush to splash the history.

It was easy enough to repair—hide could be scraped—but

I must wait until the paint was dry. My peace and focus, in any case, had been shattered, and there was no hope now of a steady hand. I sighed and sat back on my stool. The half-finished manuscript held no more charm for me than three-day-old porridge, so I brought it in and weighted it on my bench to finish drying. A second trip to bring the rest of the tools in also allowed me to fetch my cloak and Nathr.

Strifbjorn bent close to Mingan's ear at the south end of the hall. I was too far away to hear the conversation, but I saw no need to stare like a child, and looked around for anything else to occupy me as I crossed and recrossed the hall. The Raven Banner caught my eye; I stopped my fingers from absently rubbing Nathr's smooth, cool pommel.

There are times when the last people one wants around one are one's beloved family.

Ulfenfell beckoned. I hiked up the rock-scaled trail past the scholar-tree and a stand of white birch with their bare branches catching the late autumn light like fingerbones. Higher, firs and cedars clustered beside the trail. I saw the tracks of deer and wolves as well as smaller beasts, but no tracks from the gray-booted feet I knew used this trail as well. *Might as soon call him the Grey Ghost, for all the trace he leaves of his passage.*

A cold thought, and I shivered. This was his wood, his mountain. Ulfenfell, rising stark and green and silent from the very edge of the sea. His demoness dwelt on its heights. The Imogen was another one of those mysteries from before the First Day, a creature bound to him by some ancient debt or magic, a winged avatar of appetite and fury. I had seen her twice: once on the First Day, a shadowy glimpse of a thing like a feathered razor, and again many years later, when she was called to war for the first and only time. A living scythe. Our weapon of last resort.

We had made sure never to need her again. I could imagine nothing that could stand against her, except perhaps the Wyrm, the Bearer of Burdens itself.

I paused to listen to the cold wind scraping branch on branch and rustling the desiccated leaves. It was not yet noon, but under the shadow of the conifers twilight ruled. I lengthened my stride, bending into the slope as it became more extreme. Something slipped away from me through the underbrush—a deer or a boar, I thought at first, but those crash or rustle, and whatever this was glimmered cloud-white and silent, just a flash. I stopped, one foot raised, hoping to catch another glimpse, but there was nothing more.

An hour along, the wind brought the distant ring of voices— two men, arguing, and a woman calm and coaxing. There was no threat in their tone, although I could not make out the words, and no *swanning* urged me to hurry, so I left them to their own pursuits. The wind was cold in my hair as I climbed.

Some time later I found their footsteps on a cross trail— they had come upmountain from the village of Dale, probably with the dawn, and returned along the same a few hours later. Squirreling, probably, or after bigger game.

I stood on the silent shoulder of the mountain, watching the sunlight slide between the ferny branches of the firs to dapple the hard ground. I took a breath seasoned with the scent of ice.

Then I spun in place and walked down the side trail. Not homeward but toward Dale, nestled among the roots of the mountain.

The Wolf

When I leave the hall, I smell her before I see her, a scent that should be perfume. I know it is not. She awaits me beyond the birches. I stop when she comes into sight. "Heythe."

"Hello, Mingan." She steps from the shadows of an ancient red oak to greet me. Afternoon sunlight silhouettes her, tangles in her amber hair, glitters from the gold threads and jewels of her necklace. "Or do you prefer 'Wolf'?"

Her face lies in shadow, but I can hear the smile in her voice.

"As you wish it, Lady."

We're of a height. As she comes toward me she tilts her head to one side, so I can see her features.

I would back away growling. Were I not a man. Or the masquerade of one.

She stops, hand extended. "I would not try to trap thee, Master Wolf, bind or change thee. But I ask thou considerest my offer."

"What offer is that, Lady?" Her scent wreathes round my head. Musk, and a field of pungent flowers. Heady, not sweet.

She holds my gaze, lets her hand fall fluidly to her side. "You have Strifbjorn's ear. My presence threatens his power." She shakes her head, turns her eyes aside. She takes a half step closer that is matched by my half step back. "But you are his friend."

"You wish me to witness to him?" I need not force my chuckle. If I would do so, Strifbjorn would not hear me.

"No. I want you . . . to serve as a liaison between us. To hear my thoughts and his thoughts, and with your own judgment bring us to compromise. Is that so hard a thing?"

It's sense, I think, while we live under the wings of the Raven spread wide on the Banner behind her chair. "Have you spoken to Strifbjorn?"

"I need someone to smooth over the rift created by Sigrdrifa." She shakes her head. She sighs. "She's not the sense to grasp a sword by the right end. Wolf—"

"Aye, my Lady?"

"I'll treat with you. Do this thing for me, which costs you naught and serves your brethren, and I'll see what I can learn about . . ." Her fingers tap her own white throat, and the nails that click on her necklace might scratch my flesh, by the shiver they draw along my spine.

I cannot breathe to speak. As if she twisted my damned collar with those damned white hands.

Again.

Her bones, so fragile. Moving under the skin of her wrists. I must not clutch my throat. I *will* not.

And I will not give her Strifbjorn, even for that. Even for freedom. Not Strifbjorn.

But perchance, anything else.

She smiles, shakes her head again, brushes my panic away with the unfurling of her hand. "I may have resources you do not."

The collar chokes me still. My voice rasps. "You . . . would vow to make the attempt?"

"I never . . . the Aesir bound us all, one way or another. Whatever you did, in the end—it was not unprovoked." She touches my sleeve. I tremble. "You deserved better, and your sister and your brother, too, than to be cursed for a prophecy and an unfortunate paternity."

"I do not recall, Lady," I say—although her words stir answers in me, to questions long-fallow and sharp as shards of ice. "What is it that you would have me explain to him?"

She sighs, as she is sighing much. "I don't propose to treat humans as cattle. But we take thralls in tribute; we kill in battle; we kill in defense of the innocent and our own lives. How is it different to take our enemies' mortal strength before they die?"

"It is wickedness."

"Why is it so?"

"Because . . ." *we know it to be. Because we know what the kiss is for, and that, it is not.*

But. Kissing Strifbjorn was wickedness, too.

Heythe watches me before she smiles. "It seems poetic that the strength of our enemies should be made to serve us."

She reaches again, strokes a finger down my cheek. I know her disquiet, pride, resolve . . . and another thing. A thing I've only felt under Strifbjorn's hands.

Desire.

I know her surprise only when I feel it in her, for her face gives no sign. She adapts quickly, her voice under my skin. *Is that so surprising, that you should be desirable?*

Yes. My hand, innocent of its glove, catches hers. I move her fingertip from my face, but still we are skin to skin.

Still, she speaks aloud now.

"I think"—softly—"that I would like to kiss you again, Master Wolf. When you are not trying to batter me into unconsciousness."

She shakes free as I stand, silent, watching her sky-blue eyes. She smiles and drops her gaze, as if suddenly shy. "But,

I think, after you have made your decision. One way or the other. If you want."

Not choking, this time, but my tongue won't shape words. She steps back, tosses her braid from side to side like a very young girl. After a stretched moment, she says, "Consider my offer."

And with that she brushes past me and continues down the trail back toward the hall.

I watch her retreat, turning my neck but not my shoulders, and when she has vanished behind trees I climb on. The distant scent of angry men colors a bitter wind, but they are not near and there is no blood-scent. I could attend them, but instead seek my pack.

Their scent leads me off the trail. I pick across a grove of young ash trees that have claimed a decade-old burn scar on the eastern side of the mountain, making my way toward the sea.

I do not smell him. But among the ashes, I see him.

Pale as a streak of winter sun slanting between branches, he stands fetlock-deep in winter-crisped ferns. His head is turned, to track my approach, the dully gleaming fluted spiral of his horn like carved and polished seashell. I freeze and he snorts, steam jetting from dark red nostrils in a muzzle white as the sand on the shore.

We stare. His eyes are enormous and dark, glitters of light in them like sparkles on a nighttime sea. Hardly daring breathe, I crouch among fallen leaves. Making myself small.

He is there like the sea is there.

Startle not. Startle not, my beauty.

He steps forward, tossing his forelock about the root of his horn, and his beauty does not strangle me. Muscle catches light along the curve of his neck, under the shining scarred hide of his shoulder. Oh, his scars. His many scars.

Healed pale marks among the ivory coat hearten me. They recall bites and kicks from equine teeth, cloven hooves. An old, canny stallion, and in his life there have been enough of his kind in the world to give him a fight for the mares.

I thought they were a myth from across the sea, but here he lingers in the failing sunlight, shaggy with winter's approach, mincing through sere undergrowth to examine me more closely. Not so cautious as a horse or a deer, and far more silent; before long the steaming breath fogs my face.

He breathes across me, and it smells of hay and moss and the lichens he's been gnawing from the tree bark. And then there is his scent. I know not how I missed it, for he stinks, rank musk like a civet. A warning; this is no meek grazer, but a beast wily and wicked-horned. Thistles and a brown maple leaf are matted into his beard. He bows over me as I crouch lower. Small. Small. Light glints on the impossibly fine point of his horn. He sights along it like an archer along an arrow, trains it on my eye.

"Silken-swift." The stink of him is like both goat and lion. "You grace me."

He shakes his head. The horn swerves from its killing angle, returns.

I might fence with him: Svanvitr's edge might be one of the few things in the world that could withstand the unworn spiral blade. It is sharp as if stropped, and there is no sign it has ever been damaged, though the scars are so thick along the crest of his neck—where another stallion might clench his teeth— that they show the pink of skin.

"I stalk thee not." Those old wounds try my heart, and before I think of the risk of doing offense I address him as a brother. "Neither will I hunt thee. Walk from here safe, under my ward though I be unworthy."

Mist wreathes his muzzle again. He steps forward, and now the horn is so near I cannot see the tip. There will be pain, a moment of pain. And then nothing, when the horn passes through my eye and enters my brain.

But he tilts his face aside so the horn only draws a line of blood like razor-kiss along my temple. His face presses mine, brow to brow, white-gold tangles falling into my eyes.

Blood trickles down, staining his creamy muzzle.

Unworthy? I think not, Wolfling. Pure as the will of the pack, thou art.

Thou dost speak?

Ah yes. He lets me appreciate the stupidity of my question for a moment. I wince, but have to argue.

Neither in body nor in soul am I pure.

And I feel him laugh. *Pure in love, pure in intention, pure of heart. The other is no matter. Like thee and me, 'tis but a metaphor given flesh. Guard thyself. Thou shalt be tempted, and thou wilt be made to choose. Thy path is not clear before thee.*

His muzzle is soft, the hide and hair on his temple coarser, oily. Greatly daring, I place my palm against his cheek. *Choose?* I ask. *We're not for choosing, einherjar. We're for doing the will of the Light.*

Aye. He blows out another sweet breath. *All things change, and always. Wolfling, speak to thy brother. Wolfling, look to thy pack.*

He dances back a step, shakes out his tangled mane, wild as a bull elk again. *Forever, and forever, and forever*, he says, though now I touch him not. Whirling on his hind legs, he is gone among the ashes as if he never was.

The Warrior

The long trestles could be taken up in sections when not in use, and stacked against the side walls of the mead-hall near the bottom end, where the niches stopped. The benches the brethren left intact, though the thralls moved them back from the center of the mead-hall, against the row of rough-hewn, smoke-darkened interior pillars that helped support the span of our post-and-beam roof.

Now Strifbjorn stood beside the eastern one, leaning back, shaking his head. Yrenbend sat before him, elbows on his knees. Herfjotur lounged next. She had kicked one foot up on the bench and was cleaning her fingernails with a knife, flicking each nail paring into the rushes.

"My steed has no counsel yet," she admitted. "But you may rely on our support."

Strifbjorn liked Herfjotur. She was solid, sensible and ferocious. And he liked her valraven as well: a steady sort, and more interested in einherjar doings beyond his relationship with his rider than other steeds. Strifbjorn should not need the reassurance of their approval. But it did him no harm.

"Thank you, Bright one," he said, without irony.

Yrenbend sat staring, lost in thought. Strifbjorn could not tell if he heard. But Herfjotur looked up from her toilet, giving Strifbjorn a pale, thoughtful stare.

"We know you, war-leader." A dismissive flick of her knife.

"The Lady . . . There is service and there is service, and though the Light is silent, you have served the Bearer of Burdens as long as we have known you."

Not in all things as he should, but Strifbjorn could not say so. He shrugged, accepting the compliment with the best grace he could manage.

Yrenbend turned and stared at her, frowning. Perhaps he was listening after all. "And there's an interesting question." A narrow line between his eyes deepened as he spoke. "Why is there no guidance? Why should the Light be silent on such matters?"

There was an air of the rhetorical in his question, as there often was. Yrenbend was quick of wit: Strifbjorn sometimes thought everyone bored him, except for Muire and Brynhilde. But Strifbjorn waited him out, and at last he relented, smiling tensely.

"Intervention," he offered, a word dropped like a weight.

Herfjotur set down the foot she had kicked up, scuffing the rushes about restlessly. She slipped her knife into its sheath and sat straight and silent for some time before she answered. "You mean to say the Dweller Within cannot speak to us because it is . . . opposed by something?"

The Wyrm acted through the brethren. They were its extended hand, fisted or open. But there were rules to bind it as well, and one was that it could not intervene directly unless it were paid for with a willing life, or it relinquished its immunity, sacrificed its immortality and took itself from the realm of myth. By placing itself on a mortal level, it would become subject to mortal laws.

It could then be made to bleed, or die.

Yrenbend was going where Strifbjorn had suspected. "If

the Bearer of Burdens intervenes, it could meet retaliation. From Heythe's giants . . ."

He need not finish. They'd seen not a sign of giants. But the Raven Banner did not lie.

"Unsettling." Strifbjorn chewed the edge of his thumbnail. The unfinished pillar caught at the fur of his cloak, tugging at his throat as he stepped away. Of course he thought of Mingan.

He'd walked three steps before he caught himself and turned back. Herfjotur still watched. Yrenbend glanced at the door, but no one entered. He looked back at Strifbjorn and made an encouraging gesture.

"Because it hints that what we'll fight—Heythe, her ominous giants or another problem—is enough of a threat that the Bearer fears to expose itself."

"What does that mean?" Herfjotur asked.

Yrenbend answered before Strifbjorn could. "It means we're expendable."

Herfjotur laughed. She stood and patted Yrenbend on the shoulder. Strifbjorn watched the muscles flex in her forearm. "We always were," she said. She pointed at the wall. "Besides, the Raven portends victory."

Mingan returned after full dark, wolf fur streaking his sleeves and cloak. He strolled casually across the hall and ended, seemingly at random, beside Strifbjorn. Strifbjorn stood near the unkindled fire trench, staring up at the torn and blood-spotted banners nailed to the beams overhead.

"Catinhame Ford," he said, following the war-leader's gaze to a green flag blazed with some foreign heraldic beast in white. "I remember."

They'd met a human host at Catinhame—dark islanders with names such as Tadg and Connla, a beautiful folk with purple-black skin, wielding greatswords and fierce in their kilted plaids. The broad, rocky ford had run red with blood; they fought well. The children had returned four swords to the sea at the end of it, one of which was the blade of Herfjotur's husband. But after three days of battle the invaders had been turned back. Brynhilde and Sigrdrifa guarded the surrendered survivors home, and sang a blight out of the corn.

It was easier than it could have been; they had been driven by hunger to conquer. The children had fought other battles less tidy.

As if distressed by Strifbjorn's silence, Mingan said, "That *will* be remembered."

"Not if we fail," Strifbjorn said. Strifbjorn caught Mingan's considering glance on the edge of his vision. Mingan knew what Strifbjorn was thinking.

"Love," he said, so softly his lips barely moved, "Heythe came to me in the wood today."

The piece of him Strifbjorn wore inside became a needle, stitched through his soul and tugged a thread hurtfully tight. Strifbjorn knew—how couldn't he?—that he would never be enough for him. All Mingan's longings and his sorrows were there under Strifbjorn's heart, only waiting to be taken out and examined in the light.

"And?"

He thought his voice stayed level, but Mingan's nostrils flared. He scented Strifbjorn's distress. His head swayed from side to side—not quite a negation, more a gesture of thought.

"She requested a mediation between you and her." With a gloved thumb, he worried absently at the side of his neck above the shirt collar.

"And what sort of bribe did she offer you?"

He turned to face Strifbjorn. Strifbjorn didn't look at him directly, but he saw the hurt expression in his Light-filled eyes. "I am not to plead her case with you, Strifbjorn. She requests only that I . . . help seek an understanding."

"I see." Strifbjorn did understand, when he could sense past the uncomfortable tightness of jealousy in his throat. "Giants. Do you believe her?"

Whatever Mingan had been about to say, the question arrested him. There was no fire laid in the trench; the hall was cool. The low sounds of conversation, a hammering from the smithy, the thralls singing in the kitchen as they prepared a meal filled his silence. His voice held wonder and worry when he spoke at last. "You propose that she is capable of *lying*?"

Strifbjorn hadn't thought of it that way. But it was, wasn't it? What he was suggesting. Einherjar, waelcyrge, did not lie. Could not lie, not and remain in the Light.

"Well," he answered, "I'm not assuming a damned thing yet, and that's—so far—my only decision."

6

✴

Blame not blindness where passion binds
Witching wiles weed-twine the wise
Where fools walk unwaylaid
                    —*Hávámál*

The Wolf

Above the cliff over my shoulder, the sun sets. I see it not. I move along the foot of the Ulfenfell on the narrow strand, stare at the ocean. From the mountain, my pack is calling.

They sing to me, as my brothers sing, but I cannot go to them. My task lies here with Strifbjorn, with Yrenbend and the rest. Unbidden, my thoughts settle on the quiet historian. When I turn them back, they circle on and fret after Heythe's offer, the strangling cord at my throat, the heat that burns under my breastbone. I will be on fire until I die, on fire and never burning.

I taste salt on the wind. The moon rises over the sea, not gibbous but larger than a sliver. I walk until it's high in the sky, casting a fall upon the water. Miles I walk, far from the mead-hall, until I come across the tide-washed causeway and under the lights of the fishing town of Northerholm.

There are still mortal men whoring and dicing about the town's three dockside taverns. It will do them no harm to be reminded of the nature of the world.

I step to the surf-edge. Waves wet the toe caps of my boots. I pitch my voice low, recite an old spell. "By moonlight, by earth and by ocean, Bearer of Burdens, I summon you."

Moonlight like mercury puddles on an ocean lain smooth. Faint cries ring from the docks. A pillar of neck rises, shedding glowing water, reeking of salt rot and ocean bottoms. It sways heavily, starlit eyes gleaming in a tendriled head—translucent, wrought of starlight and air, but the wind of its gestures dusts my skin.

The voice of the Dweller Within is soft and sure. LITTLE BROTHER. SUMMONED, I COME.

"It was thee summoned me, my brother." All I wish to say—of Strifbjorn, of Heythe, of the unicorn and of the pack—is lost in me. I have not words for the things that close my heart like the ribbon closes my throat, that all-but-stop speech and thought. "How may I serve?"

WITH THY HEART AND THY BODY, TO THE FULLNESS OF THY ABILITY. THOU ART THE FIST AND THE OPEN HAND, LITTLE BROTHER.

"Heythe?"

OF HER I MAY NOT SPEAK, UNLESS THOU OFFEREST SACRIFICE. THOU MUST THINE OWN WAY FIND, AND THE WAY IS CLOSE.

"Mere speech of her would be an intervention?" A foolish question, already answered.

The Serpent regards me wisely. I breathe myself full of sea-scent, and bow my head.

"I have been indiscreet, Brother. I have failed you."

Its benediction is a cool wall of mist. THE TIME FOR GUIDANCE IS ENDING. THE TIME OF CHOOSING HAS BEGUN.

"I regret . . ."

Nay. Regret not. Choose, and act and keep thy troth over all. It bowers me. I crane back to regard the whiskered jaw, the softness between the scales. What I may not reveal is your danger.

I can no more than hint at Strifbjorn. If I were a true child of the Light, I would confess, forswear, atone. But I am a wolf in einherjar's clothing, and my jaws are bloody.

"Even where I have pledged it unwisely?" I ask.

Have you?

I swear the great creature winks at me, tilting its long jaw. And then it slides into the looking-glass sea, and the men along the docks make their noises of fear and awe once more.

I turn and draw Svanvitr, saluting the men impulsively. The blade sparks like dry leaves blown into the flame, foxfire running her length, casting my shadow long on the strand behind me. A cheer arises from the dockside: they are too far to see the darkness of my hair, or the detail of the cloak that is gray and not indigo.

They might not cheer so, otherwise.

With that heavy on me, I douse Svanvitr and sheathe her, turning back up the beach. Turning away.

Still, the cheers ring in my ears for a long while.

I know Heythe's waiting for me before I see her. Her green herbal scent rides on the sea breeze, all out of season in the biting chill. Her scent alters like another woman's hair, and yet I always know it for her. I could step into shadows and dodge her. Run to my mountains and my pack. But longing binds me sure as my collar.

I mince closer like a wolf in doubt what den it enters. Heythe rests on the rough-hewn stone steps leading to the top of the bluff, one elbow propped behind her, looking out to sea. The night washes her of color. Her hair is pewter, her clothes all gray, her irises opaque and dark.

She sits up as I approach but remains blocking the stairs.

"Master Wolf." Her smile crinkles the corners of her eyes pleasantly. "How nice, you happening upon me."

And I am no longer certain if she was waiting for me, or merely enjoying the ocean and the night. "Evening, Lady."

She pats the step beside and below the one she sits upon, but I stand fast. She arches an eyebrow and does not repeat the gesture. "A lovely night."

"It is." I turn away and stare at the rippling waves.

She holds the silence a few moments. I can all but feel her cup it in her hands. Her breathing slows.

"I almost died out there," she says, exquisitely soft.

"But how can one such perish?"

"I came a long way, and I was—you have heard—pursued. The journey was not easy." From the corner of my eye I see her shake out her hair. "My falcon cloak brought me over the sea, but did not last to land. I'm a strong swimmer, but not that strong."

"I warrant, you are lucky. That Strifbjorn happened by, and that you are, as you say, strong."

Seeing that I will not come to her, she stands. She comes down the stairs and halts just outside reach. She shivers. "I owe him a great deal."

Though I turn, now her eyes find the tossing water.

She wears a surcote over a kirtle, the whole rope-belted. It is a modest costume, one not suited to the winter's chill. And unlike myself, she feels the edge in the air. I draw my cloak from my shoulders and drape it around hers.

She protests. I will not hear her.

"I need it not. The cold does not touch me."

Strange that a goddess should shiver, but what know I of goddesses? She smiles again, and draws it closer, fingers tightening on thick fabric. The silver chain of the clasp dangles free, swaying between her breasts.

I look away.

"Have you thought on my offer?"

Cold air cools the fire in my belly. "I have thought."

"And?" She slides a gray-sleeved arm from under my cloak, closes the distance to rest it on my upper arm. She leans in to me, nostrils flaring. Does she test my scent?

"Aye," I say. "I will do this thing. But I will not betray my war-leader."

She smiles. "He's more than your war-leader, Wolf."

I pull away, pulse racing against my collar. "What mean you?"

"He's your friend as well."

"Aye," I say. There is no heart in me, to make my voice sound alive. "As well."

She might be toying with me. She laughs; she might also be sincere. "Mingan. You look quite wild. You're not selling your soul, wolfchild, only aiding your master."

"My master. Yes." And I say I hate their fear of me, the mortals, the other einherjar. But now I face a fearless woman, one who I know can defeat me. And I am angry that she will not be cowed. I begin to turn, to brush past her, and halt. "By your leave, my Lady?"

"Of course. Your cloak?"

"Keep it until you come inside."

She dimples prettily, clutches it closer. "Thank you." And turns back to the sea as I hurry up the steps, feeling I go with tail curled tight between my legs.

The Historian

Although Dale was not far down the mountain, I had already all but walked the brief winter day out when I got there. It was a market day or some human holiday, which explained why those men had been wandering the Ulfenfell. Some stalls were still open to the slanting light of a westering sun.

Chill came with evening, and my measured paces carried me along a frozen, rutted street fronted by rows of thatched or bark-roofed cottages, each with a narrow window or two. Single doors, elevated to provide for snowfall, led out directly to the thoroughfare. I hadn't come to Dale in many years, and with the exception of a house torn down here and a new one built there, it didn't seem much changed.

There wasn't usually much here among the humans to intrigue me, and I couldn't say what twinge of the spirit made today different. It didn't come on a *swanning*, nor the summons of a perceived death. Rather, a nagging like something left undone and unremembered picked at the back of my mind.

The creeping sensation was reinforced as the villagers thawed away before me like snow in spring sunshine. I was not accustomed to the doubtful glances and the quietly withdrawn children, or the way the street cleared out before me. Furtive watchers tracked me through unshuttered front-room windows; a prosperous-seeming woman in a blue surcote hurried across the high road to escape me.

Something had happened here which should not have.

In the square, I stopped before a greengrocer's stall that was not yet shuttered and made a show of examining his apples: a half-dozen varieties, streaked or speckled, red and green or gold.

"A dozen of these, Master Grocer, if you please." I showed him the ones I wanted. The strains changed so often, over the centuries, that I never could remember the names.

He wouldn't meet my eyes when he gave me the apples in a sack. When my fingers brushed his in passing a coin, he flinched and dropped it. Then he apologized profusely while I ducked down and recovered it from the frozen ground. "Your pardon, Bright one."

"No apology required," I said, and slipped the coin into his apron, for his hands shook as if palsied. "Master Grocer, look at me."

He did, after two cringing attempts, trembling. "Bright one?"

"Be not afraid. My name is Muire. Tell me what endangers you, candle-flicker, and I will set that danger aside. I vow it on my sword, Nathr."

He took a breath and looked deeply into my eyes. "I'm afraid of you, Bright one."

I . . . recoiled.

I would not have welcomed it, but I might have expected minor rebellion or unease, although he did not seem the type. We who defend the world must always live in it. But *fear*?

Of me?

"Afraid?"

He nodded, eyes closed. I rolled my shoulders against the weight of my baldric and chewed on my words before I spat them out. "Pray tell, Master Grocer, *why*?"

"Another waelcyrge was here." He stopped speaking, and I waited him out, quietly eating an apple until he started again. It was crisp and sweet with the frost, juice like wine running down my chin. I sighed and offered him another coin. He stared, as if it glowed with heat, and glanced around.

"Carter hits his woman a little. Hit."

"My sister intervened?"

He shrugged with big, expressive hands. "She could have thrown him out and married again, see? Pretty enough, one little girl. Good cook and a hard worker, but she stays. You know?"

I spat out a seed. "Her choice?"

"These things are . . . , what they are." The shrug widened into helplessness. "The Bright one—she came through yestereve. Heard some shouting and went into the house. Dragged Carter out in the square, not fifteen feet from where you stand, Bright one."

"What did she do?" I dropped the core in the gutter.

"She . . . ate him."

I stared, stricken, but he seemed to take it for a demand to talk on. He blanched, and stammered. "And when Carter's wife ran out to defend him, she struck the Bright one and . . . she ate the woman, too."

It took me a long time to find my voice. "What do you mean, Master Grocer, when you say '*ate*'?"

His hands pinwheeled about each other and he stepped back, from my expression or the intensity of my gaze. Reflected starlight paled his face; my eyes must be afire.

How dare they?

"The Bright one—begging your pardon—put her mouth over Carter's mouth. Kissed him, sort of. I don't know her name, Bright one—I'm sorry."

How dare they?

Mortals had difficulties telling my brethren apart. "And then?"

"She almost seemed to—well, Lady, she just *sucked* the life right out of him, if you rightly know what I mean. And then she looked up, and her eyes weren't really *silver* anymore."

I leaned forward. He was taller than me, but he cowered. "Not starlit? What did they look like?"

He paused, afraid to give a wrong answer, and I waved him on. His words, when they came, seared me. "More like steel. Except, stained, you know? Sort of . . . tarnished."

"Oh, no," I said. "No, no, no. No, no."

I was halfway back to the mead-hall when I realized that I still clutched the sack with the eleven apples in it in my right hand. The grocer's final word rang in my head like the toll of a bell. *Tarnished.*

The Wolf

The night falls away as I enter the mead-hall, for all I would rather climb to the edge of the ice field and summon my sister, who could ease the ache in my heart. But it is not good to become too reliant on her kiss.

My brethren are assembled, although there is no formal council. Strifbjorn sits in his place at the head of the bench. The fires flare in the long trench. The rushes have been swept out and replaced with pine boughs, so the hall smells as it did for Menglad's wedding. The smoke from the fire and the scent of mead combine with evergreen sharpness in a strangling pall. None of my brethren—drinking in a strange silence—seem to notice.

I pace the length of the hall and swing my leg over the bench, beside Strifbjorn.

"Brother." I greet him as Skeold brings me drink.

Firelight turns his hair to copper. "Where have you been?"

"Having conversations." I drain the horn, sweetness cloying. "I shall tell you later."

"Ah." He's silent for a little while, watching our brethren move about the hall, clustering in knots for conversation. "You've left your cloak somewhere."

"I loaned it to the Lady."

Another angled glance. His tension speeds my heart as if it were my own, the drive for some direct and concrete action. I drop my gaze. *All I have to offer thee, my brother, is more negotiations and compromises. And no clean answers.*

"I see," he says, and then impulsively claps me on the shoulder, harder than he might normally.

I drop my voice low enough to carry to no other ears. "You are angry."

"Of course I am." He shakes his head. "Do you think you can play both sides of this and walk away unscathed?"

A sigh slips away from me. "I *hope* sides need not be chosen, Strifbjorn. That is the accommodation I will try to reach between Heythe and yourself."

He leans in to my ear, further lowers his voice. "We'll speak more later."

"Meet me on the trail." I stand to go. But am halted when the banded doors burst wide on their wooden hinges and our littlest sister stumbles in, falling to her knees among the pine branches. I vault the long trestle, Strifbjorn a step behind, but Yrenbend and Menglad reach her first.

Menglad waves her husband back when Arngeir, too, strides forward. Muire gasps for breath. We gather in a silent circle, Menglad helping the Historian to her feet while Yrenbend fetches mead. He tilts the horn to her lips. She steadies his hand with her own to drain it.

When she has had what she will, though, she throws the horn aside with enough force that it splits against the wall.

It is not fear that transfigures her.

It is fury.

I turn to follow her wavering finger. Sigrdrifa's eyes widen in startlement. Muire, though, unsheathes her sword and takes one heavy step. "Sigrdrifa, were you in Dale yestereve?"

Sisters fall away from the accused waelcyrge as Muire advances. The Light of wrath that flares in Muire's eyes, that flickers the length of her blade, is only a hint of her courage.

She's no match for Sigrdrifa with a blade. All know it.

Sigrdrifa does not even lay her hand on her sword. She stands straight and meets Muire's challenge with a cool laugh.

"And were I?"

"Some justice was carried out there that was not justice."

With sword-tip, Muire prods Sigrdrifa. Menglad, behind her, steps forward if to intervene. Yrenbend halts her with a hand laid on her sleeve.

"Explain yourself." A trickle of blood stains Sigrdrifa's shirt. "Level your charges, if charges you have."

"You slew a man in Dale last night, and his innocent wife. Both through means we term abomination." Muire's voice is a low snarl, her eyes live wells oozing of silver fire.

A gasp rises round the room, and is met by Sigrdrifa's mocking smile. "You challenge me?" Confidence, arrogance, in her light, cool voice. Even I might pause.

But Muire seems as if she could not care. "Trial by combat? Aye. Yes, I do."

"No!" Strifbjorn steps recklessly between the waelcyrge. He slaps Muire's blade aside. "No combat. No trial. Not tonight."

Unbelieving, they turn to face him. He jerks his fist toward the south end of the hall, the black-stained Banner unstirred by any breeze. "While that Raven hangs on that Banner, and while I am war-leader in this hall, there are no quarrels between us. Not until the war is fought. Understand?"

He holds first Muire and then Sigrdrifa on the barbs of his stare until each, in turn, looks down. An exasperated breath puffs his cheeks out. He snarls at the taller. "Excellent. Sigrdrifa, may I suggest you take a walk? Muire, Mingan." He glances around the room. "Yrenbend and Menglad. With me."

Rage drips from his stiff shoulders, apparent in the rigid set of his spine as he leads us to the south wall under the Banner. He speaks not, nor does he look back to see if we follow. At last he turns and faces us four.

"You three I trust to hear this," he says, indicating Yren-bend, Menglad and myself. "Muire, tell your tale."

Quickly and in a spare style, she gives us details of a crime committed. As she speaks, wrath swells Strifbjorn—or perhaps, the vaulted ceiling lowers. His breath is a growl by the time she finishes. Muire herself fights tears, rage dropping out of her like sunset draining the sky.

I could embrace and comfort her, had she not flinched from my touch before. But Menglad bridges the void and wraps her arms around Muire's shoulders, pulling Muire's face into her shoulder. It's only a moment before Muire controls herself and straightens, but in that moment Strifbjorn's eyes flicker to mine.

"Go there," he says. I nod, and turn away, seeking the shadows where my pathway lies.

The Warrior

Mingan vanished into the shadows, while Strifbjorn's heart thumped in the hollow of his throat. Mingan had meant to tell Strifbjorn something, and now Strifbjorn would have to wait to hear it. And a challenge stood still between Heythe and Strifbjorn: wits, not swords.

Unfortunately, not Strifbjorn's strongest suit.

He laughed at the truth of it, which drew a strange look from Menglad. "Thinking," he said. "Muire?"

The Historian stared still at the shadowed corner whence Mingan had vanished, but her name seemed to draw her back as if from far. "Aye, war-leader?"

"Sigrdrifa. It was she?"

"Who else? She did not deny it."

Strifbjorn looked at Yrenbend, who shook his head. "Too soon for a judgment." But the line between his brows told of more to say.

"And?"

"There are witnesses. We could bring her before the village."

Menglad rocked onto the balls of her feet. "Let the humans judge her?"

Yrenbend shrugged. "They won't be able to claim it wasn't a fair trial. Of course," and he grimaced, "such a decision would be under the purview of the Lady."

Muire rubbed temples with forefingers, head ducked. "Historian? You've a level head . . ." *usually*. "What think you?"

She looked up. Her eyes were bloodshot, and the Light glittering at the backs of them waxed chill. "If she's done this thing . . . *tarnished* herself"—the word stuck in Strifbjorn's heart like a dagger—"there must be ways to tell. And there were, indeed, witnesses. The whole of the human village, in fact."

Yrenbend, ever so casually, rested his left hand on Hjalm-meyjar's hilt. Menglad mirrored him, actually going so far as to draw Skogul from her sheath and examine her smoke-dark crystal blade. The waelcyrge, when she finally looked up, caught Strifbjorn's eye. He understood the message.

She was ever-faithful, and where she went Arngeir would follow.

"Tarnished," she said. "Ugly word."

"Yes," Muire answered. "Ugly happening."

Yrenbend reached out deliberately with his right hand and slit his thumb on the tip of Skogul's blade.

Blood, red and thick, ran down the bevel, dripped one glistening drop at a time into the white pine needles carpeting the rammed-earth floor. Menglad jerked the blade away and wiped her hurriedly. "Yrenbend!"

"That's what you talk of shedding," he said quietly. When he looked up he caught Strifbjorn's eye, not hers.

"Aye," Strifbjorn said. "I am. Lady or not. . . ."

Muire's breath came a little more quickly. She said, in bitter sarcasm, "Lady, no matter what. Right?"

"Would you follow me off a cliff, Historian?"

"The right cliff," she answered, a trace too fast. She gnawed the inside of her cheek. "We're not meant for this, Strifbjorn."

"Not meant for what?"

"Free will, deciding life or death. Policy. We're here to right wrongs and raise the humans to adulthood. How, then, if we are not . . . adults ourselves?"

Strifbjorn's gaze flicked unbidden to the corner Mingan had stepped into. "Some of us are more adult than others. And there comes a time when your parents cannot direct your life anymore."

He gestured over his shoulder to the glowering Banner. "Is this one of those times? You were eager to oppose Sigrdrifa earlier, for all she would have killed you."

Muire snorted. "Sigrdrifa is not the Lady."

"No," Menglad put in, polishing her blade on a bit of cloth. "But the Lady may support her." She gestured toward the door. "And, by the way, seems to have returned."

Strifbjorn's gaze followed the gesture. His neck tightened. Heythe still wore Mingan's cloak wrapped around her shoulders for warmth, clutched with one narrow white hand.

Strifbjorn's fingers fisted; Yrenbend put a cautioning hand on his shoulder. "Lady," he said. Then he sucked the blood from his healed finger, slipped the flute from its case with his other hand and walked toward Heythe with a skirling tune following his steps.

The war-leader sighed and looked at the two waelcyrge. "No more counsel?"

Menglad did not look back. Her eyes followed the tall Lady as Heythe met Yrenbend halfway up the hall. But Muire looked Strifbjorn dead in the eye and shook her head. He blinked at the shock of seeing her, suddenly, as an equal, not a love-struck girl.

"Right," he said hoarsely. "Then I'll see you all in the morning. I have an errand to run."

Yrenbend distracted Heythe. Strifbjorn made a straight line for the door.

The Wolf

I pause in the world between worlds, sheets of ash swirling about me like autumn leaves, cinders crunching under snow. From safety I can test the scents of the human village, filtered through the veil into dead Niflheim. One scent in particular seems a likely prospect.

Rannveig, the woodcutter's daughter. I turn in the shadows and seek her.

She sleeps in a loft above the packed-earth floor of her father's cottage, under the roof where the scant warmth of banked coals collects. The rest of the house is dark and still, except for the faint sound of her father's snores rising from his own bed by the fire. The cottage has no chimney, only a pit hearth under a hole in the roof. Two sheep, a shaggy goat and a bony milk-cow share the byre at the back of the dwelling. A long-coated dog lies against the railings, her feet twitching as she dreams.

I step from darkness, kneel on the narrow ledge beside Rannveig's bed. By my own pale light she lies revealed in slumber, sweet as a child, yellow hair tangled around fingers pressed to her mouth. I brush the strands away. She blinks, startles, jerks upright. Before she cries out I still her with Ansuz drawn upturned against her lips, the letter with branches downswept like a fir. Her lips shape words. Her eyes widen as the words make no mark on the smoky, beast-sweet air.

I bend low and speak against her ear. "Hush, child—I will harm thee not."

Her nostrils flare and she flinches against my glove, but she does not struggle. She nods, pressing three fingers against her mouth. I reverse the rune, making her heated breaths loud. "Soft," I whisper. "Lest thy father awaken. Dost understand?"

She nods again, shivering in her high-collared nightdress. I lean back, offering space, and try to soothe her with a smile.

"What do you want, Master Wolf?" She pitches her voice so low even my ears strain to hear it.

"Killing was done here, not long since. Didst witness?"

Aye. Just the shape of the word on her mouth. She presses her fist against her lips again.

"Wouldst recognize the murderer?"

"Yes, my Lord. . . ."

Not "Bright one." Never do they call me that.

The reflected glow of my eyes on her pale skin increases. She shrinks back.

"I pledge thy safety, lass. Wilt come with me, though 'tis a hard road, and frightening?"

She shakes, but it does not stop her throwing aside the covers and offering her hand. "Aye, my Lord."

I miss my cloak a moment, for I would wrap it about her shoulders against the chill of Niflheim, and too of the night outside. But all I have is the embrace of my left arm to pull her within, so the heat of my body can warm her. "We go," I say into her hair, and take her into the dark behind her little bed.

She quakes against me, stifling a scream, and I tighten my grip until she swallows the sob hovering on her lips.

"Where are we?" she asks, the words half-choked. She gags on char.

"The shadowed road."

"Niflheim," she whispers, and seems as if she will take a step away. "Where are all the souls?"

"Long gone. The gates stand open, the bridge unwarded. Midgard is wasted, and where the dead of Valdyrgard go . . ." I wonder if she sees me shrug by mine own light, or feels the movement on her shoulders. Cold. The cold must burn her; already, she quakes like a withy.

"Oh."

I had not expected—*regret*? "Thou art troubled?"

A brave smile as she turns back toward me. "I had hoped . . . to see my mother here."

"Ah." A long silence. Her bare feet curl into hooks on

cinder-studded snow, so her weight rests on the sides and not the soles. I lift her off them, set her feet on my boots as if teaching her to dance. "What became of thy mother?"

She huddles. I fold my arms about her, for once grateful of the acid fire at my heart. "Childbed fever. My brother, too. A waelcyrge healer came, but she could do nothing."

Because there was nothing to be done, I thought. Shy of asking for a marvel, and those came not free of risk. *So fragile, these candle-flickers.* Rannveig's father's wrath comes plain before me. We have gifts men cannot fathom. Is it a wonder they wit not our frailties, either?

"I regret it." I must set her on her feet again to lead her to the edge of the shadows, but when we have gone as far as we must, I let her step onto my boots again. She balances against my sleeve, leaning forward to peer through worlds into the hall of my brothers.

"Oh," she breathes. "Oh!"

Yrenbend and Muire have brought forth their flute and fiddle, and Ulfgar the blacksmith has a drum between his knees. Others have formed lines, face-to-face, and they dance through the flames of the fire trench while Brynhilde chants. Music casts light over the whole of it, her words and the mead-hall.

Sigrdrifa is not to be seen, but Heythe sits at the end of the hall, and laughing converses with Herfjotur. My cloak is thrown over the arm and the back of the Lady's chair. She leans back on it, unbound hair spread across gray wool as if her pillow.

I turn away and seek out Muire, bending into her fiddle, sparks of light flickering blue at her fingertips and the cap of her bow. Her face is alight. The music is a river to her, and

Yrenbend's flute skates over the fiddle as if on that river's ice. I draw a long, frosty breath.

"Is this where you live?" The girl's eyes shine.

"Nay. But these are my brethren. Was it any here?"

She takes care on the faces, staring each to each. But then sighs "no" at last. Her shiver is all but a palsy, her cheeks frigid when I lean my face to hers. Despite the loan of my stolen heat. And yet I need her eye.

"Canst withstand the cold a little longer?"

She presses close. "Aye, Master Wolf."

We seek Sigrdrifa. Her trail is easy, scent distinct and sharp with anger. In Northerholm she stalks a vacant pier, hurling shells into the sea.

"Her?"

The girl is chill not just at hands and face now, but her flesh cold under her gown. "Aye," she murmurs, a long moment after. "Her."

I hurry her to her bed.

Too cold. Even in the half-warmth of the loft, her teeth chatter. I catch her eiderdown up and wrap us in it, draw her against my chest, sun-hot beneath my shirt. "Thou didst well. Brave lass."

The nonsense one murmurs to a horse or a child. *Kenaz*, I sketch against her forehead, for warmth.

In time, she relaxes in my arm, the tops of her ears pinkening. I would step back along the narrow ledge and leave her by the bed, but as my arms unfold— "Master Wolf," she whispers, and kisses me softly on the mouth. Shivering anew.

Candle-flicker, I sorrow, and endure the kiss a moment.

"Nay, lass," I say. "Better a mortal husband for thee."

"One like Carter?" Her step forward matches mine back. I am halted by the edge of the loft. She comes up. "Your world is bright, Master Wolf." She reaches to my face, the eiderdown falling from her shoulders.

An outraged shout rises from thrashing bedclothes by the fire. We have awakened the woodcutter. "Not my world, lass."

I toss her—half-gently—into her little bed. And walk through the shadows, away.

The Historian

I set my fiddle in the case and smoothed the foreign red silk cloth over the eight-stringed fretboard—four for the melody and four to resonate. The face of my fiddle was dark red wood, inlaid with mother-of-pearl and ivory, and the neck and pegboard were intricately carved.

I closed the case and secured the latch with a click as footsteps rustled through the pine boughs toward me.

"Bright one, may I speak with you?"

I looked up to Heythe's translucent blue eyes and her open smile. She spread her hands and smiled wider.

"Lady, of course," I said.

"Walk with me?"

I followed. She linked her arm through mine and led me from the hall, along the cliff above the ocean, our twin trails dark through the frost-kissed grass. Heavy clouds hung high; a pale glimmer of moon shone through. Songbirds had fled; insects were dead with the frost. The dark and silence were complete, and I saw the path ahead by the reflected light of my own eyes.

We walked awhile in stillness before she stopped in place and turned to me, releasing my arm. "Muire. Skeold told me what you did. It was a brave thing."

"Pardon, Lady?"

There was no light in *her* eyes, but her necklace shone in the dark. I could not see if it caught my glow, or held its own. "Calling out Sigrdrifa. Very bold. I am impressed."

Impressed would not be what I would have expected. "Doesn't she support your proposal?"

Beyond the darkness of the cliff, I heard and smelled the ocean although it was invisible below.

Heythe flicked her fingers, arrogant dismissal. "I certainly didn't ask her to do what you think she did. That's what I want to talk to you about, actually."

"Oh?"

The waves sang into her silence, but she seemed at last to gather her thoughts. "Tonight has proved I need wiser counsel," she said, making a small helpless gesture. "If Sigrdrifa did this thing, then I will deal with her as she has earned. In the meantime . . ."

Fat white flakes began to drift between us. They struck the frost-silvered grass and clung. Their hush trailed between us while we watched. Childlike, Heythe caught a flake on her tongue and ate it; we burst out laughing.

"Winter is here." She spread wide her white-kirtled arms, the Grey Wolf's gray cloak swinging slack from her shoulders. "Better yet, after it will come spring."

I didn't understand her excitement, so I glanced down. The snow collected, only a patina on the soil so far. "In the meantime, Lady?"

She shook flakes from her hair. "I want you to consider your counsel, for it could shape policy. You have a good reputation with your sisters, Muire"—*I do?*—"and more, I like your courage and discretion."

"I see." *Discretion.*

I thought of what I had told Yrenbend I overheard between Mingan and Strifbjorn. I had been truthful when I said I walked away quickly. Our kind do not lie, but . . . we are not constrained to tell everything.

It should matter that he loves another, I thought. *It should matter that that other is the Wolf.* I wasn't sure if it did, if Strifbjorn would nonetheless consider me.

I made a show of my defiance, though, fists by my thighs and chin lifted. The rising wind brought the faraway cry of a wolf, and a bitter smile across my lips. Heythe raised an eyebrow at my expression, but waited quietly.

"My first advice would be to find whoever committed the abomination—Sigrdrifa or another—and punish her."

"Death?"

"Would you have her pay a weregild?"

"I will do this," she says. "How may it be prevented from happening again?"

"We are not accustomed to being called upon to make ethical choices, my Lady. We are accustomed to being guided by the moral compass of the Light. Punishment will serve as a warning to most. The rest—you must simply forbid them. Which would help you also to heal the rift between yourself and the warleader, and reunite the children of the Light."

"I'd first thought to marry him," she said with a widening grin. "To cement things. But I suspect we would make better allies than bedmates. The Wolf, now—what do you think of him?"

"For marrying?"

She nodded. "What else?"

I swallowed. "He has . . . a demon consort. A weapon. He feeds her on . . . something. His soul, his grief, though I little understand it. In return, she serves. To marry him would be . . ."

"To share him with his demoness? Ah well." Heythe scuffed the toe of her blue kidskin boot through the gathering snow. "I've shared with worse. Thank you, Muire. You have been invaluable, and I hope . . . we can speak again?"

"Yes, Lady."

Strifbjorn, I thought. If Mingan married, then Strifbjorn could, too . . . and then perhaps Heythe was not so uncompromising as she had been painted.

And perhaps I was being manipulated. Of course, that was a possibility, too.

7

Wolf weaned on   red war's carrion
Sanguine smears   the seats of gods
Sun scarred black   storms follow after
Would you know more?
                                    —*Völuspá*

The Wolf

Bare branches lace dark against moon-smeared clouds. I perch in the fork of an apple tree, remnant of a homestead long abandoned. The wind knifes through my shirt, tugging fabric. I must reclaim my cloak.

But later. After Strifbjorn.

And until he comes to me, I entertain my not-brothers.

They come to my call, wary and restive. The red bitch and her mate prowl circles around my tree. I swing to the ground and crouch, and the pale cub creeps to me, curls against me, his back pressing my knees. My glove between my teeth, I stroke his ears, scratching through winter-harsh coat. *Why such fear, cub?*

What I give is not words exactly; what he gives back is not words at all. A river of scents and sights, sounds and textures—the world, wolf-witted. He stands, whines, presses his nose into the crook of my arm.

And gives me the scent, the outline of two men, as from a

low angle and tilted crazily. They might tumble forward or back at any moment. So frail are we.

Two men. The woodcutter and Hagrim the Baker, whose name Rannveig gave me. His arm is in a sling.

The cub catches my snarl. *Trespassing in my wood.*

No. No wrath, no rage for territory. That is not a safe thought, for the wolves or the men. An they do no harm, they may walk where they list. And there is kindling to gather against winter, game to slay and smoke. But still. This is my wood. My pack. *Cub, the pack must stay in the summer range as long as the snow does not fall. They must not wander the sheltered valleys.*

He sniffs my face, his tail wagging lazy agreement. He turns and trots away, leaving me with a chill that draws no heat from my swallowed fire.

Men should not wander where wolves are, when wolves are where wolves belong.

Strifbjorn's scent vanguards him, and my pack become mist and shadows before he strides into sight. His head is bowed, broad shoulders slumping. I await him, one shadow that does not melt into the trees. The light kindling in his eyes when he sees me cannot conceal his grief and worry.

"Mingan." He closes the distance between us with three quick steps. "What news?"

"Sigrdrifa." I force a smile through my frown of concern. Ungloved, I clasp his hand. His hurt and thought and love spark across the touch.

Jealousy. And more. Lost, he feels, and stretched like a cord ready to snap.

"Ah," he says. "The provocation?"

I shake my head, my fingers closing tighter on his wrist. *Not enough.*

Could it ever be enough?

I know the answer he expects. It is not an answer I can offer him. I am thinking of the girl in the loft, her cold, dark life and how the bright mead-hall called her.

There are cities in the south—Freimarc, Drusban, Eiledon, Ayrie, peopled with tens of thousands. I wonder how a mortal girl of courage might make her way in those cities, and what such a girl could become. I understand such things but little.

But I know the face of one who is shown her chains.

I could rescue that girl from the muddy village of Dale.

Could it ever be enough? Strifbjorn asks twice. I withdraw my hand and pull up straight.

"Perhaps."

His brow furrows. He reaches out once more, laying his hand—this time—on my shoulder, where the cloth of my shirt comes between us. "Mingan . . ."

I step back. "Before you ask, I told her yes."

"Yes?"

"Yes, I will play the go-between. She says—" I touch my throat, and step back again. I don't need to explain.

"If she can," he says, meaning *if she can get the collar off*, "you should."

I wish he would pursue me, but instead he stands planted, oak of battle, glaring at the tips of his own boots. "I'm not sure there can be a mediation."

I lean my head to the side and study him—the straight nose, strong jaw, the worried pale eyes. Handsome beyond the meaning of the word, he has always before seemed to me as a thing carved of supple wood. Now I see in him a brittleness that frightens. "Should it not be our task to avert that, if possible?"

He licks his lips and at long last meets my gaze. The first flakes of snow speckle his queue. "There are principles I will not compromise," he says. "Don't make me choose between you and them. Oh, Hel. Mingan, when this is over, I may marry. I may play the dutiful child of the Light. . . ."

His voice trails off. He lifts his shoulders and crosses the few feet that separate us, but stops before he touches me.

"Sigrdrifa," I say, circling as wolves circle. "You must punish her, Strifbjorn."

He turns aside. "Your proof?"

"A mortal witness." Challenging. "A village full."

"After the flyting. If I still have the authority."

"Now, while you are certain you do." If he will not touch me, I will touch him. I grab his shoulder. "Now, brother. There must be penance. The other children are not *choosers*. They will follow who they think is strong."

We stare. He catches my chin in his palm. "You will always be the world to me." His voice is hoarse with the vow. "No matter what happens. And I beg you, understand me. Understand what I must do. And stand by my side."

Do not make me choose.

Mute, I nod. Strifbjorn kisses me roughly, on the mouth. Turns. Stalks away.

I watch him go, pain welling in my breast like a river under the ice of spring, so cold and so tight that even the burning pales. I throw my head back. If I were still a wolf, a real wolf, I would cry into the night. But the sorrow and hurt and all the sharp brittle love dam in my throat, will not flow free. I cannot howl.

I sob, and it chokes me.

When Strifbjorn is gone, my wolves come from the forest. The snow falls faster now, whitening dark branches.

The Warrior

The snow followed Strifbjorn down the trail like that last, soft sound of Mingan's. Broad flakes caressed his neck before they melted. By the time he came from the shelter of the trees, his sleeves and cuffs were wet through, the long guard hairs of his cloak frosted white.

I am losing him, Strifbjorn thought, *losing them all*. When he tried to push the thought away, it would not go. Apprehension tangled in his stomach, leaving him queasy and troubled.

It snowed harder in the meadow, big wet flakes clumping on the ground in piles and furrows. He shuffled through, letting snow cling to his boots. Wind stung his cheeks. Ahead, two figures crossed from the sea-cliff to the door of the mead-hall. Strifbjorn knew one by the gray cloak slung around her shoulders and the other by her height and slight build. The chill in his belly settled deeper while he watched Heythe open one side of the door and hold it for Muire to precede her inside.

Strifbjorn paused, considering the closing wedge of firelight behind the door, thinking of what Muire might know—what Mingan suspected she knew—and what she might have told Heythe. And then he thought, *You must trust someone*.

He shook his head. There was no one he could afford to trust. Not the little historian. Not Yrenbend, not totally. Not even Mingan. Squaring his shoulders, Strifbjorn walked on.

The mead-hall was quiet. Yrenbend and a waelcyrge named Bergdis were playing at draughts at the north end of the hall. Strifbjorn nodded as he passed. Yrenbend caught Strifbjorn's sleeve, a gold Lady glinting in his other hand. "She's pled weariness and claimed your bench," he said.

Strifbjorn had no doubts of whom he spoke.

"She sleeps?"

"And eats, apparently. She dined earlier."

That surprised the war-leader. "Whatever did you find to feed her?"

Turning back to the board, he placed his Lady on a white square. "Your pardon," he said to Bergdis, and then turned back to Strifbjorn while she studied the board. "The thralls keep the kitchen warm for their own needs. They eat better of a day than many in Dale do on feast-nights."

"Ah," Strifbjorn said. "Excellent, Yrenbend." A waelcyrge brought Strifbjorn a drinking horn. He nodded thanks before she returned to her sewing. Around the hall, Strifbjorn could see some of his brothers and sisters at draughts, or playing knife-and-peg or knucklebones. Skeold sat at the foot of the dais upon which the Cynge's chair rested, embroidering the hem of a gown, and Muire emerged from her niche bearing cloth for writing, pens and colors. From other niches, Strifbjorn heard soft sounds of conversation, lovemaking and what-have-you. His brother Hrothgar tuned a harp, seated on a stool in the corner farthest from the fire.

Strifbjorn's charge, and Strifbjorn's family. He turned to cast his eye over the lot of them, the length of the hall. *I'll get us out of this somehow.*

He slung his leg over the bench, sat beside Yrenbend and smiled at Bergdis. "May I play the winner?"

The Wolf

Sigrdrifa no longer paces the dock, but I find her scent there and follow her through the narrow streets of Northerholm. So large a town, it boasts three taverns—two more than Dale, which has not even an inn. Cold wrath takes me as I dance from shadow to shadow, a brave girl's shiver still a memory on my skin. Sigrdrifa is hunting.

And I am hunting her.

A large town—there is not just the high road to search, but several others—but her scent lingers. So before dawn I find my sister lounging against a piling along the waterfront below the tavern called the Keeping Gull. She watches the fishermen, who are already putting out to sea, though the east is barely gray. Sigrdrifa watches them, and I . . . watch her.

What Strifbjorn will not do, I shall.

"Candle-flickers," I say into her ear. I enjoy watching her jump and clutch the hilt of her sword. She whirls, but when she sees who stands at her shoulder her eyes narrow from surprise to rage.

Her furious hiss matches the sound of the sword wrenched from her sheath. "Come on Strifbjorn's errand like a cur?"

She's a strong one, Sigrdrifa, long and lean, with reach on me. I come inside it, Svanvitr in my right hand, angling her blow aside more slowly than I should. The cut lays flesh open to the bone across my upper arm.

"Thou hast scratched me, cat."

But strong as she is, I am stronger. Quick as she is, I am quicker. I beat her blade aside, glide up. I wish to step inside her reach. She must keep me at a blade length.

She laughs at me and rises to my casting, belittles me in her turn. "First blood. Wilt summon thy demoness now, and let a woman fight for thee?"

Our blades clash, rise and fall. The beach is stones and shells; they rattle and crush underfoot. I drive her toward the water, away from the shelter of the pier. If the men watch, they watch in silence.

Glide and sidestep, move smooth over the turning pebbles. Touch, provoke and dance. Our blades peal like crystal bells. Svanvitr flares to light—sharp, blue-white, so we duel in a ring of cast shadows, as if a sundial chased our nimble feet.

But Sigrdrifa's sword stays smoky-dark. I mark her cheek.

"I need no aid for such as thee—," I say. The collar turns my voice to gravel, or perhaps it has always been so. I have worn the ribbon so long I can't recall how I sound without it.

And I was a wolf then, anyway.

I turn Sigrdrifa's blade and grin. I lunge. She steps aside. She feints, moves in a whirl of ermine-trimmed cloak, parries. She's good.

Not good enough. No tricks, no brilliance or fakery. Just once, she is too slow, and I am inside her guard. I have her blade out of her hand and the point of my own under her chin.

"Bastard," she hisses.

I can nod at the compliment. "An legendry be true, aye, and borne of my father's body rather than my mother's," I answer. Now that she is captive, I can afford respectful tones. "And on to your own bastardy. A witness says you killed last night."

"I claimed justice, aye." Her eyes are dark as the night behind the stars. Svanvitr dents her throat.

"You killed for one who was not slain. And then killed the one you claimed to carry vengeance for. What justice is that?"

"You would slay your sister for a candle-flicker?"

My hand clenches on the wire-wound hilt of my sword. I would, aye.

But her life is not my life to take. I am not war-leader. Nor am I Cynge, or Lady.

I step a step away. "Not tonight. But forget not, Sigrdrifa, that it could happen."

She opens her mouth. With blade-tip I touch her lower lip so the bright blood springs up from that place.

"Hush. I've naught to lose. And it would please me to put an end to you."

She licks the blood from her mouth, in a fury that leaves her shaking. Her eyes flicker after her blade, and I could pray she reaches for it. But she nods, drawing her own blood, and I let Svanvitr slide from her throat.

"I won't ask for your vow," I say. A further insult. "But if I find thee hunting men, sister, thou shalt wish I'd sent thee to the embrace of thy victims."

I step away and sheathe Svanvitr. She speaks not. But when I turn I feel her gaze like a rapier in my back.

This last trip through the shadows exhausts me, and even I feel the cold. *Too much in one night.*

So far can I push, and no further. I crave Strifbjorn, but would he welcome my presence? He is at the mead-hall. Tonight I cannot stand the pretense.

I step from the shadows, north of the Ulfenfell, miles from the mead-hall. The coast is rockier here. The north slope of the mountain drops to a fjord-runneled stretch of coast which ends in a wall of ice half a mile tall. Greater mountains lie beyond the ice field, sword-edged in the darkness, catching the faint light of the stars.

The snowstorm is only on the south face of the Ulfenfell. Here, at the edge of the glacier, lichen grows on the till washed from beneath by summer melt, and icebergs calve into the northern sea. The glacier sucks dampness from the air, so the wind is not raw but knifelike, and there is only enough old snow on the stones to render them treacherous.

A broad neck of land points into the sea like an accusing finger. The moon has set. The east fades from silver to ice-pink as I choose a path on the ice-rimed cliff edge. Gray directionless light reveals the mane-tossing stallion sea five hundred feet below.

Sigrdrifa, aye, mocked me. And 'tis ungood to call my demon so soon again. But pain compels.

"Imogen," I whisper.

In some little while I turn south to witness her dark wings rowing, stark against the watery sky. She lands before me, her wings gusting loess and snow. Her eyes shimmer with morning-cold radiance.

"My Lord. I did think you would not summon me so soon."

She is needful as an infant, deadly as a knife. "Imogen. Do you hunger?"

She cocks her head, black-furred face intent, feathers soft. "Always, my Lord."

I close her wrists in my hands and draw her in.

The Historian

My eyes burned so I could barely discern the letters on the roll of close-woven cloth before me, but I clung to my brush. I'd laid quills and knives on the rough wood trestle-top beside the sheet of thick leather that smoothed the surface for my work. Candles and a chipped stone lamp and the dim light of my own eyes gave almost-adequate illumination, though if I had been acting intelligently I would have waited for daylight. But frustration drove me to quiet my brain by busying my hands.

Unfortunately, it also drove me to shaking so hard that I didn't dare touch the brush to the book. The knife-angled runes of the poem I was illuminating swam in my vision; a tear dripped down my cheek. I jerked my head back; it fell fortuitously in the margin.

But more water burned my eyes; I scrubbed it away with the back of my left hand and tipped my head back, breathing through my nose. The brush, laden with lapis pigment suspended in egg-white and grease, trembled in my hand.

I could do as Heythe asked. I could choose not to choose, even, and I supposed in time it would be just as if I had chosen her. After the flyting, it would be easy; she would be our Lady unopposed. And I could have what I wanted—

At the bottom of the trestle, Strifbjorn sat playing draughts with Yrenbend. Bergdis, who won the previous game, had retired her shield and adjourned for a walk in the first snow with her husband. Heythe had appropriated Strifbjorn's bench and apparently slept.

My hand wavered over the letters, but they blurred and danced before my eyes. I shook my head—*useless*—and set the paint-loaded brush in a water-filled bowl. It was too easy to walk away; I just stepped over the bench and fled past the ominous Raven Banner and through the narrow rear door. Snow blew across my face as I crossed the small alley to the kitchens.

We had more thralls than we knew what to do with. Most of them slept in the low cottages clustered against the lee side of the mead-hall, but the privileged ones lay here, on pallets warmed by the banked cook-fires. As I entered, Thorra the cook sat up and pushed her blanket down. "Bright one—"

I halted her with an outstretched hand. "Don't stir. I'm here to boil water."

I broke ice on the water-butt, filled a kettle and set it on a hook over the coals. While the water slowly heated, I used the silence and precious near-privacy to think. Without Strifbjorn before me, without Heythe whispering in my ear.

Heythe was the Lady, and I owed her fealty. She'd as much as offered me Strifbjorn, like a choice bone thrown to a faithful dog. I knew Heythe would promise me a place by her chair, a seat in her council. To her, I would not be the littlest sister, the quiet one who was not much of a fighter.

I blinked the sharp tears back again, sniffling. Thorra's blankets rustled.

And then there was Strifbjorn, whom we had followed since

we came from the sea, and who stood half a step away from open rebellion of the goddess we awaited for centuries. And I loved him, with a love that grew rather than fading, as if each brush-stroke of our recent history limned his mettle brighter.

But it was not love that drew me to him, for what I felt for him could never be requited. He had nothing for me except the quiet reserve he offered all my sisters. His heart was given, and he was true.

And Strifbjorn was right, and Heythe was wrong.

The water began to boil.

"Bright one?" Thorra asked, hesitantly, solicitously—as if she could not for another instant bear my sniffling.

"It's all right, Thorra. Rest; you have a feast to prepare to-morrow." The flyting—a contest of wit and insult—would begin at sunset, and I suspected that Strifbjorn had no hope of winning. Quickness of tongue had never been his strength. Rather he led with a powerful arm, a fine quiet understanding and an unspoken devotion to each of us.

Our whispers had awakened one or two of the others; bright eyes peeped from blankets as I broke birch twigs and crumbled mint into a deep wooden bowl. I lifted the kettle from the hook without benefit of a rag. Thorra hissed and glanced away, but the heat could not harm me, even when I judged the brew steeped enough by its scent and strained the twigs out with my fingers.

The wet wood made aromatic steam when I cast it in the fire.

I winked at Thorra and carried the infusion out. Snowflakes melted in the steam while I wrested the postern door open.

Strifbjorn stood over my book, and did not notice my return. I stepped back into the shadows by the door, closing it silent as I could. He touched a spot on the manuscript with one weapon-callused fingertip, raised it to his lips as if to taste. Difficult to judge, at that distance, but I thought he closed his eyes.

My breath shallow enough to hurt, I held my bowl carefully in both hands while he read, painstakingly, the lines of poetry. A smile touched lips as he did so—not cruel, or mocking, but thoughtful.

Then he looked up and saw me standing by the door. The expression fell off his face, replaced by a neutral mask, and he nodded once, politely, and turned and melted away.

I could not run after him, with so many of my brethren in the hall. So I leaned against the rough-hewn logs in the darkness and drank my tea, casting sidelong glances at Heythe's empty chair. The Banner behind it ruffled in the drafts that came through the turf-chinked walls.

Did I think she might be lying?

She was no waelcyrge. She felt the cold; she needed rest. She might lie. But the Raven Banner should not.

I finished the infusion, set the bowl beside the kitchen door for a thrall to collect, and—picking up a pen, ink and a scrap of writing-cloth in passing—I went in pursuit of Strifbjorn.

And as simply as that chose rebellion.

8

With warlock words   thou didst work
Witchcraft in   womanish ways
                              —Lokasenna

The Wolf

I bide dawn and morning in the icy waste, breathing cold air and solitude. The snow catches me at midday: colder here, and the ice has taken most of its water so the flakes are more like pellets. The heat of my skin still melts them, though.

At sunset I walk into the blue-lit shadows of the glacier and through the long, cold passage beyond. I pause in the dark folds of our blue-and-silver banner, furled behind the Cynge's chair. Fire has been kindled in the trench, the broad trestles scrubbed to shining and set along both sides of the hall. My brethren file in.

And Strifbjorn?

Strifbjorn slumps on the steps below me, elbows on his knees, staring at his hands. I watch the rise and fall of his shoulders as he breathes. The braid I plaited shines in the light of hundreds of torches and candles, catching red highlights off the sunset through high windows still unshuttered against the night.

I breathe the icy air of the shadowed road, and step into

the light. He doesn't notice me until I sink beside him, my hand on his arm. "Brother." I try to put enough warmth into my voice to bridge the ragged gap between us.

He looks up. "Brother," he says. "You'll stand with me?"

"I could not stand against," I say, squeezing his shoulder lightly. "Strifbjorn . . ."

He looks up at me, starlight pooling in the backs of his eyes, shimmering there like unshed tears. "Aye?"

I lean close into his ear. "Thou art my true and only family. I vow I will never do thee harm."

The relief in his eyes is terrible to see. Can he have doubted me so deeply, when he holds me in his heart?

We've kissed. He *knows* me.

And thus, if he doubts me, his doubt is justified.

But by the same token, I know his strength, his love. His faith. I solace myself with that knowledge, the knowledge of what he has risked for my sake, the fidelity of his love.

Cold comfort, but comfort.

"Brother," he begins—but whatever he might say is interrupted as Menglad wanders close. Limping, he finishes, "It is good to have you with me."

The broad doors swing open and Skeold enters. She crosses the hall and dips a curtsey before Strifbjorn, self-consciously. "War-leader, the Lady sends that she is ready."

My glove slides from his sleeve as Strifbjorn stands, a picture of fluid strength. He towers over both Skeold and myself. "Thank you," he says.

She lays a deft hand on his arm, where mine rested. "Strifbjorn?"

"Aye, sister?"

She takes a breath. "I look forward to the end of this argument, brother, when we can stand once more together against whatever enemies may come."

She spins on her heel, shattering dry pine boughs, and strides away. I rise from my crouch. "Art ready?"

"I'd better be," he answers. "Order the feast served, Mingan, if you will?"

He walks away before I can answer.

The feast is laid with ceremony. When full dark has fallen, we take our seats except for Heythe. Custom demands her late arrival. Even Skeold and Sigrdrifa are at their places on the cross-bench. Strifbjorn does not eat, although he idly sticks the point of his knife into the food on our shared trencher.

I can do naught to comfort him.

Instead I count heads. Count what I am coming to think of as *our side*—Yrenbend, Brynhilde, Bergdis, Muire. Menglad, Arngeir, Herewys . . . Perhaps three hundred and fifty out of ten hundred or a little less, and not even all the hundred-odd who look to our own mead-hall are with us.

It will not be an easy challenge.

I want to leap up when Heythe enters through a wide-flung door, but instead I slide my knife into the butter and feign blindness. She is robed in silver, a creamy blue kirtle peeking from underneath her surcote. Her necklace shines on the white column of her throat, and a spray of diamonds adorns her brow, glittering in the firelight like ice festooning birch twigs.

Strifbjorn leans over and whispers in my ear. "This is going to be fun." I don't need our bond to hear the fury in his tone.

"See that you win it."

He draws back. The chill shine in his eyes tells me he has no intention of cutting any deals with her—now, or ever. "I'll see that I do."

He raises his eyes at last, as the Lady sweeps to a halt before us. She draws a single breath in deep and seems to dismiss Strifbjorn with a look, although he does not honor her by rising. Instead she surveys the room, imperious, addressing her words to the einherjar and waelcyrge and not our warleader.

> "Heythe they call me, and Gullveig also:
> Burned and reborn, traveling roads most fell
> Across wide waters, through windswept darkness,
> And yet I am spurned, by the lord of this hall?
>
> "Promised I was, prophesied coming
> To stand in the shelter of the Ulfenfell.
> And yet this Strifbjorn my counsel refuses?
> Refuses me further the loaf and the ale?"

She turns to Strifbjorn, raising an accusing finger. The edge of her gaze catches mine. I am reminded of the needle point of the unicorn's horn. I *see* it, burned before me in the air. I must blink to drive it away.

Visions. She has the power of raising memories.

Strifbjorn pales under her gaze, so I wonder what spook she has called into him. Her smile curves in mockery as he stands. But he faces her unflinching and declaims, making my heart fierce and glad.

> *"Guest you cannot be,*
> *Lady or stranger—*
> *One claims a kin's right;*
> *The other's a liar."*

A gasp runs the length of the table. Heythe rocks a half step on her heels. My breath hisses between my teeth: a blunt attack. I would have saved such for the end.

He smiles, leaning forward, and presses the momentary advantage.

> *"Nor your honor may*
> *Surely we ken—*
> *Secrets and shadows*
> *You weave at your whim."*

Nicely done, to call her on her witchery. That's a splinter under a nail, I wot.

But Heythe laughs, low and seductive, and with a long arm sweeps the room.

> *"Weak I am and woman; witchery besuits me—*
> *What warrants war-leader, to womanish ways?"*

I am a fool to knock the bench back and jump up. I slap one hand on Svanvitr's hilt in the sudden breathless silence of the hall. The word she used was *nithling. Faggot.*

But Strifbjorn . . . never looks away from the Lady. He smiles and tips his head as if to praise. His hand on my shoulder is gentle, urging me into my seat.

I sit. A silent snarl bares my teeth.

> *"Weak I am not, and warrior; whom I bed besuits me:*
> *That my duty lies undone, no one in truth can say."*

I slide down in my seat. Oh, aye. Whom *he* beds. And who beds him, does that matter?

But his hand lies light on my shoulder, and after shocked silence the hall is laughing—*howling*—as he picks up her meter and turns her direst insult back on her. And little Muire, head thrown back, laughs violently, Menglad leaning on her in a weakness of glee.

The witches. *That's* who ghost-wrote Strifbjorn's verse. But those final lines must be his own voice. His skill has shocked his helpmeets.

He is more than any of us suspected. More than we *granted*. I am shamed.

Heythe searches the room for welcoming faces, startled by the laughter and the sanction it implies. I think she is bewildered by Strifbjorn's sudden and public acknowledgment. *They knew already.*

I must laugh myself at all the stealth and despair. But a chill settles into my throat a moment later, choking the mirth at its source.

But they don't know about the kiss. Does Heythe?

I must sit straight and proud under Strifbjorn's hand, though I be cold with dread.

But Strifbjorn's grin is feral. He leans forward, mastery in his grasp, riding the laughter of our peers. Heythe swings from side to side, but finds only mockery. *Is that the best you can do?*

Near the cross-bench, Sigrdrifa is on her feet—Herfjotur and Skeold drag her skirts to restrain her.

And Strifbjorn smirks and shakes his head, raising his voice so his scorn can be heard over the merriment. I close my eyes and down my drink.

"Heythe. You promise us an enemy. I see no evidence, unless she be thee. The Raven could warn of thy arrival as easily as the advance of any revenant giant."

He leans back, as if to sit down beside me and finish his drink. "What you counsel is the true abomination, and I will not have it in my hall."

The laughter peaks. Heythe staggers, steps back. Half a breath fills my chest, but I choke it back, unwilling to count on victory.

And Heythe turns away.

I touch Strifbjorn's thigh beneath the table. He settles back—

And then we are both on out feet, along with half the hall, pulled up by a crash and the sound of tearing cloth as Sigrdrifa kicks over the trestle in front of the cross-bench. She strides through the ruin of the feast. Torn skirts drag in gravy and aspic. She snatches Heythe's arm and yanks her back, but she snarls at Strifbjorn.

"You talk of abomination?" She strikes the table, overturns a bowl of ale. "What do you call what you've been doing with *him?*" Her finger wavers in my direction, but she will not meet my eyes.

Strifbjorn spears meat on the point of his knife. "I believe I've answered that question to everyone's satisfaction."

His voice is quiet. In such silence, it carries.

Sigrdrifa spits into the pine boughs. "I heard nothing of the kiss."

My wooden bowl shatters in my hand, and this time Strifbjorn does not stop me as I rise. For a moment we stand shoulder to shoulder, confronting the Lady and her cur.

"I am not," Strifbjorn says, each word a drip of acid, "going to dignify that."

Sigrdrifa laughs, delighted, while Heythe steps away, wearing a stricken grimace. I could pity her. For an instant.

And the hall falls into silence so complete I hear pine sap popping in the fire. Yrenbend, on my left, slides away.

"Oh, really?" Sigrdrifa claps her hands together, suddenly bright and assured again. "What does it cost you, Strifbjorn, to say no?"

Into that hanging silence, a voice rings across the hall. "Unless you cannot." Bergdis stands from the cross-bench, picking more carefully across the ruins of the meal than did Sigrdrifa. I barely see her, for on the bench behind her is Muire, face buried in her hands, gone from triumph to grief in an instant.

Bergdis comes to stand before us, sorrowful and angry.

"Indeed," Heythe echoes, voice shaking. "Just say her nay, Strifbjorn."

Her gesture takes in Sigrdrifa, the mead-hall and the sea. "We will believe you."

And Strifbjorn draws a breath. I see the word's shape on his lips. A lie, bitter and brutal—an abrogation of our contract with the Light. The silence deepens, as if even the fire and the wind outside held their breaths.

"I cannot," he says at last, and—catching me to him while

I stand in stunned slackness—he kisses me hard, futilely, on the mouth, before all the hall. And then turns and strides around the edge of the table. Shoving Sigrdrifa aside, he stalks toward the door.

It is a long stunned moment before I gather myself enough to follow, a moment in which I cannot even hear my brothers and my sisters breathe. Heythe meets my gaze, and something shatters inside of me under the pressure of her regard. Whatever the vision is that she would give me, I shove away—hard—and swallow down like bile.

I feel the weight of all their stares. I stiffen my spine and follow Strifbjorn into his exile.

The Warrior

Mingan caught Strifbjorn ten feet up the trail. Once they were out of sight of the mead-hall, dignity permitted him to run the few steps between. He grabbed Strifbjorn's arm in fingers like an iron cuff and turned him. Strifbjorn stumbled into a drift. With another band of weather, it was snowing again.

He seemed about to speak, but could not for a moment, and in that moment, Strifbjorn's checked tears overflowed. His cheeks stretched when he threw back his head, but no sound passed his lips but a thin, exhausted whine. He fell to his knees. Snow soaked the shins of his trousers.

"It's over," Mingan said, kneeling beside him, catching his wrists in his hands when Strifbjorn might have struck at Mingan or at himself. "It's over."

"We lost."

"Not yet."

Strifbjorn tried to shove him away, but though he out-weighed Mingan, Mingan held on and pushed back. Snow melted around the Wolf, soaking his clothing, and he seemed not to care in the slightest. He still hadn't reclaimed his cloak.

Strifbjorn wondered what Heythe had done with it. Min-gan's touch calmed him, and once he could breathe without pain he stood and moved away.

Mingan remained kneeling in the meltwater, looking up at Strifbjorn. "I'm free," Strifbjorn said, as if it were a discovery. "We can—"

"We can die," he said. "Unless you mean to let her twist them into devils."

Hard and stern. And what Strifbjorn needed. He was wrong. Still he argued. "I have no power over them."

"Strifbjorn."

"I'm sorry," he said, hoping Mingan could understand how many ways he meant the sorrow. Strifbjorn could have argued more—they made their decision; they did not want his help—but as it was not Strifbjorn's choice to lead them, so it was not Strifbjorn's choice to leave them. He looked away from Mingan, out into the forest. Mingan must have understood, be-cause he stood and walked through the rumpled snow to stand beside Strifbjorn.

"Sorry?"

Strifbjorn glanced at him sidelong. He was looking away, dreamy, as if the rustle of the falling snow were a whisper in his ear. "Mingan. Sorry to have made you an outcast as well."

He looked at Strifbjorn then, eyes gleaming, lips half-open to show the points of his teeth. In his eyes was the killing laughter of wolves. "Outcast?" He moved a step closer, his heat and scent hanging on the breathless air. "Only with thee, Strifbjorn, and with the pack—only then am I other than outcast. You have robbed me of nothing. Nothing at all."

Strifbjorn was caught on his eyes like an insect snagged on firelight. He leaned closer even before Mingan reached up, buried his glove-clad hands in Strifbjorn's hair and pulled him into a ferocious embrace.

Too close to the hall, Strifbjorn thought, and then he thought, *Oh, who gives a fuck?*

Mingan tumbled Strifbjorn into a snowdrift beside the ground-sweeping boughs of a spruce, amid a scatter of hastily discarded clothing. The snow crystals, at first melting on his skin, at last cooled it to the point where he felt chill when Strifbjorn laid the palm of his hand against Mingan's back. Mingan was no more gentle with Strifbjorn than Strifbjorn was with Mingan, until the end, when Mingan knelt over the war-leader-no-longer and pressed lips to lips soft as the snow that was still falling over them, and Strifbjorn filled him and they filled the air with light.

There was a taste of sorrow on Mingan's breath that was not familiar, and a resolution—cold, also, as that falling snow— that Strifbjorn was too tired to question.

He said nothing after, except "Wait for me here." And then he dressed himself and left.

Herfjotur came to Strifbjorn as he waited, perched on a granite boulder alongside the trail. The way was too overhung for her steed to bear her, so she slogged afoot. She stopped when she saw him. "Brother," she offered in a neutral tone.

"Sister."

She came closer, close enough to touch. Strifbjorn stood, out of respect. Flakes of snow tangled in her braid. "I'm sorry to have failed you, sister."

She laughed, not meeting his eyes, and punched him lightly on the shoulder.

"Idiot," she said. "You realize, of course, that"—words failed her, and her gesture took in the mountain and the mead-hall and the whole dark cloud-wrapped sky—"some of us are willing to follow you no matter what."

"The Lady won the flyting," Strifbjorn reminded.

She shrugged. "I'm not above treason in a good cause, Strif-bjorn. And Heythe . . . is a good cause. If I won't bloody my hands for her purposes, it seems I'll bloody my hands opposing them."

"You talk about slaying our brethren. And most likely dying in the attempt."

She patted the hilt of her blade. "I remember Yrenbend's demonstration," she said coolly, although Strifbjorn heard the pain beneath it. "I also know they are as free to choose as I."

"Ah," Strifbjorn said, thinking of Yrenbend.

"Yrenbend agrees with me. Menglad, too. I know not how many others."

"We'll lose," Strifbjorn said. "We'll die. It's only about a clean death now."

"I know," she answered. "Send word when you are ready for us. I'll see how many I can bring."

The Wolf

I hunt.

Something mad sits in me—a thing I recognize from long ago, although I do not remember with a sapient mind ever feeling it before. I step into the cold, charred shadows, and recall—with the brutal force of a blow to the body—that I have been here before, in this darkness, many times. There was a dog that howled. There was a woman whose face was divided, purple from white.

I know this place. *Knew* the name of this place, in another time, with the mind of . . .

The mind of a beast. Dim and sorrowful. Trapped and panicking. I claw at the collar, sag to my knees. Gasp glacial air, flakes of soot rising around me, disturbed by my fall.

Burned, all burned and cold and empty. This was my sister's realm, a place for dead souls deemed unworthy. I remember the smell of it under the char. And I remember a chain, and a rock, and a blade driven between my teeth for a gag, and the taste of my own blood running down my throat for a thousand years.

I sprawl prone, hiding my face in my hands, and choke on vomit and blood and the taste of scorched hair.

I know what Heythe broke, in my mind. A wall, a mirror, a mystery. Shattered now.

Everything.

She has given me back everything, and I do not want any of it. I recall a ship clinker-built of the torn nails of dead men, and the hot taste of god-flesh and the bitterness of injustice. My father's rough hand, and my sister's pity. My brothers, monsters also: the eight-legged stallion, the legless world-girdling Wyrm. Treacheries and tricks—all recalled by scent and sensation more than thought, recalled with the dim wit of an animal and the hopeful heart of a child.

I choke on soot and strangle on the collar, tasting the heat of a star between my teeth, hearing in my ear the words that Heythe herself spoke. A prophecy she gave before the old world died that doomed us all: me to my rock and my sister to her rimed wormy hall and my brother to depths of the sea. And our half brother bitted and blinkered, saddled and spurred, made to bear the all-Father on his back as a final insult to our sire. And that all-Father himself, the lost Cynge . . . Well. I remember why he won't be coming for us, now.

He won't be coming because I ate him.

As Heythe prophesied I would.

W hen I rise up from the ice and cinders, my breath, at last, is quiet. Tears have streaked the soot down my face. I feel their salt-stiff crackle on my cheeks.

I taste my own smile, and it is terrible. This cannot be what Heythe intended when she gave me back my memories, for I have recollected myself—and what I am is so awful that my old name is still a word of nightmare, centuries later and a world away. *Suneater.*

Oh, I remember now.

Words have come back to me, words that are not new at all, but were cast in prophecy long ago.

I clutch them close to my burning heart, where they cannot spill out again, and go hunting Heythe, the witch.

She stands beside a red mare in a field not far from Northerholm. The horse is sweated, steaming in the cold air. She tosses up her head and fights the bridle when I step out of the shadows and the wind brings her my scent. Her Lady turns to soothe her, a hand on her muzzle, giving me her shoulder as if she trusts me. She still wears my cloak.

"Heythe," I say. "Gullveig. Mardoll. *Lady.*" The wolf in me keeps me a wary arm's length from her. I remember the last time, and her hands under my collar. "You have so many names."

I want to tear her throat out with my teeth, crunch the glittering strands of that necklace between my jaws. There are two wolves in me: the monster, and the simple beast. The Suneater's lust is upon me, raw and hot. Under it, drowned in it, I know the purer intention of the wolf that is only a wolf. I want to taste her blood, and . . . despite Strifbjorn's touch still lingering on my skin, I want other things, too. With an urgency that dismays.

"As many names as I had deaths, Wolf," she answers. "I see you have your memories."

"Yes." My voice a snarl through bared teeth. "Thank you." The only gratitude in it is mocking.

She does not turn away from her mare. "The Aesir used us all poorly, Wolf. But I am not of the Aesir, and never have been. They raped me, too. Snatched me from my home, held me hostage. Stole from me my husband. I was but a prize of war." Her forehead rests on the red mare's mane. She takes a breath. "The ones who chained and taunted you, the ones who earned your wrath, are dead."

I open my mouth again, and poetry spills out of it.

"Fetters burst; the wolf will rage:
Much do I know; and more can see
Of the fate of the gods; the mighty in fight.
The sun burns black; earth shatters in the sea,
And hot bright stars; from heaven are hurled.
Now do I see; the earth in foam
Rises green and renewed; from the waves again—"

My voice chokes off with a growl. "Your words. Your curse. Your prophecy. I know what you are, tricksteress."

She turns back to me, the mare quieting, and smiles. "Only because I showed you. Hush, Wolf. Peace. I was prophesied to be here, and you yourself prepared my place for me. Surely, things . . . can be arranged to suit us both?"

"Prophecies do not always come true," I remind her. "As I stand here before you, when you spoke my death, aye and the deaths of my brother and sister, too."

"Ah, yes," she says. "There is that. But here you are. Perhaps I am not so skilled at prophecy." And then she grins. "I *did* put the all-Father's throat in your teeth."

"What makes you think we can still converse—after tonight?"

"The flyting?"

"Sigrdrifa's display. Or will you maintain that was her own idea?"

Heythe shakes her head. "Sigrdrifa . . . you and Strifbjorn are each worth ten such as she. Do you understand?"

"You deny that was your doing?"

"How could it be my doing? I didn't even know, Mingan. How could I have known?"

I taste the wind—so much warmer than the wind off the shadowed road, the wind between the stars. The Suneater struggles in my breast—but his rage will not serve now. You can drive any animal mad, if you fetter and torment it. The Suneater has been chained all his life, so chained in me that I had forgotten him. The very flesh of my body is his chain.

Now am I also complicit in his slavery.

"Swear it." My tone, startling me, is soft and precise. "Swear that you were ignorant."

"I swear," she says, her eyes steady on mine. "I care not whom you love, Mingan, or who loves you. If you choose to return and live under my rule, both Strifbjorn and yourself are welcome."

"And if we do not?"

Her eyes seem to rime with ice about the edges. "Then do not oppose me. I'd rather see you live." Her fingers fumble at her collar, and she slips the cloak from her shoulders. Its heavy folds drape her fist. "Here," she says. "I kept this for you. Thank you."

I take it. Her fingertips brush my glove. I know she sees me shiver, but she turns and mounts her horse. One hand raised in farewell, she reins the mare around and rides away.

In me, two wolves howl. One is sane and sorrowing, and the other is as mad and old and merciless as the sea.

The Historian

Sigrdrifa was still picking herself up from among the pine needles when I kicked her in the face. She sprawled backwards, both hands raised in defense; I reached over my shoulder and slid Nathr into my hand. Out of the corner of my eye, I saw Yrenbend come up behind me, his hand also on the hilt of his sword. I glanced over at Heythe, and the Lady took a step back and turned away, pointedly looking at the door she edged toward.

Sigrdrifa was on her own. As she tried to get up, Yrenbend put his boot on her chest and pushed down hard. Menglad and Herfjotur came up on either side of me.

Around us, those of our brethren who were somehow still seated rose. Bergdis stepped forward as if to intervene, and Yrenbend just raised an eyebrow at her. "I'm probably not going to kill her," he said mildly. "As long as she's helpful."

Fury rose cold up my throat. My fist clenched on Nathr's hilt. *I* might kill her anyway.

Bergdis dropped her gaze and stepped back. "Watch your step, Yrenbend," she said as she turned away.

He glanced down at his boot on Sigrdrifa's chest and smiled. "I'm watching it now," he muttered. Herfjotur, turning to survey the room, barked a laugh.

Sigrdrifa didn't struggle, but her eyes turned to the side, to Skeold and the rest of her faction. Skeold and three einherjar began to walk forward.

Herfjotur raised her hand, and an unexpected gust of wind disordered my hair. Her steed towered above and behind us, his shoulder higher than my head. He spread wings that brushed the ceiling of the mead-hall and tossed his alabaster manes. I cringed away, accidentally crowding Yrenbend, but my weight was not enough to shift him when he was braced.

Menglad grabbed my belt and steadied me, staying clear of

my sword arm. I could not have been more grateful for that quick solid touch.

Herfjotur's face was stern, her one raised hand seeming to be the only thing that held back her steed, or—conversely—the brethren gathered behind Skeold.

The Light was dead and dull and silent in the back of my head, and I could not hear the music at all.

I remember thinking, calm and quiet, *Oh. So this is how it ends.*

"So," Yrenbend said, slowly, "where exactly did you get that piece of information, Sigrdrifa?"

She spat at him, her eyes blazing like lanterns. They were cold infernos, brighter and harsher than they should have been, a savage light that cast stark shadows across Yrenbend's features and picked out the red in the gold of his queue.

He leaned forward, putting weight on his foot. She gasped. "I said I wouldn't *kill* you," he pointed out, politely.

"Probably," I added. "So tell us, please?"

Her eyes swept aside, in the direction that Heythe had gone, but the Lady had already effected her departure.

Sigrdrifa paled. She looked back to Yrenbend. "I followed them," she said, her voice breaking around it, the Light in her eyes flickering to darkness. "I spied on them."

She was lying. I could not take a breath around the implication of that, and so I denied it: She was a child of the Light. She could not be lying.

"Why?"

"The Wolf . . . threatened my life."

Most of our brethren seemed to be leaving the hall, or going about their business. Ten or fifteen still stood in a loose semicircle, observing, not interfering—whether in caution of the steed bowering us with his massive wings or out of approval for our actions I did not know.

I kicked her in the side, below her ribs. Yrenbend glanced at me, pursing his lips, but said nothing. "And Strifbjorn refused you."

"Like he refused you, runt?"

I almost kicked her again, but it would have given her too much satisfaction. "Exactly like that." I smirked. "Except I didn't stick a knife in his back."

She made a rude gesture, as well as she could with her elbows braced on the floor. Yrenbend shot a glance at Menglad. "Are we done?"

"I think so," she replied, and Yrenbend took his boot off Sigrdrifa's chest. He'd left a muddy footprint on the immaculate white of her surcote.

I smiled.

Herfjotur put a hand on her steed's right-side neck, holding his mane, and led him from the hall. The rest of us followed her, Yrenbend directing a glare at Sigrdrifa that kept her on her elbows until we were outside.

"I'm going to look for Strifbjorn and the Wolf," Herfjotur said, and started across the meadow toward the trailhead. Her steed whinnied after her. Whatever she answered was unspoken. He watched her go for a moment, both heads raised and turned, and then seemed to shrug and shake himself. Hoofbeats drummed hollowly, echoing against the mountain, as he trotted to the sea-cliff and fell into flight, untroubled by the wind and the blowing snow.

More snow was falling, so Menglad, Yrenbend and I

walked around behind the mead-hall and stood in the lee, among the huts and lean-tos where the thralls kept house.

When the howl of the wind grew quieter I leaned on the mud-chinked wall and kicked a heel against it. Yrenbend leaned beside me, his arm pressing my shoulder comfortingly, and Menglad stood across from us. Eddies furled her cloak around her like the wings of some strange raven.

We stood and stared, one to the other, for a few minutes before she sighed and folded her arms across her bosom. "What now?" she said, eventually.

I shook my head. "You don't think she'll . . . force us to . . . rape souls, do you?"

Yrenbend said, "Did you want an honest answer to that?"

"Yes." Menglad drew her knife and began cleaning her fingernails, plainly for something to do with her hands.

The set of Yrenbend's shoulders was as defeated as the tuck of his chin. "I don't see how she can *force* us. But there are only two choices now. And I don't believe what Sigrdrifa had to say for herself."

"I don't see how that follows," I said.

He shook his head. "I'm sure she did eavesdrop. I'm equally sure that Heythe put her up to it."

"So how did Heythe know? I—" Too much, and I bit it off midsentence.

Yrenbend was too clever to let it pass. "You?"

"I knew. They were . . . very discreet, Yrenbend."

"But you found out?"

"I was . . . looking for privacy. And stumbled over something I shouldn't have. But most of us don't walk up the mountain unless we're looking for the Grey Wolf."

"Ah." He seemed to think about that for a long moment.

Menglad finished with her fingernails and wiped her knife on her trousers before slipping it back into the sheath.

"So how would Heythe have known. For certain?" Yrenbend came up hard as if someone had snapped his reins. "Sigrdrifa lied."

My lips shaped words twice before I managed to give them voice. "Lied? How do you know?" *I thought so, too. How could she have lied?*

"She's no huntress. A warrior, yes—but Mingan would have smelled her coming."

I raised an eyebrow. "Mingan didn't smell me."

"Muire—you may not appreciate it, but your woodcraft is probably surpassed only by his. What you just said—most of us don't walk up the mountain, but you do, and Mingan does, and Strifbjorn does. Sigrdrifa . . . doesn't step out of the mead-hall if she can help it." He chuckled. "Some of us notice your skills."

"Oh." I dropped my foot and scuffed the boot through crisp snow, which was accumulating faster now. "So how did Heythe find out to tell her?"

Yrenbend was thinking hard. I recognized the expression, the tension in the line of his jaw, the half-folded hand upraised for temporary silence.

"Strifbjorn," he murmured.

Menglad's brow furrowed even as mine smoothed. "He breathed for her," I said.

Yrenbend nodded. "Yes." And turning with a sudden, liquid motion drove his fist wrist-deep into the bark-shingled log wall of the mead-hall.

The Wolf

Strifbjorn is in brighter spirits when I find him. He has dusted the snow from a boulder and sits there, his bearskin spread across the rock as a pad. Footprints neither mine nor his mark rutted snow. A trace of scent still lingers. "Herfjotur."

"Pledges her support, and as many of the others as she can bring." He stands and comes to me, rests a hand on my shoulder. "You got your cloak back."

"I spoke with Heythe." The wolf in me leans into the touch of his hand—pack-touch, leader-touch. The reawakened Suneater growls low in my throat, untrusting of the kindness that leads to chains. I close my eyes and take the scent of my lover deep, step into his clasp. The barbs in what Heythe said about serving my master only prickle the Suneater, and the insolent pride of a man.

The wolf is more sensible. First and always, the pack.

Strifbjorn smooths an escaped strand behind my ear. "What ultimatums did she have to offer?"

I shrug, my cloak swinging from the movement, brushing my calves. I step away so I may look him in the eye. His hand stays on my shoulder. "She offers a place by her side to both of us. She claims she knew nothing; she wants us to return. . . ."

"And follow her leadership? You told her nay."

I place my right hand over his own, let him see me smile. It's cold and dark inside me, despite the furnace of a swallowed sun. "Are we going to war?"

He swallows, and then he nods. "We'll die doing it, Mingan. There aren't enough who will rebel."

He will not like what I have to offer; I offer anyway. "We have the Imogen."

That freezes him as the snow never could. "Against our brethren?"

"Against Heythe."

"Oh, no."

"Think on it. It may be the only chance." My poor sister. Hunger her plate, and famine her knife and a cold grave to sleep in. But a goddess to dine upon. That might fill even the Imogen's belly.

The justice of it would suit me.

He looks away. His hand slides down my arm. I let him go. "We could leave," he says. "We could go south."

"And what? A cottage by the sea, fish and forage and braid hemp rope?"

"Why not?" He snaps. I stare. He says it again, softer. Coaxing. "Why not?"

He knows why not. And when I meet his eyes, he gnaws his own mouth and looks down.

"Come," I say, and start up the trail toward the denning-tree.

The wolves should have gone down the mountain when the snow came. They cannot run over it like the great cats do, or men on snowshoes, and the game flee to the valleys in winter, too. I expect the denning-tree to be lonely and chill; I think we will make a nest among the roots and wait out the night.

If I were still a wolf, I would know sooner. If I were still a wolf in truth . . .

My father had five sons and a daughter. Four of us were bastards and monsters, the Grey Wolf and the Wyrm and the centipede stallion, and the half-dead girl whose hunger could never be fed. But two were well-made, born in wedlock, pleasing the eye.

Our father adored them.

And of those two, the all-Father transfigured one into a wolf, and fed him on the flesh of the other and then bound my sire beneath a mountain with the guts of his own dead son.

So there is justice in that, glutted on the body and bones of the all-Father—who was no father to me or mine—I should awaken reborn as a man.

. . . yes. We *can* bite down on a grudge and grin around it until the end of time.

I remember the taste of that grudge, the crunch of those bones, the shock of my transformation as we crest the trail. The cold scent of blood raises the fine hairs that would be hackles, had I not been forged into this man-shape.

Other scents layer under the blood, man and wolf and piss and spilled bowels, and risen hackles become a snarl and the wild unchanneled flare of starlight. The Suneater snarls in me, feral but cunning. I sprint through snowdrifts, off the trail, into the cedars and then still, still as a feather hung on an updraft. Strifbjorn, startled, must follow—I hear him wallowing through the snow, tangled on a dog rose that is naught but a briar in wintertime.

No wolf, Strifbjorn.

Nothing but an angel, he.

I pause in the shadows and the falling snow, and all I can smell is blood.

The Suneater moves through the falling snow like a part of the storm. He seeks his enemy on hushed steps, a wraith with a silver stare. But the enemy is gone, and I step from among the cedars and through the thin stand of white birch and into a clearing awash with blood, blood and trampled snow, the clean new fall drifting across like a sheet dragged over the dead.

I cannot tell them apart.

Boar-spears and arrows, and some of the blood is men's blood, but not enough, not enough at all.

It will never be enough blood to sate me.

Strifbjorn finds me. It must only be moments later. He finds me kneeling by the bodies, piled like so much meat under the naked boughs of the copper beech, and I cannot tell them apart.

He comes and pushes my face into the fur covering his shoulder, turns me away from the bodies of my not-brothers, the bodies of my friends, stripped of their deep plush coats, their scents and their individuality. Stripped of their lives and their laughter.

Punished, I know—because I know the men whose scents pollute the clearing—punished for my sin.

My unforgivable sin of leaving a man alive.

Strifbjorn tries to hold me. But inside me the Suneater blinks eyes like molten rock. He grins, tongue a tide of blood lolling over ragged yellow teeth. He knows where embraces lead, and laughter and promises of comradeship.

I shove Strifbjorn aside and stand, walking away, back into the woods at the end of the clearing, following all the man-trails trodden in the snow.

The whole pack. Every one of them is dead, and skinned and lying under a gathering drift of bloody snow next to my lover, who sits in that snow with his head in his hands and cannot weep, any more than I can.

I circle the clearing. The growl low in my throat tightens against my collar. My fur should be abristle; my eyes should glare yellow in the dark. I remember the taste of hot blood and hair and meat. *I will rend them*, but it is not a thought framed in words. Rather a knifelike jag of intention.

The wind blows snow through the bare branches, covering the scents of the men, the blood of the wolves. I turn as if I could see the cloud-wrapped peak of the mountain through the storm that enfolds it, but all there is, is gray. I breathe in the silence and the cold. It has no power to comfort me.

I come back to Strifbjorn. He has not moved from the spot where he knelt down beside me. I stand beside him, behind him. His eyes are closed. I am looking at the bodies of my friends.

"Is this all of them?" he asks finally, in a small voice.

"By count," I say, "but I cannot tell them apart."

"We should leave," he says, climbing to his feet as if his joints pain him. His eyes slide from the dead wolves, where I cannot stop looking at them. The red bitch, the grizzled old male, the snow-colored cub not even old enough to choose a mate. I cannot tell them apart.

"Enough," he says, tugging my arm. "Enough. Come with me. There's nothing you can do for them."

I cough up a laugh and spit it into the snow. "Leave. Aye. I'm going to leave."

"North," he says.

"West," I answer, and he looks at me in surprise. The wolf

inside me bares his teeth and howls a mourning promise. The Suneater blinks once. Mad wolves are silent. They are in perfect harmony, perfect accord. "I want you to help me."

"Anything." Big hands gentle as if reining a nervous horse, he turns me away. Blood and ice cake our boots and our leggings.

"I'm going to kill them," I tell him, the words on my tongue like iron splinters. "And I want you to come."

9

✴

Who invokes Hel from her ice and anguish?
Ice-burned and storm-frozen
Dew-shrouded, I am aeons dead.
—*Baldur's Dreams*

The Warrior

No matter how he turned Mingan's words in his head, Strifbjorn could not make them fit sense. "You can't mean that."

"Can I not?" His hand jerked spastically, at the pitiful huddle of corpses already half-drifted. "You deny me requital?"

Strifbjorn couldn't believe it was Mingan speaking. It was as if he were inhabited by something ancient and fell. As if a cold wind from the north possessed him, one colder than the one that filled Strifbjorn's nostrils and stung his eyes.

He glanced up, seeking counsel. But the stars were hidden behind the storm.

"No . . . I . . ."

Who could stand and regard a man surrounded by the bodies of his innocent family and deny his right to redress murder? And yet—

Strifbjorn cleared his throat and tried again. "Brother, your wrath is justified—"

Mingan cut him short with a chopping hand and spoke

softly. "It is not wrath. There is nothing righteous in it. I was more contemplating sack and slaughter."

"Who do you mean to kill?" Vengeance was what they were for. If he claimed justice, Strifbjorn should not stop him. If Strifbjorn could limit him to just vengeance . . .

Mingan grinned at him, more wolf than Strifbjorn had ever seen him, snow riming his hair, his deep-set eyes ablaze in a face cold as stone. "I was thinking of starting with Dale."

Strifbjorn felt his face go as cold as the Wolf's. His musk clogged Strifbjorn's nostrils, already thick with the nauseating scent of blood and bodies. "You can't."

"I understand you will not aid me." Mingan brushed past Strifbjorn and started down the mountain. Snow crunched under his boots. The wind sang through the trees, blowing the flakes of snow horizontal.

"Mingan. It's *wrong*."

He neither stopped nor answered.

Strifbjorn tried again. "If you do this thing, you are no better than Sigrdrifa."

Mingan turned on him, snarling, and took the seven steps back. His fingers knotted in the fur of Strifbjorn's cloak. In his hand, the clasp snapped. He cast it aside. Strifbjorn caught his wrist, braced his back foot and slung him into a snowdrift. Mingan went down on one knee, rose again, turned—and Strifbjorn stepped in front of him. "No."

His hands curled in claws, his eyes gone dark and bottomless. Strifbjorn raised his fists and Mingan sprang, not battle-mad but as if to lunge past.

Strifbjorn stepped in front of him again.

He did not stop. Strifbjorn scrabbled, grabbed hold of his

shoulder. Strifbjorn knew Mingan's strength of old, but his heart still shuddered in his chest when the wolf clutched his collar and, one-handed, casually lifted him off his feet. Mingan brought his face close to Strifbjorn's, and Strifbjorn thought for a moment that Mingan might break his neck.

It would do no good to strike him now. Strifbjorn hung limp in his hands as a puppy shaken by the scruff.

"Mingan. If you . . ."

He knew, already. Strifbjorn couldn't threaten him. He had nothing to bargain, because Mingan had already decided. He was taking nothing with him where he was going. No pack. No soul. And nobody's love to clothe him.

For a moment, though, he stared at Strifbjorn clear-eyed, and Strifbjorn hoped. And a moment later Mingan laughed and threw him across the clearing. He hit hard, bounced and rolled into the snow, sliding until he struck the bole of an oak.

"I have not so quickly forgotten my vow to harm thee not," he said, more to the mountain than to Strifbjorn. He spun in place and trotted into the snow.

By the time Strifbjorn found his feet, Mingan was gone into the shadows, beyond any pursuit that might have reached him in time.

Strifbjorn had no way to burn or bury the wolves. The ground was hard as steel under the drifts, and they were wolves, anyway: the best he could do was drag the freezing bodies apart, into the woods, and bury them in the drifts. They were already stiff with the cold, blood freezing in sticky crystals that melted into a clotting mess, caking his hands and arms.

Scavengers would have to see to their mortal remains.

Afterwards, Strifbjorn scrubbed snow on his clothes to try to get the blood out of the white fabric, but he was stained. He picked up his cloak and beat the ice from it as best he could.

Then he sat down on the curving root of the beech tree where Mingan had combed out his hair, and leaned his head back against the smooth, silver bark to wait for his lover's return.

In the morning, or perhaps the morning of the day after that, Strifbjorn stood and shook the snow out of his hair.

He wrapped his fur cloak tight around his shoulders and started walking north. Herfjotur and her steed could find him if they needed.

And if they couldn't, he was sure he didn't care.

The Wolf

I run through dead shadows, fleeing the ghosts that pursue. Four-legged ghosts lolling tongues and forgiving yellow eyes. I do not deserve their forgiveness.

I choose blood.

I wait for dawn. When the sun casts rose highlights on the snow, I stand at the slope leading from the edge of the forest into Dale. The village lies nestled like an egg in wool in the deep-drifted valley. Snow falls still, so I see the cottages in glimpses when the snow is blown aside. It's up to my knees now, warming the winter earth. The clouds pale to silver. The shadow of the mountain falls upon them from above.

The village slumbers still. In the snow, they will sleep late, save their fuel, until the animals rouse them.

I put my back to the mountain and the wind. My cloak billows forward, fouling my arms. I would hang it from a branch, but I won't need my sword.

"Imogen."

Through the snow she comes. Flakes curl from the draft of velvet-black feathertips, until she settles beside me and casts a wing across my shoulders.

"My Lord. Your pain is very great."

"I feel no pain."

"Lord?"

I do not look at her. My eyes are fixed on the shadowed village before us. "Nothing hurts me, Imogen. Do you hunger?"

"Aye, my Lord."

"I am not your Lord, sister. I am your brother." My left hand lifts. One gloved finger points to the village, its dark cottages, its single street. "There is your meal. As many as you like. But leave this house and that one alone."

"Lo—brother?"

"Those are mine."

She stares at me with her great gold eyes, and I signal her forward. Her wings leave feather-tracks in the snow as she leaps into the air. A moment, three wingbeats, and she is gone beyond the snow as I walk toward my first claim. Hagrim. The Baker.

I don't expect to hear screaming. My sister is always hungry.

Two wolf-pelts are tacked to the side of the house, spread wide so they will freeze flat until summer. One is gray as soot, tipped with silver and copper highlights like sunlight on storm-clouds. The other is soft, thick, almost as white as the snowflakes adhering to the guard hairs.

I don't bother stepping through shadows to enter the house. It's simpler to tear the wide plank door off its leathern hinges. The baker leaps from the bed beside the well-banked fire, a wood-axe upraised in his hands. I throw the door into the snow. Dim morning lightens the room. Two children scream in the loft. There is no sign of a woman.

The baker swings at my head. I parry the haft with my forearm. It shatters against the bone, and the bone snaps, too, but I—*I feel no pain*—take him by the throat. The children's whimpering reminds me of the whimpering of wolf-cubs. I raise their father into the air, my fingers as tight on his throat as the collar that cuts mine.

He gurgles. I smile. I could speak, but there is nothing I wish to explain to this murderer, this mortal, this candle-flicker. I drag his mouth to mine, flooded with self-contempt. *How, that this squalling thing could have been permitted to wound me?* He screams, shoving, biting, pounding my face with balled fists . . . and then, as I drag the soul from him with his protesting breath, his fingers uncurl and he begins to pull me close, whimpering like a lover, pressing his cold, meaty face to mine.

Strength pours into me like liquor, like sunlight, like honey swirled in tea. He grips my hair, my collar, his scent and his touch offensive, and from the flavor of his exhalation I know I have taken enough, and he is dying and I must stop before I take the last of his breath and with it the geas of vengeance.

I drop him to the rammed-earth floor. He falls clutching my boot, begging for the kiss. My gorge rises. I kick him away.

The children in the loft cry like puppies.

Like the puppies I left on the mountain, they do not cry for long.

The Imogen is finished with her morning's work by the time I am done. The snow is sprayed with blood, scattered with sucked-clean bones. Each cottage stands silent and empty.

I walk past their gaping doors and silent windows until I come to the house of the woodcutter.

Rannveig and her father huddle in the snow beside their doorway. The Imogen stands over them, wings spread wide. She smiles as I approach, glittering a mouthful of needles. Not a spot of blood marks her; not a feather has fallen out of place.

"You have done well." She leans into the caress as my fingers trace the seashell outline of her ear. "Pretty Imogen."

She purrs like a cat at the praise.

The woodcutter stands. He puts his daughter behind him. "Devil!" he cries. "I told her you were a devil."

There is no satisfaction to be had in making answer. I kill him before Rannveig's eyes.

I expect her to bolt during that kiss, but she stands straight against the bark-shingled wall and lifts her chin to look me in the eye when I drop her father at my feet. She's in her night-dress, barefoot in the snow. "Your wolves," she whispers.

Still I answer not, but my footsteps halt at the sound of her voice. She studies my face, trembling like a catkin when you blow across it. The vast indifference of the storm rises over us. Gusts plaster her shift to her shape.

I lift my foot with an effort. The Imogen watches avidly, longing, no doubt, to claim this one last life.

"You poor thing," Rannveig says, and minces toward me like a determined doe, snow packing under her cold blue toes. Her father had a pelt tacked to his door, too, oak-leaf brown with a golden undercoat. Blood has frozen around the edges, and if I look away from Rannveig, I must notice.

"Your eyes look strange." Her voice has fallen to a whisper. "So dark, Master Wolf."

She steps over her father's body, stifling a sob, but grimly reaches up to touch my face. I shy, flinching from the caress.

"I'm sorry," she says. "My village. If you . . . if I do whatever you want . . ." But the Imogen's wings come down, and when Rannveig looks past me, she sees what she could not see before. "Oh."

"There will be no bargaining."

Strange, how soft and plain her voice is. As soft and plain as my own. "They're dead?"

"All of them."

"It doesn't look like enough blood. For so many people. How will they know who they are, to bury them?"

"No one will bury them."

"But I . . . oh." She takes a breath, as if only now recalling that she must. "I never should have brought you the cake. It was my fault, wasn't it? That's why you . . . you saved me for last."

"Yes."

She swallows hard. Then she closes her eyes tight and tilts her head back, lips parting and closing slightly, like a resting butterfly's wings. I bend over her, my braid falling over my shoulder. She smells of wood-ash, goat's milk and unwashed girl. I taste her breath and feel the hunger, the Suneater's rage, flare up in me. Her blond head is framed by the door-hung pelt. I have never been so *hungry*.

The Imogen shifts and croons. Snow creaks under her weight. Wind soughs through the empty cottages, rattling doors and thumping shutters. The morning grows brighter, and Rannveig trembles, cold to the bone.

Her breath tastes of strength and summer and innocence and roses, of the sea, of hope, of the fresh-turned loam. It tickles my lips, strong as brandywine, sharp as the bitter, blood-scented air. It's not enough blood. And the baker's breath, and the woodcutter's, has awakened something in me, something as ravenous as the Suneater I always was and always was meant to be. The wolf, the man. These were only ever guises.

And the girl . . . she's a yearling doe, a succulent coney hare. Lovely and insignificant. I exhale slowly and bend over her. Shaking so I have to hold her on her feet, she crushes her eyes shut in whatever emotion grips her.

Her lips are chapped and peeling, human and flawed. She sighs as mine come down, but then stiffens in panic. Her eyes fly wide, her hands splayed flat against my chest. She shoves at me, panting.

I think of the cub, of the red bitch who would sit with her back to mine in the dappled shade of a summer evening. If she had lived out her life to its fullest, she might have hoped for as many years as this human child has already squandered.

I hold her fast with one hand, and with the other I reach up and tilt her face roughly. *Hush, candle-flicker. I will make this more pleasant for thee than thou dost deserve.* My gloved thumb slides down the yielding resilience of her cheek. The softness pleases me, and so does the way she tries to writhe away from the touch of my mouth. The capability I have to hurt her—or choose to do no harm—that pleases me as well, with a kind of acrid satisfaction. It's filling, and fulfilling, and while it is bitter it is also *sweet*, surcease for that emptiness I always took for loneliness.

But oh, I know the truth of it now.

She opens her mouth and screams with all the fury in her. Her breath rushes down my throat like a draft of wine, heady and strengthening. I breathe her deep, and—

With a reversal so sudden I am made light-headed, she leans into me, the arm I have not pinioned sliding up and around my neck. Her mouth falls open, seeking, and she relaxes into my touch like a lover might. As Strifbjorn would, when he gave himself to me—

I won't permit that thought to linger. I have chosen other things.

The breath comes from her on a long, surrendering sigh. Strength flows through me like warmth from liquor. Her own is failing: her knees buckle; her eyes close. I lift my lips from hers before she passes, and she whimpers, ever so slightly, curling her dying face against my throat like a wolf-cub.

Don't stop, she begs. *Never stop. . . .* Her curled fingers slide down my shoulder, her arm hanging limp as her head lolls back on her neck. Almost gone.

The strength I have robbed from her, from her father, from the baker and his cubs—that strength possesses me, power like a stag in rut. Power like the star that burns behind my breastbone. And then through it, swelling, consuming . . . the darkness, the cold icy nothing that is the voice of my pack, which I will never hear again. Tarnished-silver, both molten and cold as the wild blue ice to the north. It will consume me. The wolf in me knows, pure and holy in its intention, untainted by the bitterness of the man, of the Suneater. *I am three souls, one heart. What justice is there?*

The wolf in me is the angel, and the wolf knows pity. *Let the girl die.*

But no. *She shall live with this as well.*

I lift her gently now, cradling her in mine arms like the child she is . . . and I give her something none of my brethren have given a human before.

I give her my kiss, and my sorrow, and the grief that eats me like a worm gnaws the root of a tree. I give her the Suneater's fury, and the anguish of the wolf and the suffering of the man. I give her my breath, and my kiss and my pain.

And then I drop her in the snow beside her father's corpse, and I turn, and I walk away.

Silent as a hunting owl, the Imogen has vanished in the snowfall. Perhaps Rannveig will freeze.

It would be a kindness.

I walk in spirals through the forest, the new strength on me as if I were ridden by something old and wild. Snow falls and falls: I leap up and run across its surface on light feet like a snow-hare's.

The pack, I remember—*Strifbjorn will have left by now*—and go to see to the bodies.

But he curls under the span of the copper beech, wrapped

tight in his cloak, heedless of the snow drifting. Waiting for me. I halt in the shadow of the cedars. The bodies . . . the bodies are gone.

Strifbjorn has cared for them for me.

I whimper, a wolf-cry for succor, for the attention and guidance of the pack leader. I step forward . . . I mean to step forward, and something binds my boot to the snow. I look down. I am ice-caked and blood-spattered, and I try again to lift my foot and step into the clearing.

Strifbjorn does not shift. He sits staring, snow falling over him as if frosting a statue, and I cannot go to him. I cannot. He is the pack, and the pack is dead, and I have forsaken what remains of it. Faithless.

My crimes are beyond forgiving, and still there is not enough blood.

Where I cannot go forward, I can leave.

I know not how long I walk, nor how far. A silence takes me—wolf-mind, a space without thought or remembrance, all endless motion. One foot, and then another foot and then another. Hiss of storm through tree boughs, crunch of snow under my boots. Small animals flee. They know a predator. The mountain is a memory behind me and I have walked the storm out when next something snags and focuses my mind.

Something that does not flee.

His cloven hooves break the crust of the snow, but he does not flounder as a deer would. He prances, the ivory of his coat like a stain on the snow. Tossing his matted mane, flared nostrils wet and red as blood, and the white sclera of his eyes shows me his fury.

Once more. Again.

I drop to my knees in the snow. Gloved fingers fumble the laces at my collar. I bare my throat to him, turning my head aside. He snorts and levels his horn. I close my eyes.

His annoyance and amusement press like a knife into my breast. The tip of the old stallion's horn bears down on into the thin pearly ribbon of my collar, dimples the skin behind it—but even a unicorn's horn cannot part that thread.

Do you not know a messenger yet, Wolfling? Did not your brother the Wyrm send me to your side? And did you not then go to it for counsel?

I have failed it, I say. *I cannot escape this story.*

But you eluded fate before. He paws the snow, and the pressure of the horn drives my collar into my skin. Red blood trickles over the ridges and hollows of my ribs, and still the horn cannot part the silken ribbon. *Am I not proof enough that nothing must be as it was foretold? Are you not proof enough of the delusiveness of prophecy?*

My fault. He says it is my fault.

He is right, and it is my fault, and I could have stopped this before it began.

"Put an end to it," I whisper.

I told thee to look to thy pack, he answers. *Live then, and be in the future less innocent.*

I hear nothing else. But when I open my eyes he has gone.

The Historian

Two days after the flyting, the storm broke into a bright, clear morning and I fled the crowded confines of the mead-hall like a partridge flushed from a coppice. The snow lay too deep for walking, but I needed silence and the deep woods over me.

And if I were Strifbjorn, I would have weathered the blizzard in Dale.

The valley road was drifted deep, but the high trail over the mountain—though shorter—would be harder work on skis, and the drifts and billows were too deep to wade through. Travel was faster in wintertime.

I dug my poles in and made good speed cross-country.

Snow hung heavy on the fir trees. The black edge of another stormfront rose up dripping from the east, but I judged I had until midafternoon. The clouds looked to be well out to sea, and sunlight fell so brilliant on the snow that the shadows under the firs gleamed blue. Only the hiss of powder under my skis broke the hush.

Skiing from the ferny embrace of the conifers into the sheltered valley, I was struck by the silence hanging over Dale. Snow had not been cleared from the doors of the houses—any of the houses.

I drove my poles deep and halted, breath curling from my lips in silvery filaments and fantastical whorls. The scene lay perfect before me, snow bowing branches to the ground, graceful as the line of a lady's skirts. No smell of smoke tainted the air, no *swanning* of an imminent death.

Just breathless stillness and a buried village.

And then I spotted a single lonely smoke-curl rising from a house at the far end of town.

I skied down the high street, remembering the hustling marketplace of only a few days before. The cottages were cold, doors ripped wide. Snow drifted over roofs on the windward side, but windows stood staring open.

I wondered what the snow hid, and I was glad not to know.

When I closed on that still-warm cottage, the poignancy of woodsmoke pierced me with all the things it should mean: home, and warmth and safety. Snow lay halfway up the wooden door—but there was a door, and that was something.

I thrust my poles into a drift and squatted to undo my bindings. I leaned the skis against the cottage and climbed the snowbank, taking care, for it was slippery. I tapped upon the door.

I didn't expect an answer: the latchstring had been drawn inside and I guessed the door was barred. In a moment, however, footsteps rustled through hay or pine boughs. I put my hand on Nathr and shuffled backwards through the snow.

The door swung in, and a young girl—fair-haired as one of my sisters, if not quite so lovely or tall—stood framed in the dimness, only the red light of coals in the fireplace behind her. Her eyes were glazed with fever. Her silence lay like a mantle across my shoulders. A goat bleated in the byre behind her.

She stepped back, barely, clutching the door for support so it creaked on the leather hinges. I half-hopped and half-slid down the high-piled snow into the cottage, and brought half of it with me.

She did not speak; I was not even certain she breathed. Her cheeks flushed bright against a livid pallor. Blankets from the bedstead trailed behind her, caught to her breast with a trembling hand. A shaggy dog big as a sheep pressed herself to her leg, brown eyes worried in her rough gray head. She whined, the tip of her tail quivering just a little as she assessed me.

"Child, where is everyone?"

She opened her mouth, closed it and fell into my arms.

The illness was on her like a passion. I know not where she found the strength to stand and open the door, the courage to walk so far on feet that had been gnawed by the frost. She'd lost toes, and the bedclothes stank of gangrene.

I commandeered the cottage for a chirurgery—boiling water in an iron kettle over the fire and dosing her with herbs, trickling goat's milk into her mouth from a rag, bathing her to break the fever that had her shivering like a captured hare.

She mumbled and cried in her delirium, quieting only when I lay down beside her and gathered her into my arms. "Mam," she whispered, and cuddled close. "Mam, I don't feel good."

It was an odd sensation, a child calling me mother, and not one I ever expected to know. That was one of the reasons marriage was so central a part of our rituals: those rare children came only to pairs who shared their spirits deeply and often. There were never so many of us, children of the Light, and not even enough babies born to replace the ones who perished. Fortunately, we were not easy to kill.

At midafternoon on the first day, the storm I had glimpsed on the horizon broke over us with a hiss like serpents. I risked a peek out the door and found frozen rain sheeting down like a wall of glass, freezing to everything it brushed. Hastily, I dragged my skis inside, before they could glaze to the snow, and leaned them against the wall beside the door.

I sat that night beside the girl's bed, tending her livestock and feeding the dog, which paced worriedly about the cottage between naps on her bed of straw just outside the byre. Every so often she crossed to the girl and nosed her hand out from under the covers. Once or twice she stirred, and once she cried out words that I could not understand.

The night stretched long. "So what's your name, then?" I asked the dog, and she looked at me and thumped her tail before coming over to rest her head on my knee. Near midnight, trees in the wood began exploding under the weight of the ice. In the spring, there would be clearings where seedlings could push up to greet the uncertain young sun.

In the morning, I had to break the door open. I caught my breath at the vision that met me: a world of crystal, glittering like a lens held up before a candleflame—too bright even for my eyes. The air I gasped was frigid. I closed the door in a hurry, not for my sake but for the girl's.

The second day passed much as the first, except I got some broth into her to go with the milk and there was no storm. The third day was no different, and I daydreamed through most of it with her head pillowed on my scant bosom.

On the fourth day she awakened, and her eyes were clear. Her lips parted; she licked them, grimacing at the pain of a dry tongue meeting fever cracks. She tried to speak and croaked.

"Lass, wait." I brought her warm water from the pot pulled up beside the fire, with honey and herbs stirred into it. Her hair was like straw when I brushed it from her face.

I cradled her head in my other hand while she drank from

the cup I held, until she raised her hand to signal enough. I lowered her onto sweat-damp ticking and sat on the stool beside her bed.

"Now tell me what transpired."

She took a breath, but her face contorted and she started to sob. I held her through that as well, the brave candle-flicker, until she could speak through the tears. "We angered a spirit," she said. "And he killed everyone."

"Except you."

She nodded and then choked, her hand rising to her mouth.

"What's your name, lass?"

"Rannveig the woodcutter's . . . Rannveig."

"Tell me about your spirit. How did you anger it?"

"He rescued me from my father's . . . *friend*. In the forest. And then when I went to thank him, they must have followed me. And they killed . . ." Her voice trailed off, her fingers plucking at the eiderdown.

Patience. She was doing her best. I thought her brave. "What did they kill?"

"A pack of wolves." Her eyes closed tight, and I did not know if she meant to remember, or hide from memory's sight. "And he came back with a demon, and . . ."

"Oh, no." I laid my forehead in the palm of my hand and moaned. "No. Oh, no. So he took his vengeance on the village." *The greengrocer, the babies in carriers. The woman in the blue skirts who crossed the street out of fear of me.*

"Yes."

"And he spared you?"

Both her hands clenched in front of her mouth, the right

one dragging the eiderdown with it. "Not spared," she whispered. "Just didn't kill."

I forced my voice to gentleness and called the Light up in my eyes. Just now, it might resemble the tossing light of a storm more than the glow of a summer night. "Please explain."

She breathed deep once, twice. "I wanted him to kiss me, before." Another breath, taken and held, and the expression on her face shaded from terror into longing. Her voice grew ragged and caught. "And he did."

"And then?" The dog shoved her tousled head into my lap. She did not growl me away from the girl, but I thought it was an effort for her.

Her jaw tensed. I thought she chewed her cheek, and slow tears rolled through her lashes almost gently. "And then he gave me his pain, and left me lying in the snow beside my father. I would still be there if Bo hadn't come looking for me and made me come into the house."

"Bo?"

She ruffled the ears of the worried dog. "Bo."

My heart ached—not for the Wolf, for what he had done here was beyond my capacity to meet with pity. But oh. Oh, Strifbjorn.

"Where is your father, Rannveig?"

She looked at me as if I had grown wings. "Under the snow by the door, Bright one. The Wolf killed him." Her frostbitten hands knotted before her chest, and she shuddered. Blackened flesh cracked, showing pink beneath. She seemed not to notice. "I wouldn't have minded, if he had killed me like that. But to leave me alive, with this . . . this in me. Oh. How he must hate."

The Warrior

By the time Strifbjorn started moving, the snow was too deep for walking. He floundered through drifts until he found a spruce, its branches bowed under its salt-white crown. He slipped in under its bower, where there was a depression in the snow, and placed his hand against the bark.

He sang to the tree. He hadn't the power with music that Yrenbend or Muire did—his voice was more suited to supporting than leading a wreaking itself—but his skills were adequate to small tasks. The tree shivered, awakening under his touch. He cautioned it back to near-slumber—sap flowing at the start of winter would be disastrous—and in chanted words explained what he needed.

Light traced spirals up the spruce from Strifbjorn's fingertips, swirling like coils of smoke. The bark writhed, peeled back from pale wood beneath. In moments, long pale slats grew like ribs from the trunk. Strifbjorn leaned into the song and a perfect pair of skis dropped to the snow. A rustle above and two strong, straight limbs marked with swellings three inches from pointed ends daggered into the drifts. Poles.

He sang the wound in the bark closed and thanked the tree. Then he sat in the snow under its branches to see what he could improvise for bindings.

He skied north, mostly, along the seacoast and away from the Ulfenfell. He would have vowed not to return, but he knew it for a lie in advance of the telling.

He had a great deal of time to think. Didn't it seem odd that the villagers trapped the wolves so easily? The whole pack, all at once and together? That none escaped? How many men or what magic would that require?

Strifbjorn skied from bare-branched foothills into the cold desert places farther north. Hillocked ground gave way to tundra, less thickly blanketed by snow. Any snow at all was unusual this far north: the thirsty ice usually drank all water from the air.

The deaths of the wolves seemed odd indeed. He meant to understand it. The relentless rhythm, the hiss of his skis, parted the numb silence that had wrapped him since Mingan left. Pieces and shards began to fall into place. With them came a cold, old, patient determination. For the sake of his love, and his brethren, and the poor mortal candle-flickers Heythe so easily discarded. For the wolves, and for the world. She would not be rid of Strfbjorn this easily.

That passion came with a flaring of the Light through his veins, burning a dire conviction.

It was wrath, and it was holy.

With the darkness of the evening, a freezing rain began.

10

Whence cometh the sun
The smooth skies bestriding
Once Fenrir hath her consumed?
—*Vafþrúðnismál*

The Wolf

The ice storm does not catch me until I emerge from the birches. Bitter rain soaks my cloak, slicks my clothes to my skin as I cross the meadow. My boots break a crust on the snow. It matters not: I am numb at the heart already.

The rain steams on my skin.

I come the long way around. I wish to look upon the hall of my brothers as I approach it.

Look to thy pack. I failed one family.

I will not fail another.

When I enter, the mead-hall is crowded, benches arrayed along both sides of the long trestles. My brothers and sisters sit or stand gossiping and dicing. Many from other halls came for the flyting, and more have flooded in, drawn by the word that a Lady has returned to us.

The talk gutters as I enter, my cloak black with rain. Every gaze that seeks my face slides away again as if from ice. Tendrils of vapor rise from my clothes and hair. A ripple of silence paces me the length of the hall as I stride, head high, to stand before Heythe's chair.

Yrenbend does not hide his face as I pass, but nods once as if in recognition of an equal. I do not choose to see him. I am the Grey Wolf, the Suneater, and I have no equals. I have masters, and I have prey.

Heythe rises as I ascend to her chair. Skeold stands beside her, her hand on her black crystal sword. But I let my hand fall far from Svanvitr's hilt, my fingers relaxed.

"Master Wolf," Heythe greets me, resplendent in blue robes traced with gold embroidery, her surcote and kirtle cut low across her bosom to display the glitter of her necklace against skin white as silk. Her hair drips crystal. In the torchlight, she shimmers.

"Lady," I answer, and hear the collective intake of breath behind me as I drop to one knee. "Permit this one to serve."

She never hesitates, nor do her eyes so much as widen. Her hand falls on my bowed head, blessing and sanction. Fingertips strong and light outline the curve of my ear, slide under the five-strand plait to ruffle the hair on my nape. The low whimper in the back of my throat is a cry of submission that might have shamed me once. But no longer.

Done with that caress, absently completed as fondling the ears of a favorite dog, she tilts my face to look me in the eye. I can feel the brethren watching as she bends, the floor-brushing sleeves of her surcote falling about me like the curtains of a tapestried bed.

"Master Wolf," she says, her voice soft luxury, "you are wet to the skin, and filthy with blood. I bid you use my chamber.

Go and undress; make yourself warm and clean"—as if steam were not rising from my plastered shirt—"wait for me there. I will speak with you when you are comfortable."

Her pointing finger directs me to a curtained niche. A shiver that derives not from ice-rimed hair or clothing rattles my teeth. Strifbjorn's bench. Which the Lady has claimed for her own. I nod, swallow and go where I am bid. It is a long walk—the length of the hall a second time. As I step into the alcove, I hear the pitch of conversation swell.

I have been in this niche only once before, when Heythe choked me insensible. There is just enough room beyond the tapestry for a bench and a wardrobe. I strip off my shirt, boots and cloak and hang Svanvitr on the wall, but I leave the leathern trousers on despite clotted blood. A thrall arrives with warm water and bathes me. He unbraids my hair, combs and washes it and combs it again. There's no reason to stop him. None that makes any sense.

But once I've let him pull my plait apart, nothing else he asks of me can matter. I let him take the clothes for laundering, and the filthy trousers, too.

My skin prickles, and I might slide under the furs and the eiderdown, curled up small around the ache in my belly—but the bench smells of Heythe, layered over the scent of Strifbjorn, and that is more than I can bear. Worst is the way the raindrop light from my collar fills up the niche once my shirt is unlaced and set aside.

I find a dark scarf laid on the dressing-bench and wind it

about my throat to contain the glow. Then I lean back on the bench and close my eyes, numb as a drunken tongue, and try not to listen to what I can hear of the conversation beyond.

Heythe leaves me until sunrise, when the storm has ended and the shutters are thrown back from the high windows above, letting wintry sunlight spill into the hall. I know she's coming. I hear the faint scrape of her chair under the talk, and the way the voices of my brothers swell for a moment, then fall silent.

She brushes the tapestry aside and steps past, allowing it to swing shut behind her. The illusion of privacy. But nothing can be said here that will not be heard by anyone passing close.

She is radiant in the dawnlight, her hair as golden as the wires of her necklace, her eyes as bright as the sky glimpsed through the windows above. Her gaze travels over me, lingering. A slow flush caresses my chest and my face.

"Master Wolf," she says through the curve of her lips. She shrugs her mantle off and lets it puddle on the cold earthen floor. She unpins, too, the net of crystals from her high-piled hair. Strands wander downward as she moves.

"Lady. I thank you your hospitality." I have never been ashamed of nakedness, but the way she examines me leaves me sweating.

"You've sworn to my service," she replies. "It is but your due, my duty."

"Aye. And how may I serve you, then?"

"Oh, you may begin by unlacing this surcote. I find I can hardly breathe in the damned thing."

She turns her back. My fingers tremble on the laces, but I

manage the knots at last and the gown falls at her feet in a stiff rush of linen and golden thread. She stoops in her kirtle to pick it up, her shoulders and buttocks straining the fabric. I glance away as she stands and hangs the gown in the cabinet against the wall. She does not turn to me until she has stepped out of her boots and slithered the kirtle over her head.

She wears no shift, and her intent gleams in her eyes as she comes to me. "I have wanted this since first you laid hands on me, Mingan."

I think she will kiss me, but she lifts my hair aside and talks on, her voice low and soft as she unwinds the black sash. I cannot exhale.

"Let me see you without pretenses." The length of cloth unfastened, she draws it slowly into one hand. Her hand falls back to her side as she judges the shiver that runs through me.

So close the air moving between us strokes my skin like feathers, and yet she does not touch me, quite. She looks at me with expectation in her eyes. I brush fingers along the wires and jewels of her necklace, hunting the clasp by feel under the fall of unpinned hair. She stops me with a touch on my wrist.

"No, Wolf. So long as you wear your collar, I shall wear mine in sympathy."

She smiles, and steps into my arms, her skin cool as linen sheets, her mouth wet and chill as it runs through the unshaven prickles along my jaw, down my throat past the collar to my chest and lower still.

In the morning, I plait my own hair.

The Historian

Once her fever broke, Rannveig recovered rapidly. Two days later, after I assured myself there were no other survivors— human or animal—in Dale, I turned my attention to the task of getting her safely to Northerholm with her dowry. She wouldn't last a winter alone in the village, and I couldn't take her back to the hall.

It took most of a day. I made my way to the fishing town, and paid for a sledge to be sent for her and her livestock and goods, for her lodging through the winter and feed for her beasts.

Then I returned to tell her that she wouldn't be ruined, at least—she had property of her own, if she ever chose to return to Dale, and the beasts would dower her in Northerholm or fetch enough in the spring markets to see her south to a city. I gave her such coin as I carried, and she took as well what her father had in store.

She moved through it all with a dreamlike absence, a sorrow so deep on her that even if I touched her skin I could not touch her heart. Music could bring neither smiles nor tears to her face, and when the men with the sledge came for her and set her there beside her sheep, her goat, her dog and her bedstead and tied the cow behind, she only turned to me and raised a hand in thanks. The short day of winter was ending behind her.

It was all she could muster. It was enough.

My thoughts lay dark and still. Mingan should have killed her. It would have been a kindness.

But she had had the strength to drag herself into the cottage, bar the door and rekindle the fire. She had the strength to drag herself from blood and death and the worst the Grey Wolf could devise, and for that she deserved a chance.

She could still become a seeress. A sorceress, a witch.

I did not think she would marry.

I leaned against the cottage wall, binding on my skis. My poles were where I left them. I started home, skiing in darkness, more than six days after I left.

The hall was alight when I skied into the bottom of the meadow, the night clear and the stars blazing overhead like jeweled earrings thrust through a cloth for display. Moonlight gleamed on untrammeled snow. Closer to the hall, black shadows fell in the ruts. I stopped for a moment to take it in, the wind bringing me the distant noise of my brethren.

Despite Heythe, despite Sigrdrifa, despite the destruction wrought on Dale—I felt in that moment a part of something bigger than myself. A brotherhood, a great and knowing thing that somehow I still believed would prevail. Love and pity and hope buoyed my mood.

I dug my poles into the snow and ice and glided down the hill toward home.

I slipped in through the postern door, my skis and poles tucked under my arm. I meant to stow them and join the festivities once I had washed and changed, but rather stopped in the shadows just inside the door.

Heythe sat on her gilded seat before the Raven Banner, a gleaming white mantle cast over her sea-green gown. *She must have amassed quite a trousseau.*

It amused me, in the moment before I registered the dark-clad shadow who lounged beside her, one arm draped over the back of her chair. She turned to him, her hand possessively on his waist above the sword-belt. He bent to her in the fire-dancing darkness and she spoke into his ear while my gorge rose up my throat. The line her fingertips traced down his hip spoke more than every book rolled up and stored in my niche.

Oh, Strifbjorn. Betrayed and betrayed. And no hope that the Lady would punish Mingan for his crimes. I closed my eyes. And—feeling another's gaze upon me—opened them again. The Grey Wolf was staring.

Whether he noticed me returning the gaze, his eyes flickered quickly away. His attention might have been drawn by something as simple as my movement in the darkness, and he might have seen and dismissed me as the least of his brethren.

What shocked me into stillness was his expression. I had expected . . . sorrow, or grief or perhaps dark triumph. But his face was slack and still, almost in repose. A death mask, and his smile held a distant, lordly amusement: the predator's appraisal of the prey. His eyes burned in exhaustion hollows. The light in them had not dimmed, but it was a new, harsh light, such as might sear flesh from bone.

My hands prickled numb with fear. But under it I found a slow, shadowy thing. Disdain.

For Sigrdrifa. For the Grey Wolf. And for the Lady I had once anticipated serving, a fortnight and a lifetime ago.

Heythe touched Mingan's arm again. He swayed to her, and she spoke against his ear. He smiled, a cold smile with no juice in it. And then stepped down from the dais, obedient to whatever instruction his mistress had given.

I watched his gray-cloaked shoulders moving through the press of bodies, and then I went in search of Yrenbend.

The Wolf

The storm heralds a break in the weather, holding five days cold and clear, and with it the frost of winter ices me also. I stand behind Heythe's chair in darkness like a hand on my soul, or I move through the shadows of the mead-hall like the ghost I am becoming. My brethren's eyes skip off mine. When I pass their talk falters. They eye me with dread and disgust. The Suneater returns the stares with mockery. There is no pain in the rejection. The pain is far away. When I step into the shadows and watch them from that cold and distant road, I hear my name whispered in corners, speculation and—once little Muire returns from her errand, her errantry—some hint of truth.

So I learn that the woodcutter's daughter lived.

Even my new allies, Heythe's most loyal—Skeold, Sigrdrifa—show me fear after that. I overhear Herfjotur in fevered conversation with Bergdis, in sunlight under a snow-drenched spruce, and learn that Strifbjorn has vanished into exile.

Heythe brings me to her bench in the evenings or the afternoons. She teaches a commerce lingering and artful, that carries no memory of a more furtive, passionate lovemaking.

Nothing hurts me, and though her hands wander cool across my skin, nothing touches me. When she is done and while she sleeps I watch her, the Suneater plotting, or I wander the shadowed path. Nothing tires me at first, while the liquor of the souls

I have drunk is heady in me. I have not been so strong and wild since before the collar was wound about my throat, in another world, on the other side of a star-strewn void.

It is all an education, in more than the arts of making love.

Heythe thinks she owns me. And as the days pass, if I am honest with myself in the distance that has fallen over me, I feel her caresses like a brand whenever her eye passes over me.

It is an education in manipulation, in domination, in control—and I drink it up like wine, along with the secrets and the plots my brethren whisper in the shadows, forgetting I can hear. I keep their secrets.

I am here for you, O my brothers.

I am here. For you.

The Warrior

Strifbjorn ran out of snow before he reached the mile-tall ice cliffs looming on the horizon, so he turned west and inland. He didn't count the passing days. His awareness narrowed to the hissing under his skis. The blood on his clothing browned and flaked, stains patterning his trousers and shirtfront. Sometimes his thoughts chased each other in miserable circles. More often, as time went by, he was aware of nothing but the blind white emptiness arching up over him, and that was good.

The northern wastes spread endless and empty. Strifbjorn glimpsed caribou and a white bear, his namesake, but neither humans nor another like himself. On the third or fourth or fifth day, Strifbjorn found himself on his knees in the snow, his right ski snapped, with no recollection of how he'd gotten there. He braced himself on his pole, levered upward . . . and fell to the side. Though he pushed and struggled, there would be no rising. He'd exhausted himself.

Rounded rocks—a layer of glacial till—prodded him through the snow. The children of the Light did not sleep, not unless they were wounded. But Strifbjorn wished then that he could, could sleep and never wake again.

He pulled his head into the shelter of his cloak, yanked his boots from the bindings and hid from the brief winter sun.

Hours later, the thunder of vast wings roused him. He blinked and rolled stumbling upright, Alvitr in his hand before he recognized the moonlit silhouette of Herfjotur's steed. He was barely earthbound, wings still furling, when she slid down his shoulder and came running to Strifbjorn like a child.

Strifbjorn held Alvitr wide so Herfjotur would not impale herself on the blade, and the waelcyrge threw herself into his arms.

She pounded his back for a moment, weeping, and then stepped back and punched him in the nose.

Strifbjorn went down on his ass, blood gushing down his face until he focused enough to heal. He thought inanely that it wasn't like a little more blood would damage his shirt at this point. And that she hadn't pulled the punch.

"Light, Strifbjorn, where the Hel have you been?" She grabbed his swordless hand and hauled him up. His blood smeared her glove.

He gestured along his back trail, a single furrow reaching into darkness. You could see it for a long way, under the moon. "Skiing."

From the look on her face Strifbjorn thought she was likely

to hit him again. Instead, she shook her head and sat down on a snow-covered rock. Her stallion tossed his heads and pawed the snow, responding to her emotion.

"Things are bad," she said, after a little.

Strifbjorn found another boulder nearby and dusted it off before he sat. He left his cloak lying in compacted snow. The clasp was broken anyway. "How bad?"

She kicked her rock with her heel. "Really bad. Mingan . . . Strifbjorn, Muire says he . . ."

She can't say it, so he filled her silence. It was one of his duties, to do what the others cannot.

It *was* one of his duties.

"How many did he kill?"

Her eyebrow notched higher. "All of Dale: Fifty or so. One survivor."

"Oh."

"He raped her."

It was three deep breaths before Strifbjorn could speak. Even then, his voice broke. "He . . . raped . . . ?" He could not—no. *He was* mine, *and he would never—*

Herfjotur could not lie. She put her head down on her knees and knotted her hands on her braids. Strifbjorn saw her scalp pale, so hard she pulled her own hair. She moaned.

My fault. All of it my fault. I should have—

"Oh, Light," he said, and sank his teeth in the back of his hand. "He . . . I . . ."

She shook her head without lifting it, as if it was easier to keep speaking with her face pressed to her knees. "Not like that. But he . . ."

No. That was no better.

"Forced his kiss on her? Oh. Bearer of Burdens." Horror took Strifbjorn's breath away. The thing he had not accepted came home all at once, brilliantly, with the painless flash of a knifeblade plunged between his eyes. Mingan was lost.

Not just to me, but for all time.

Strifbjorn stood. He crouched and picked up his bearskin, shook off the snow.

"Strifbjorn?"

He bent the clasp more or less together with his thumbs. "I'll kill him myself." She did not rise, and he knew the news only got worse. "Did you hear me? I said I'll kill him myself."

"I heard you, war-leader."

Light, don't call me that. "What else is there, Herfjotur?"

She swallowed hard. His hands, his face, his arms—like so much senseless flesh hung on him. He could not feel at all, and he was grateful. "What?"

"Heythe. She's sent the children out, about their tasks. I've been seeking you since I could get away. She told them to use their kiss as a punishment, Strifbjorn, and I don't know how many will obey."

"Right," Strifbjorn said. "Who remains at the hall?"

"Some two dozen. And there's more about Mingan."

His knees failed. He sat back on the stone. *Get it over with, Herfjotur!* "Tell me."

She weighed her words silently. It was like having the skin stripped inch by inch from his face.

"He swore fealty to Heythe. And—Strifbjorn—she's bedding him. Quite . . . flaunting it. Just as if they were married."

"I see." A revelation unfolded in his mind, the shape of bloody bodies piled in the snow. The impossibility of the villagers, alone, planning and carrying out such a hunt—the unlikelihood that they would dare anger the spirits of the mountain.

"Blood and the cold of Niflheim," he cursed, hatred on his soul like nothing he had known.

"What?"

He was on his feet again, fists clenched white. He stared at her boots and thought of air coming in and out of his lungs, counting breaths until he could speak. "Heythe. The wolves. Damn her. She planned it. She broke him, Herfjotur, and she took him away from me, and I was the blind bloody fool who let her do it. First the children, and then Mingan. She's got us at each other's throats, and I warrant it has nothing to do with any giant army from over the sea."

Herfjotur lifted her head. "Can you be sure?"

"I can never be *sure*. But I'm as certain of it as I've been of anything." He looked up from the snow. "I need you to get me into that mead-hall. Will you risk it?"

She needed that. She needed direction. A job.

She needed him.

She gathered herself and stood, dusting snow from her seat. "For you, war-leader?" she said. "I will risk whatever you need me to."

The Wolf

On the evening of the seventh day, we meet in council. The *Althing*. Heythe takes her place at the head of the hall. Skeold and I flank her chair. The Raven Banner flickers against my back, rippled by the draft through the wall. Arngeir—stiff and hostile—sits in what was Strifbjorn's place, Yrenbend in what was mine. Arngeir, at least, will be trouble for the Lady, and the Lady has my oath.

Yrenbend alone still will meet my stare. He regards me steadily, his hair shining red in the torchlight over the planes and hollows of his face. His lips shape words while Heythe looks away, down to the cross-bench, with a small crease between her eyes, as if counting the waelcyrge there. *I hope you know what you're doing, brother.* And then he turns away to Arngeir, as if nothing had passed between us.

Sigrdrifa brings ale to Heythe and myself. Skeold steps down from the dais to wander the hall. If the venom in Sigrdrifa's look as she hands me the horn could drip into the drink, I would be convulsing on the floor. But I salute her with it, and speak in a voice that only she and Heythe will hear. "Habit of stepping into thy place, haven't I?"

Heythe does not glance up. Sigrdrifa turns her head and spits into the pine boughs, then wheels and strides away.

"You'll have to kill her," Heythe says, out of the corner of her mouth.

So easily, she sets this other aside. It's no surprise. "After the battle, my Lady." I tilt my head at the Banner. Heythe offers me her hand and I support her to her feet.

"After the battle." The hall falls silent as she rises.

I step into the shadows behind her chair, just watching. Yrenbend seeks my eye. I shake my head. I swore to serve her.

If there is treason in the hall, I will choose not to know.

If there is—and I choose not to know if this is so—Yrenbend is at its root.

I think now that I will someday kill him. The Suneater smiles with my lips, remembering the taste of blood. I have always liked Yrenbend—intelligent, unflinching, strong.

And yet there is no pain.

Heythe takes a breath, surveys her small kingdom. She doesn't trouble herself to rule it, leaving whatever decisions must be made to Skeold and Sigrdrifa. She takes no interest in the daily business of the einherjar.

I wonder how it would have been, if Strifbjorn had stayed. I think of yellow hair through my hands.

I tell myself there is no pain.

The Lady's eyes meet with Arngeir's, especially, and those of Herewys. Ulfgar the smith pushes back from the table as if to rise, his bearded face wreathed in a frown. A tense ripple runs the length of the hall, rebounding and returning like a wave in a washtub.

"Brethren," Heythe says, her voice ringing clear, "it is time to take up our great task again. This has been a season of turmoil and upheaval for the children of the Light . . . but that must now come to an end. I charge each of you to go back into the world, to take up your burdens and wait for my summons."

Her voice falls on our ears with rich and sonorous tones, lulling and exhorting. Her eyes flash as she throws her mantle back, golden embroidery blazing in the torchlight. At the crossbench, I see little Muire scribbling with the quill and inkpot that are always on her person. Charmed, I could laugh, if the Suneater were not watching; she is writing on the cuff of her kirtle. *For posterity.*

She does not look up as Heythe takes breath and speaks again. "There is a war on the horizon." She gestures floridly over her shoulder, toward the Banner I stand before. A rustle among the crowd. Voices murmur among the stirring of cloth. "But we cannot permit that war to interfere with our duties to the world and to men. You know what I have asked you."

The rhythm of her words washes me. I study the others. There is Brynhilde, leaning forward, nodding tightly but unhappily, and Yrenbend watching her rather than Heythe, as if immune to the spell of Heythe's words. I barely hear, so far-flung is my attention. And yet I step up to stand at heel behind her, a carrion crow at the beck of a songbird. *Sorcery?* I wonder, remembering the cataract of remembrance in which she washed me.

My brethren nod, frown. Most of them. Menglad Brightwing bites her lip and looks down, leaning to speak to Muire, who nods like the others but still does not look up, even when she dips her pen and turns her wrist, still writing. I stand behind a wall of ice—clear as rock crystal, cold and unyielding. Tens upon tens of them, so many they range against the walls and scatter near the fire trench, almost every face upturned to Heythe, ensorcelled by her power.

Her voice dips and sways. "Each of you will return to your tasks—but I grant you this new right, children of the Light. To carry out your retribution with a kiss, when convenient, and hoard that strength for whatever enemies may find us."

She pauses for breath, drawing my attention. Her face is white and taut beneath the rouge and jewels. She lays her hand on my arm, as if in benediction. The coldness of her touch seeps through my sleeve. I lay my opposite hand over hers.

She never looks at me, but I see her struggle to stand. She's enchanted them all. Almost all. No sorceress I've heard sing of could manage such a thing.

Even for a goddess, it has exacted a price.

She draws herself up. Through my lust and loathing, I admire her courage, for I think that only I glimpse her weakness. "Sigrdrifa and the Grey Wolf will instruct you tomorrow."

Clever, for by laying her hand on me, she turned every eye in the room to me. I know what they think.

They still cannot look at my face. Eyes slip from my defiance, resettle on the Lady. I sense them stretching toward her, reaching like waves up a cliff.

Heythe trembles. She draws breath again, and only I hear her sob of effort. The Suneater looks at her with my eyes, appraising her weakness. Prey? Not yet.

But even she has limits.

"We begin in the morning." She nods, and dismisses their attention. Their focus falls back on themselves like that wave into the ocean, and around us the tide of discussion swells. Heythe clings to my arm, white and shaking. She leans close, as if to offer me her kiss. I bend until my lips brush hers. Her arms go around my neck, and only my grip at her waist keeps her from falling. The brethren do not scruple to hide their mirth.

They have their theories, no doubt, of what wedge drove between myself and Strifbjorn. Inane as grackles. They do not see the weariness that folds my Lady into my arms.

"Carry me to bed," she whispers. "Make it look good."

Ribald laughter dogs us as I sweep her from her feet and bear her down the dais, but for once she is too tired for what I coldly term love, and I am grateful.

11

The warrior-god, wolf-destroyer
War-tempered,
Better payment bequeathed me:
My grief-gift given voice.
And to song-craft supplied he
One more measure of mettle
A heart gorged on hate.
—*Sonatorrek,* by Egill Skallagrimsson

The Historian

I did not wait for dawn, but left the *Althing* minutes after the Grey Wolf carried his new lover off to bed. It was all I could do not to turn my head and spit on the floor as they passed.

Before I left, I changed my kirtle and surcote for trousers and a tunic, and wrapped my star-blue cloak about my shoulders. Then I slid my belt-knife from its sheath and I went to work on the dress. It was the work of moments to pick out the stitches binding sleeve to bodice. I folded my scribbled cuff into a roll, careful of the ink so it might not smudge.

That done, I followed the strains of his flute to Yrenbend.

He had dragged a little bench outside, beside the door, and sat in the starlit darkness playing a fragile descending tune I'd never heard before. I leaned against the wall beside him and started binding on my skis. He played a few bars to me, eyes dancing behind the flute despite the sorrow in the music, and then he brought the tune to a close with a flourish.

He stood and slid the flute into its case at his hip. I handed him my sleeve.

"What's this?" he asked.

"You tell me, Yrenbend." I kept my voice low. "And come out here." I led him into the meadow, gliding on my skis while he floundered behind. He stopped at last, amid a bright expanse of starlight, and I skied in a circle, coming back to him. He held my sleeve up to the starlight, squinting at soot-dark ink blotting white linen.

"This is from Heythe's speech," he said.

"But not all of it," I answered. "Only stressed words and alliterations. Some linking bits."

"It's poetry."

"Worked into the text."

He looked down at me, lowering his arm to his side, the sleeve trailing from his fingers like a flag of parley. "It's not my specialty, Muire." His clever eyes went dark and thoughtful, and he frowned.

"Sorcery."

"Ah." He glanced toward the open doors of the hall, at our brethren coming out and going inside in clumps and clusters and trios and pairs, deep in worried conversation.

The Raven Banner hung behind Heythe's chair, prophesying war and victory. Heythe was our Lady, our leader, and perhaps her path was the only one to assure victory against the terrible enemy she foresaw.

But I was a poet, too, and I recognized the strains of sorcery she wove over my brethren, although I could never have matched her power. "It's a spell of willing mind, Yrenbend," I whispered. "A binding."

"She's . . . the whole hall? Such strength! Damn me, Muire . . . I felt nothing."

I chuckled. "See there?" I point at the other side of the sleeve.

He lifted it again, and examined the smaller, hasty scribble. "Runes. Your name, and mine and protection?"

"Shelter and hiding, aye. I warded us."

His laughter rang out clearly through the night. I held up a hand in warning as a figure approached, behind him, and then dropped it again as he turned and we both recognized Herfjotur.

"I'm going for Strifbjorn," she said, her voice brooking no argument. "If we are moving, we must move. He—can you make a spell that will hide him, Muire? Even from the Lady?"

I did not know. But I nodded.

Yrenbend touched my shoulder, approving. He said, "I will direct the trustworthy ones to Arngeir's hall. We will regroup there." Yrenbend's jaw tightened. "Muire says a sorcery was laid over us all."

Herfjotur touched an amulet at her throat. A gift of her dead husband. "I felt it," she said. "But my thoughts were not changed after."

"Others will not be so strong," I answered. "You were not willing to be swayed by Heythe in anything."

Her hand dropped. "Can you break her hold on them?"

Frustration a sourness in my throat, I had to shake my head. "I haven't the strength. But it will fade if they are out of her presence. And I can ward a few."

She gnawed her lip and then shook her head. "Herewys, then. Menglad, Arngeir. Brynhilde. Can you do more than that?"

I thought, chin tucked. "No." My right hand curled into a fist, wishing for the power to strike Heythe's sorcery down.

"It will be enough. Brynhilde and I on our steeds can reach many of our brethren, as they go out in the world. It's just a matter of getting to them before they do anything . . ." *irredeemable*.

Her silence hung. Then: "Will you remain here, Yrenbend?"

"It will be dangerous. Especially once Heythe knows of the revolt. But aye, I shall remain."

"I was . . ." I let my voice trail off. *It's such a small and futile hope, a tiny thing.* I was certain it would come to naught, but there was the hope that shard of decency might lie, still, in the heart of the Wolf. If it came to war, the children could possibly stand against Heythe, and against whoever she might succeed in tarnishing.

But not against Mingan, and not against the Imogen.

Yrenbend gestured me to continue.

"I was going to fetch the girl, Rannveig, from Northerholm. Set her before Mingan's eye. To stir his pity, has he any."

"My steed and I will fetch her when we return," Herfjotur said. "And you may treat with her here. Tonight, weave your wardings, and in the morning I will need a pass-unseen for Strifbjorn. Can you manage it?"

"Aye. I can manage it."

She fingered Solbiort's hilt with something like satisfaction, and gave me a curt, conspiratorial nod. "Tomorrow, then. And if not, the day after."

Yrenbend laid a hand on her shoulder. "And until then?"

Herfjotur shrugged. "Then I think you're in charge, Yrenbend."

She cocked her head skyward, a distant expression crossing her face. A moment later and the rush of wind from the wings of her pale steed swirled stinging crystals of snow all around us. The stallion appeared caparisoned in saddle and bells. He dropped to one knee so Herfjotur could mount more conveniently.

She swung up and waved, clutching the pommel one-handed as her mount bore her skyward. Yrenbend winked at me, silencing whatever useless thing I had been about to say. Together, we returned to the mead-hall, where I withdrew to my niche to sketch spells until I understood how they must work.

Before morning, I was bent over the bellows in the smithy.

For three hours I stood among the bar and scrap and the racks of tools, melting gold and stamping it into bands, working by the light of the forge and thick candles set well back from the heat. In the open smithy, the wind iced my back and the heat of the forge seared my face. I wondered how a mortal would endure. When the rings had cooled enough to hold the imprint, I tooled runes on the insides. *Menglad, Arngeir, Brynhilde, Herewys. Muire, Yrenbend, Herfjotur.*

I set the butter-bright, butter-soft gold on a scorched oak table in the corner and turned back to the forge, blowing the coals up hot once more. Thick silver softened in the glow, and with hammer-blows and main strength I stretched and bent it into a diadem, set with smoky quartz and rock crystal.

The rhythm of the work caught me up and I poured my

frustration into it, the swing of the hammer and the hiss of the bellows. When Ulfgar crept up behind me, the smith startled me so badly that I almost caught him in the face with the hammer when I spun. I gasped and he chuckled at me, turning away to examine the little pile of gleaming rings.

He picked one up with his fingertips, holding it close to his face. His time at the forge had given him admirable shoulders, and he braided his queue in five strands to keep it short and out of the fire: it hung in a round column only to the middle of his back. "Pretty," he said. "Nice work."

I nodded. "A gift for a friend." It was Brynhilde's, and I watched as he turned it over in his hand.

"A warding?"

Was he Heythe's? The worry curdled like soured milk in my mouth. Ulfgar was a friend, someone who worked the bellows while I pounded steel. A valraven, a hippogriff, partnered him. He had never married.

There is no reason why a brother cannot also be an enemy. I thought of Mingan. *A brother. Or a lover.* "Yes," I said. "We are going to war, after all."

He nodded and rolled the band between his fingers. As casually as I could, I picked up the others and dropped them into the pocket of my scarred leathern apron while Ulfgar raised my ring to his eye and peered at me through it, winking broadly. The motion folded the fine lines at the corner of his eye. I looked away, and held my hand out for Brynhilde's ring.

"May I borrow this a moment?" He tilted it so I could see the design of oak leaves I had stamped around the surface. Yrenbend's bore a pattern of feathers, and the others were marked with flowers or different sorts of leaves. "I'd like to . . ." His voice drifted off. He cleared his throat. "Show it to a lady I mean to ask a question of soon."

"Bergdis?"

He smiled. "If we all live that long."

It would seem suspicious to say he cannot take it. I nodded and waved him inside with it. "If we all live that long, Ulfgar, I'll *make* you the rings."

He returned just as I was setting the last stone in the diadem, the crystals evenly spaced to catch the music I planned to weave into it soon. "She thought the ring lovely," he said with a smile. "The Lady commented on it as well. She said to show her the next."

Ulfgar dropped the ring into my gapping pocket and leaned over my shoulder to examine the work on the silver. "Not for you," he commented. "That would suit a man's head."

"It's a gift as well."

"Ah." He laid a hand on my shoulder, squeezing gently. "Muire, it's good to see you . . . moving on. You deserve a good husband."

His words went into me like a scalpel working the edge of a wound. I tilted my head and looked him in the eye. "Ulfgar, you never asked," I said, and he grinned at me out of a face tanned to leather by the forge.

"I already knew the answer," he replied, and clapped me on the shoulder, turning as if to go.

I watched him leave. Setting my tongs down, I dug in my pocket until I came up with Brynhilde's ring. It seemed untouched, and I frowned over it. At last, I pursed my lips and whistled up the dweomer of magic around it, studying the calm blue-silver glow.

All appeared as it should.

I resolved to re-enchant it anyway.

The Wolf

Heythe tugs her boots over the cuffs of her trousers and straightens, stamping her feet into place. A cold draft disorders the fine curled hair at the nape of her neck. Amused, I watch her.

I prefer her this way, rough-clad, hair bound in a simple braid bouncing down her back. She still wears the necklace, invisible behind the laced collar of her shirt, and over the shirt she layers a sweater and a reindeer-skin coat. I toss my cloak over my shoulder and refrain from comment, although she raises an eyebrow.

The night before, she had turned to me in the darkness and whispered, "Take me to where it happened."

"What is that, my Lady?"

"Where your pack was killed."

Though my heart was a plucked string in my chest, I nodded in the dark. I don't wonder that she knows. Everyone knows.

There are no secrets in a mead-hall.

"Are you ready?" She gives me a smile I think is meant to be comforting. I appease her with a nod. "Come with me, then," she says, and leads me into the snow.

I could take her through the shadowed road, but balk. What right has she to my secrets? And, I tell myself, the cold might damage her. An odd sort of goddess, this: stronger than any mortal, any einherjar—and yet so vulnerable to physical needs and fragilities. It troubles me.

"It is far to walk in the snow," I say.

She laughs at me. "Trust in my strength, Wolf."

She pulls my face to hers and kisses me there, just outside the door of the mead-hall, her tongue cool and slick between my lips. The sun still lies low, slanting rays casting our shadows long upon the trampled snow. Someone else kisses her. Someone else lets his fingers rest lightly on the back of her neck.

She leans back, sunlight splintering through the blue crystal of her eyes. The smell of her imprints my skin, and there is a yellow-eyed wolfshadow deep in me that wants to roll in the snow and scrub myself clean of the scent. Something else revels in the touch, but it is not a clean delight. There's a perversity in it.

It's wrong, I ken, and ken as well that I deserve no better. I am tainted. There's no perversity in a wolf—only need and joy and the struggle to fulfill both. A human thing, sin and the taste for sin. A thing not for wolves, but for men and for monsters.

Heythe strokes my cheek, her touch like a razor. So sharp I feel nothing. *There is no pain*, I think, and know it for the lie it is.

The truth is that there is nothing, nothing within me but hunger and a void . . . so when the pain comes, it comes as a relief, a song in silence. It is the only thing left that binds me to earth, and the more it hurts, the better. I do not deserve the pleasure of that pain.

I could summon the Imogen. But I need my emptiness. I need my grief.

I lean into Heythe's caress.

"Watch," she says, and raises the hand that does not rest against my face to touch her collar. The jewels of her necklace suddenly sparkle through layers of cloth, glittering in dozens of shades.

She glances at the shadowless sky. And a rainbow falls at our feet, broad as a horse-path, casting stained-glass shadows on the billows of snow leading up to the tree line. It looks like a ribbon of spun candy, firm enough to step onto.

Which is exactly what Heythe does. Her hand on my shoulder, she urges me to follow. I step up onto the span, expecting my boot to find no more support than a mud puddle. But my bootnails click. Firm as stone.

"Come, Wolf." She draws me after her. "Surely you recall this."

And I do, although I have not walked this path in many years. Last time, the bridge was cool under pads as I was led to my prison.

The Suneater wants to snarl and jump back, lick his paws, but he follows his mistress into the sky. I look back only once, and see the children who remain at the mead-hall clustered below the bridge, hair gleaming like coins in the rising sun.

The rainbow fades below, lifting back into the sky as if the touch of the earth repels it. The Ulfenfell spreads out as I have never seen, an unlooked-for tapestry of granite and silver. The slate sea tosses. Velvet-green spruce and fir peek through gleaming snow and ice. The wind whips my cloak. I breathe in glory with the morning.

This must be the world the Imogen sees.

Heythe, scampering like a squirrel up the railless pathway,

turns back with shining eyes. "You like it?" Her voice is breathless and happy. She meant this for a gift.

The sight pierces me sharp as if I cast myself on Svanvitr. "Thank you, my Lady."

I mean it.

Too soon, we reach the flank of the mountain and come to earth under the span of the copper beech. The clearing is peaceful and silent, contours softened by a pall of snow. Heythe slips her hand into mine as we step off her rainbow. She might mean the squeeze for comfort.

"The bodies are scattered." I cannot bear to say Strifbjorn's name to her.

"Bring me to one." She released me.

"They are under snow and ice, Lady." *Let them lie in peace.*

"Sing one up, then."

I make no answer, but I go and crouch on crusted snow under a cedar where my lover laid one of the dead. I smell frozen blood and meat.

I lay my hand on Svanvitr's hilt. I close my eyes and begin to sing.

I haven't the voice of my siblings: Muire's pure soprano, Strifbjorn's steady baritone. My voice whispers and growls and howls around the notes, constricted by the collar. But it can brush the snow aside.

Moments later, I bear the frozen carcass of a friend into the clearing and lay her at my mistress' feet. I kneel and cannot raise my eyes.

Heythe strokes my hair with one hand.

"Poor little thing," she says, in a voice dripping sorrow, and peels her glove from her hand in a motion that looks like skinning. I taste blood.

"I wish I could bring you back to what you were," she whispers, and then she leans over the corpse and strokes her forefingers over its frozen eyes, tracing a rune across each of them and another between. *Sowilo, Hagalaz, Nauthiz.*

Life, wrath, need.

Bending, she spits into the mouth of the wolf. I whimper. She silences me with a glare.

And then another whimper—not mine—and the frozen eyelids of the skinned animal twitch.

"No. Please."

Heythe ignores me, gentling the creature's frozen forehead with a caress not unlike the one she just granted me. She stands and moves away. In the shadow of the beech she kneels, rooting beneath it as if digging for a lost ring.

My hand hovers an inch from the crying, motionless wolf, the dead wolf, the body of my friend that somehow, unbearably, begs for an end to a pain it should be beyond.

"Heythe." My voice breaks.

"Hush." When she comes back, her fingers drip darkness. She bends beside my wolf, one hand gloved and one bare, and rubs the shadowstuff into her flesh. Hot tears shiver down the creases in my cheeks, a trickle of light. Some of the tears drip onto the body of the wolf. Their ripple of light fades into the darkness Heythe spreads.

A darkness which soaks in, tightening over bone, consuming the flesh between. What stands, at last, and wags its tail, and licks my face with a tongue like raw meat, is a gaunt yellow-eyed horror like a hide hung over an animated skeleton, a monster with massive, splayed paws and jaws that drip slaver. It circles wide, and sits at heel behind my mistress.

I kneel in the snow and cannot raise my head. "What is that thing?"

"Sdada," she says. The name, I know, must come from *sceadhu*—"shadow." She smiles. "I give you your vengeance, my love, on the humans who hurt you so badly."

Her hand falls gentle on the beast's dark head, and it closes mad yellow eyes in enjoyment. I know the caress, and I know the surrender to it.

I shudder.

"Fetch me another," Heythe says.

The Historian

Later that night, I gave the rings to Yrenbend, all but Herfjotur's and mine, so that he could see them distributed.

Herfjotur did not return in the morning, however, and the next day at dawnlight Heythe took Mingan away riding on rainbows, something I had never heard of outside of alf-tales. But the next afternoon, while I fretted in the mead-hall over scraps of cloth and a saga that would not come right, a shadow fell over me. A girl's soft voice spoke in my ear. "Bright one?"

It was Rannveig, bindings from skis she must have left by the door dangling from her hand, her face bright with cold. "Herfjotur says to meet her in the wood. I am to show you." Her eyes seemed bruised, dark in their sockets. She was thinner than even at the end of her fever.

Silently, I stood and led her to my niche. She limped still, her stride awkward and unbalanced. I folded my things away and fetched my skis, my fiddle and the finished diadem, and when we were ready she led me across the meadow and up the hill. Skiing beside her, I asked without taking my eyes from the trail, "Did Herfjotur tell you what I will ask of you?"

"Yes," she said tightly. Her eyes were trained straight ahead, skis working steadily. Her tone was unwelcoming. "You want to make me a thrall at the mead-hall, so that the Wolf will see me and think on his crimes." She was silent a moment. "I am willing, though it cost me my life."

"No," I answer. "I want to make you my student."

She tumbled and fell over her skis, catching herself with her poles before I could assist. "Your student?" She turned to me, so I stopped as well.

"Do you want to be a farmwife? A merchant?"

She shook her head. "I will not marry."

"How about a sorceress?" I patted the fiddle in its case, slung over my shoulder beside Nathr.

"Will you teach me seithr?" She offered no hint if she found the idea alluring.

"I am no prophetess," I said. "No, nor a witch, either. But I can teach you music and runes and poetry."

She did not smile, but the crease between her eyebrows eased. Whether it was the promise of power or the taste of vengeance I did not know, but she thought about it carefully. "I should like that, Bright one. Thank you."

"You'll be risking your life, you do realize?"

"I care not," she answered.

"All right, then," I said. And we traveled on in silence.

Herfjotur and Strifbjorn waited in the shadow of a vertical cliff face, a high sweep of granite frosted with snow as if sugar had been thrown against it. A frozen waterfall tumbled down its height, formed in magic twists like candle-wax.

They greeted us with tight nods, and I gave Herfjotur her ring. She took it without comment, though Rannveig raised a questioning brow. "You will need one as well," I told her. "But you'll have to make your own. My strength is at its limits. It will be your first lesson; I'll show you how when we return."

"What does it do?"

"Protection from spells that bend the wits," I said.

Her eyes widened a bit. "Oh. You'll teach me that?"

"You're useless to me else."

I turned to Strifbjorn, browned bloodstains covering his arms and chest. He did not offer, and I did not ask.

"This is for you, war-leader." I held the circlet out, unable to meet his gaze, flinching as he took it from my hand although his fingers did not brush mine.

"Set this on my head?"

I nodded. And began unpacking my fiddle, for all it complained in the cold and I had to mark it with *Fehu* to protect the wood and loosen all eight strings. By the time I had it re-tuned, Strifbjorn had jammed the narrow hammered circlet over his hair, looking as if he felt faintly foolish.

He looked like a martial prince, our war-leader who had never needed a symbol of authority. We had always known, since the beginning, who we followed.

I looked him in the eye, drew a breath, set the fiddle under my chin.

Light soared from my fingertips with the music, silver-bright and crystalline, and Herfjotur threw her head back and joined in the song. Gossamer filaments of brilliance swirled around us like dye in water, drawn to the polished crystals bright in their six-sided settings. I stood before Strifbjorn, one foot shuffling time in the snow, and fixed him with a mocking, aching gaze.

I would never tell him that I loved him but this once, and not in words even now. But if we died together, outnumbered under the swords of our brethren or the teeth of a demoness, he would know.

And he would know that it was not the reason I stood beside him.

I leaned the whole weight of my power into the song, a wreaking as fine as ever I had made. Despite Herfjotur's voice bending into the song, low and sweet, I let him have no doubt of what the music was saying as it twined his limbs, coiled his throat, crowned him in blazing white light.

Guard him; ward him; hide him from sight. Watch him; keep him; bring him back to me whole—until the end of time. His eyes never left mine, and once—just once—he nodded and I saw the acknowledgment on his face. Acceptance. But nothing returned.

I was going to die for this man who could not love me. And for once, the only pity I felt was for him.

When the last tendril and flicker of Light sank into his crown, he flickered and grew indistinct. My eye slid off him like a foot off wet rock, and if I did not know to look for him I never would have seen him standing before me, six and a half feet tall and not six feet away.

I set my fiddle back in the case while Rannveig looked

from Herfjotur to myself, her mouth wide in amazement. "You can teach me that?"

"I've already started," I said. "Come; let us hurry. The spell will not last forever."

The Wolf

My wolves aren't the only wolves dead under the snowdrifts, and Heythe needs only the bones. In a hand of days we claim dozens, traveling Heythe's rainbows—even in the darkness—and singing out the dead. Not just wolf, but snow leopard, and arctic tiger and white and brown bears. The first sdadown have an amazing facility for unearthing dead things, and we scour the continent bare of corpses as far south and west as Eiledon, where the river Naglfar runs into a sea that the sun sets behind rather than rising before.

Heythe makes her fell beasts and releases them to await her call. I follow like a shadow cast. The emaciated ghosts of my pack run alongside us, yellow eyes glaring.

The Lady needs beds and food and warmth, and that means inns, and that means men and the cities of men. Twice I intervene in minor crimes and each time, hunger on my back with spurs, I slay a candle-flicker with my kiss. When Heythe sleeps in way stations, wearied by our labors, I stand guard. The sdadown take their ease in the darkness below our windows, lean specters slipping across moon-white snow.

I do not know if the men see them. If they do, they are wise enough to stay by their fires of a winter night.

The sdadown are a yoke hung on my shoulders, but I do

not protest. The time for protests is past—passed long before that final night of our travels when Heythe forbids me my place by the window and draws me into her hired bed. Under eiderdowns, between clean linens on a mattress that still smells of summer hay, she smooths her hands over my thighs, the bones of my hips. Her fingernails tick across my ribs. She cups a cold hand between my legs, presses like a cat against my heat.

I shrink from her touch. I cannot make love to her.

I curl away. She hisses annoyance and with one hand on my shoulder shoves me onto my back. The room is full of scattered light, from my collar and her necklace.

I am numb. Tingling, nerve-dead as a manacled hand. Plush thighs bestride my chest. She smiles down. "Mingan," she says. "This won't do."

Two fingers burrowed under my collar twist my dull body to life. My vision tunnels as the ribbon slices, tight enough to prick blood to my skin. My eyes burn, vessels popping. My lungs burn, starved of air. My hands claw her wrists, nails driven deep. I wish she would yank harder, drive deeper, choke me into a darkness I need never come up from again.

My prick and the Suneater . . . have their own ideas.

She hurts me. I thrash. I kick like a hare in a wire. I growl in hate and need and the sheer demeaning pleasure of being punished.

Being owned.

I clutch her and she lets me, lets me thrust her back against the bed and mount her, though my sight is fading. I bite her, paw her, pin her shoulders while she twists the collar and I move in her as if it were my last act on earth. I wish—

—it were.

She makes me powerless.

And like a mortal man, I permit it.

She is slender and delicate, and should be fragile enough to break with my hands, but when she submits to my rage I know it is acquiescence, and when I fuck her with all the hate and poison in me, so the bed shatters plaster from the wall, she laughs at my strength and chokes me until my skin breaks on the cord, until I cannot see or hear but only feel her stretching against me, thighs a vise.

I would tear her throat open in the darkness, soak the bed with her blood. But my teeth scratch at her necklace, chip on fragile wires and jewels. Her hands clench as her body convulses.

The darkness crushes me. Release scours me dry.

I wake in her arms.

She sleeps against my shoulder, frail and delicate and strong enough to kill me with her bare hands. With the one fine-boned hand that lies still entwined with my collar.

There are no linear thoughts in sleep, just the jumble and slide of emotion. I taste them as I taste her sweat. There is no way to avoid them, dark and bright and coiling—triumph, pleasure and a kind of gloating pity.

And the fine, piquant ferment of a long-anticipated, delicately-savored revenge.

12

Kin will kin-slaughter
And brothers' blades bloody
Woe, woe, all the wicked wide world.
An axe-age, a sword-age, an age of shields shattered
A wind-age, a wolf-age, the old world unwinding
No mercy to muster, no heart left unhewed.

—Völuspá

The Wolf

We return to the mead-hall in the morning. Those first dozen sdadown attend. Only Skeold comes to greet us, presenting the welcoming-cup, her expression questioning. She flinches from the undead wolves, and will not look me in the eye. The Lady, however, she ducks a little curtsey as she holds out the drinking horns.

"Welcome home, my Lady," she says, and adds, "my brother" on the end.

I drink because the Lady drinks. As we lower our empty cups, Skeold takes them from us and steps aside. Her eyes flick again to the dark beasts pacing behind Heythe, but she says nothing more.

The mead-hall is largely empty, though Yrenbend works at carvery in the corner, his tools and wood spread on a bench.

I see only a few others. Most of my brethren must be about the errands Heythe set them.

Heythe releases her sdadown from heel. They loll about the hall like so many hunting hounds before the fire. Golden eyes blink from dead faces. Heythe lays her hand on Skeold's shoulder, smiling fondly, and draws her aside.

"Come sit with me, Skeold, and tell me what has transpired in my absence. Mingan"—she smiles at the coldness I turn on her—"find Sigrdrifa, my love?"

Skeold's eyes open at the fond words, but I turn away without answering. Sigrdrifa is easy enough to locate, hacking at a pell in the trampled practice yard. My face must serve as a warning, because she only nods to me and sheathes her sword. I watch her go, the cold wind ruffling my cloak.

The cliff is only a few dozen yards further on.

I climb the rim, balancing on ice-rimed rocks, and watch the sea toss. Cold calm mutes the memory of the night before. It's not serenity so much as ice and mist over the molten stone of loss and hate. I might tumble into that seethe . . . but unless I should, it's as if I stand at a distance and watch another grieve and rage.

I gave so much into the woodcutter's daughter I'm surprised there is still even this.

My skin prickles between my shoulders. Someone watches, but when I turn and stare across to the mead-hall and the practice yard, no one moves there.

It is plain there is no peace for me here, either. I step back from the cliff.

Inside, Heythe sits in her gilded chair, head-bent with

Skeold and Sigrdrifa. The Raven of victory spreads broad wings behind the three who weave as pitiless as any Norns.

Heythe does not glance up as I enter, but the sdada lounging behind her chair tracks me with insane eyes.

I crave solitude, a lonely place, but I will not climb the Ulfenfell again. Instead I retire to Heythe's alcove, and rest on the bench in the back corner. Sooner or later, she'll want me. I huddle in anticipation, boots drawn up and knees bent, dreaming with my eyes open.

That is where I still am sitting when the arras is brushed aside and the voice of a girl intrudes.

"Master Wolf," Rannveig whispers. She lets the tapestry fall behind her. Her voice is pitched low, not to carry.

I leap up, whirling on her, back to the wall. "Go!" But when she starts to obey I interrupt her. "What dost thou here?"

She checks her step, hand on the arras. She's well-dressed and clean-scrubbed, her dark tunic mended at the elbow but thick and warm, embroidery-decorated around the keyhole collar and the hem. Her russet cloak swathes her shoulders, a contrast to the straw-gold of her braid. It is cold in the hall, by mortal standards.

"Apprenticed," she says. "Mistress Muire is teaching me a trade."

Baiting me with my sins, you mean.

We stare. She will not look down. She is smiling.

I force my voice to softness. "Seek me not again," I warn her, and she nods once, gracefully.

"I only came to see if you were well." When she leaves, the curtain falls shut behind her.

The Warrior

Strifbjorn and the others had a few days' grace before Heythe returned to the mead-hall. He used every second for politics, the whole enriched by an element of comedy. Yrenbend and Muire chose to whom they would speak. Strifbjorn moved through the hall in silence, observing the comings and goings of his brethren like a ghost, eavesdropping on their conversations. It was a slow process, careful, carried out while Herfjotur and Brynhilde spread word to trustworthy siblings whom they could find in the world, going about their tasks. Muire refreshed the spell on Strifbjorn's circlet every day or so.

Meanwhile, she instructed her new pupil in the spells of music and runes. Yrenbend likewise taught Rannveig something Strifbjorn had had no idea Yrenbend knew—human sorcery, bindings with blood and knots and silver.

Strifbjorn found if he spoke directly to someone, or intended to be seen, he could make himself plain. Otherwise, the eye and the ear skipped off him like a flat stone off still water. Despite the drama of the situation . . . it was fun, after a fashion.

And so did four days pass.

On the fifth, the Lady and Mingan returned. Strifbjorn had been standing in the corner, whispering to Yrenbend while he worked on a wood carving, when the main doors swung wide. A moment and Skeold jumped to her feet, hurrying to fetch mead for the returning travelers. Strifbjorn took a breath and stepped back into the shadows, while Yrenbend further bowed his head to his task.

Swirling shadows cast out from Heythe as she entered,

following spiraling pathways. It was a moment before Strif-bjorn's eye could be made to give them shape. Yellow-eyed beasts with rust-black hides stank of iron like clotted blood as they paced around the hall.

Strifbjorn froze against the wall, but even the one that passed close enough to Yrenbend to touch never glanced at him.

And he in turn nearly forgot the beasts when he saw his lover's face. *He's not yours anymore. You wouldn't take him back if he begged.*

But Strifbjorn still felt the wintry darkness of Mingan's expression like a kick.

Mingan followed Heythe into the room like a hunting dog at heel, and when she turned and spoke in his ear he nodded once and turned to do her bidding. Strifbjorn could bear to watch no longer. He slid through the open postern door.

The kitchen lay cold. Strifbjorn walked around it, toward the sharp thudding of bladework methodically destroying a pell. In the practice yard, Sigrdrifa beat her frustrations against the wooden dummy.

The log wall of the kitchen was rough and cold. Strifbjorn stepped from the pathway and leaned against it, letting the solid logs and bark cladding support his weight. *I swear on my troth I shall never love anyone again. I cannot bear it.*

The pass-unseen proved comforting again; he closed his eyes, bit his tongue and let the tears come. *Were we punished for our passion, then?* The cruelty took his breath away.

Strifbjorn held his breath in shock when he heard Min-gan's low, rough voice behind him.

It wasn't Strifbjorn he spoke to. The sound of bladework paused, and Strifbjorn looked up in time to see Sigrdrifa sheathe her sword and turn inside, in obedience to the summons. Mingan gave her no more notice, walking instead toward the sea-cliff with the dreamy, lost expression of one who intends to jump.

Strifbjorn stood and watched. His hands clenched.

The wind smeared Mingan's cloak sideways, snagging it on the hilt of his sword. More than the world, Strifbjorn wanted the freedom to walk up behind him and straighten the hang of its folds.

Strifbjorn's lips shaped the Wolf's name, and at that moment he turned suddenly and cast a searching glance over his shoulder. His ragged profile silhouetted against the tossing blue and silver of a cloud-streaming sky, the ocean writhing white and gray in the distance. For a second he stood poised, a wild thing from a snow-wrapped wilderness, and Strifbjorn's heart beat hard in his throat. The pain on Mingan's face cut so hard Strifbjorn took a slow step toward him, heedless of his footprints in the snow. *And if I asked him to come back, am I fool enough to suppose he might?*

Mingan continued turning, then, and his eyes swept over Strifbjorn without a skip. Blinded, too. And though he passed within an arm's length Strifbjorn did not catch his sleeve.

That night under cover of darkness, Herfjotur took Strifbjorn away.

Arngeir met Strifbjorn and Herfjotur in the paved court of his mead-hall at morning, Menglad beside him with her hand laid on his arm. They were not smiling, although Menglad stepped forward and threw her arms around Strifbjorn's shoulders once his feet were firmly on the ground. He held her for a moment, hearing the sound of the sea from where he stood. The sky overhead was painstakingly blue.

"News?" Strifbjorn asked.

She shook her head. "A few more have come. Arngeir has been on errantry, and . . ."

"It'll be ugly," Strifbjorn agreed.

Herfjotur patted her steed on the shoulder and sent him on his way. Strifbjorn met her eyes. She nodded.

He looked at the three of them, all gold and silver. *Not a one of us will see the springtime.*

"Come on," he said into the lengthy silence. "I'm of a mind to get good and drunk today."

Arngeir clapped him on the shoulder and led both newcomers into his hall. *His* hall was roofed in tile, built of stone, flagged under the rushes, and the high windows ran floor to ceiling and glittered with leaded bits of glass. Strifbjorn saw the ocean through the one over his shoulder, and a white-sand, frost-rimed beach beside a long pier stretching out into the sea.

"What do we know?" he asked when they were seated on benches on either side of the long table.

Strifbjorn sipped brandywine, the flavor a sharp reminder, and rolled his head from side to side to crack the tension out. "Too much, or not enough." The liquor loosened his tongue, and Strifbjorn drank more. "I can get three hundred of us. Perhaps four. Less than half, and Mingan . . ."

Menglad lifted the clay bottle and refilled Strifbjorn's bowl and her own. "The Imogen," she said, her jaw working.

Strifbjorn nodded. She let her red tongue slide across her lips. She held the bowl in her right hand, inhaling the fumes, and brushed Arngeir's arm. His fond glance left Strifbjorn unable to breathe.

Strifbjorn stared down at the floor. Gray slates, set in mortar: a much more modern mead-hall. Why hadn't it ever occurred to him to change things? They were good enough; the children of the Light did not require much comfort—

"What do we do?" Arngeir asked.

"We fight like hell," Strifbjorn answered. "Or we give in."

"No." Menglad set her bowl down. She breathed out between her teeth. "A clean death is better."

Strifbjorn nodded. "For me as well."

"But a clean life is better still." Arngeir laid a hand over his wife's. "What can we do about the Imogen?"

Strifbjorn touched the circlet threaded on his belt. He finished his brandy with the other hand. "If I kill Mingan, we won't have to worry about the demoness."

The Wolf

Midwinter passes with small celebrations, the grip of the ice ever tightening. Rannveig avoids me, but her rust-brown cloak reminds me of clotted blood anyway. Spring seems more distant than ever on the day when Ulfgar, who had left on errantry, braves the journey through a howling blizzard to bring us word from the southern town of Freimarc.

Heythe has provided me a chair behind her own, on the dais where her black hounds laze. When she holds court, I sprawl indecorously across it. Perhaps she could force me to feign decorum, but I think my insolence amuses her.

The knowledge is not quite enough to stop me.

Today, she sleeps, but I maintain my chair. Even from the dais I see how ice cakes the wings of Ulfgar's valraven, an eagle-beaked creature with the limbs and lashing tail of some great cat. He leads the steed inside to a spot beside the fire trench, where the sdadown rise to grant it pride of place.

Little Muire, wintering at the mead-hall with her troubling student, brings him a welcoming-cup. I study her; the sdada at my feet lifts its head and whines. Muire will not go near the beasts, nor will her student—but she has not left the hall. I wonder if she is loyal to the Lady, despite her misgivings, or if I shall kill her soon.

Her judgment of me is apparent. And matters not.

She is small and courageous as a terrier, and would stand as long against me as that terrier would stand against the undead wolf who rests his chin on my boot. I imagine her blood splashed on the bough-strewn earth. Saliva curdles on my tongue.

I turn and spit it out and rise. The sdada whines and does not follow.

When Ulfgar has drained his cup and placed it back in Muire's hand, I come forward to clasp his wrist. The waelcyrge withdraws to the table where she sat teaching the woodcutter's daughter the runes and the craft of writing.

"Tidings?" Ulfgar flinches from the heat of my breath. I smile privately. There are things to enjoy about being feared.

"Bring me to the Lady?"

"She is resting. I shall awaken her." He stands beside the fire, melting caked ice dripping from his cloak and intricately knotted queue, until I return with Heythe, who is clad in a dressing robe. I bring a bench close to the fire for her while

Ulfgar claims another, and then I wait behind her while they speak. My hand falls on her shoulder as if that is natural, and I find myself staring at it, the broad outline of my knuckles against the white silk of her robe.

When the pleasantries are dispensed with, Ulfgar drops his voice and begins to speak in earnest. "Strifbjorn is rallying the traitors."

She leans forward. Her scent sharpens. A shift of tension runs across her shoulders; my hand brushes the skin below her necklace and above her collar. I sense expectancy—not misgiving. Her excitement is not what I expected her to feel. I draw my hand back slowly, trying to hide my surprise. My fingers caress her hair—safer than touching her skin, reading her thoughts.

I would rather not know about her lies.

"Where?" She brushes my hand aside, lays the power of her stare on Ulfgar. He swallows hard. I turn aside, relieved to be dismissed. I fetch my cloak and step into the storm.

The wind is bitter, blowing to the northeast, and what sheets from the low-hanging clouds is an icy mixture of snow and rain that freezes in my hair, stiffens my cloak across my shoulders. Ulfgar was hurried indeed to fly in this.

I should stay and eavesdrop. But there is some peace to be found in the storm, and none to be had in the hall.

I have only walked a little across the crusted snow when the shadow of dark wings falls over me. My sister glides from the sleet, sheltering me beneath her pinions as she settles.

I have not summoned her.

She leans in, claws stroking my cheeks. "Hungry," she whispers. "My brother, you are in pain."

"No," I answer. I feel no pain. Only emptiness and dull sorrow, a sensation like a missing limb.

Nevertheless, her lips brush my throat. "Please?" Hissed between teeth like needles. Behind my eyes, a memory burns—the Imogen, ankle-deep in blood-wet snow.

"I will be what you need. This one?" She transforms. Blurring, growing—into the shape of a tall, broad man with platinum hair and a crooked, assessing smile.

Gasping, I backhand her across the face. All my strength cannot even turn her head. "Brother?" she whispers, in Strifbjorn's injured tone.

"Go!" I shriek over the howl of the wind. "I have nothing for you! Go, and don't come back until I call you!"

"As you wish it—" She turns and melts like running wax, drifting back to her own black-furred, black-feathered form, and vanishes into the storm. I wheel back to the mead-hall, glancing over my shoulder once to be sure the Imogen has gone.

I do not notice the brown-clad servant who steps into my path until I bowl her over.

I stoop and reach out to lift her to her feet, surprised at first when she grasps my hand unhesitatingly. But her smell comes through the frozen rain at the same moment I glimpse her eyes under her hood. They are not the eyes of a thrall.

"I told you to stay away!" I lift her by the shoulders, slam her against the log wall. Bark shingling cracks and falls away, shards of ice splintering. The girl's breath bursts out on a bitten cry.

Stunned, she struggles for air. I hold her off her feet, lean in to taste her breath. "I heard you cry out, Master Wolf," she whispers through her teeth. I shove. Her arms indent under my thumbs.

"I am under the protection of your sister," she adds when she has wind. Ice water shed from the roof drenches us both, discomfiting me, endangering her brittle human life.

She's light as eiderdown, a morsel, nothing more. Her eyes are bright on mine, muddy human gray-blue, not the stark silver of my kind or the lit blue of Heythe's.

"I know you." I shake her and she gasps, squawks, but will not stop. She says, "You're in me. You put your hurt in me. And it still didn't make it go away."

I cannot understand her fearlessness. My lips touch hers, soft as an ink-soaked brush caresses cloth, waiting for her shudder and squirming away. But I've forgotten the girl's courage, and I've forgotten the death I laid in her, poison under her skin. I taste my own grief on her lips, and the taste is bitter.

Until I taste as well her desire to have my kiss again, though it be her death, though she loathes me as only one who knows can loathe. A filthy passion.

And its mirror lives in me, when I lean my cheek into a goddess' touch.

My breath locks in my throat. My grip on her slides. She presses her mouth to mine in a mockery of love. She's cold, so cold to the touch, so cold in her heart with the ice I have grown there.

"Go ahead," Rannveig murmurs against my lips. "You've killed my heart already. You may as well have my body, too."

Writhing like a serpent, she edges higher against the wall, swings her thighs forward and clasps my hips. She grinds her sex on mine, through my trousers. "I'll be your whore if that's what you want. A whore for a whore," she gasps, laughing brutally.

She tumbles from my numbed hands. I go to my knees before her. Rain streaks and stings my eyes; water sharp with ice crystals thumps my head and shoulders. Rannveig falls harder, striking her head and shoulder on the wall, and still she struggles up while I kneel, head bowed and fists clenched.

I cannot speak. I cannot breathe. Heat flares in my chest, and if I pulled my shirt open I might see my bones outlined from within. Her teeth rattling with cold, she bends over me, fumbling with her hair and the hood of her cloak.

"I do not wish this," I hiss between my teeth.

"We don't get what we wish, Master Wolf," she answers in gallows tones. She tilts my head to the side, runs her fingers down my left ear as if caressing a dog, twists my plait around her hand. If she were Heythe, I would know what happens next.

But she stoops to kiss between my eyes and says, "We get what we deserve. Hold very still."

The pain is sharp and sudden, breathtaking as only superficial injuries can be. I yelp, too shocked to jerk away, feel a twist and hear a loud, sharp click.

Rannveig steps back, out from under the deluge off the roof, licking my blood from her hands.

I touch my ear. The flesh feels strange, hot, heavy. I think she has torn the earlobe away, but my fingers meet skin and the slickness of dripping blood, the chill of ice water—and the weighty twisted shape of a metal ring.

I tug at it, wince.

"Don't bother," she says, stepping forward and pulling my

hand away. "Yrenbend helped me make it. It won't come free. Wear it like a tag on cattle."

"Sorcery?"

She shakes so with the cold that she can hardly stand, but her strength is humbling. *I* cannot even rise.

"A curse?" I ask, again.

"There's a spell on it to see through glamours. The best I could manage. I told Yrenbend it was for me." She pulls me up, where I stand, weaving, while she laces her hands through my hair. Her fingers brush the throbbing lobe of my left ear. "I didn't tell Muire. She wouldn't have approved. She doesn't understand you.

"Mostly"—she grabs that ear and pulls my face down, kisses my mouth, gives the earring a twist that sharps my eyes with tears—"it's a reminder from somebody else who got what she deserved. You fucking bastard."

She stalks away, leaving me frozen in the frozen rain.

The Warrior

For a month and a half Strifbjorn divided his time: sometimes at Arngeir's hall; sometimes with Herfjotur on her snow-white steed, talking to einherjar and waelcyrge in the cities and villages; sometimes returning to the woods above what had been his home, speaking with Yrenbend or Muire.

Weeks passed slowly, the factions more clearly drawn every day, and Strifbjorn knew it was only a matter of time before his rebellion was laid open to the Lady. A third of the children had promised their aid, gathering in the now-crowded confines of Arngeir's hall while they debated. Heythe's faction killed, growing stronger.

Rumors reached Arngeir's hall of starveling monsters preying on livestock and lone humans. Strifbjorn imagined the yellow-eyed beasts that Heythe commanded, and wondered how many she might have. Every passing day weakened Strifbjorn's faction by strengthening Heythe and her band.

On the coldest day of winter Strifbjorn went with Herfjotur to bring Yrenbend and Muire out of Heythe's hall. *Heythe's hall.* Strifbjorn bit his lip until he tasted blood. *My hall.*

He had another task while here, as well.

The valraven's wings cupped air as he descended to land at the base of the Ulfenfell's spectacular waterfall. The muscles of his back slid and strained under silken hide. Strifbjorn braced against Herfjotur's back, but the stallion touched down like a sparrow, cantering to a halt and craning his heads about curiously at the clearing.

The waterfall trickling under the ice made a plinking sound. Ice weighed the bare branches of the surrounding birch and poplar. Snow had long covered the footsteps of Strifbjorn and the others previous meeting. The clearing and the bank were lovely and untrampled, the deep pool crisp with ice.

Strifbjorn looked away. There was a cave behind the waterfall, a granite cave with many levels.

He knew the place because Mingan had shown it to him, when the world was bright and young, and Mingan had loved him.

Herfjotur and Strifbjorn dismounted, striding to meet the

two figures who came out of the forest to greet them. Strifbjorn knew as soon as they came into the clearing that something was wrong. The taller was Yrenbend, but the woman was broader than Muire, and clad in a russet cloak Strifbjorn remembered.

"Yrenbend." Strifbjorn clasped his wrist and nodded to the mortal girl. Muire's new apprentice. He remembered her name in a moment. "Rannveig?"

She smiled without pleasure. "Bright one." She nodded. "We bring tidings."

Strifbjorn turned back to Yrenbend. "Not Muire?"

He shook his head, releasing Strifbjorn's hand. "Well. She would not come on this errand."

"She's staying with Heythe?" Strifbjorn's heart sank. He had never doubted her loyalty.

"No," Rannveig put in hesitantly. "It's . . ." She drew a breath. "Bright one. The Grey Wolf. He is not . . . well."

Ice pack creaked under Strifbjorn's boots as he stepped back. They stood on a thick layer of crust from a storm two nights past, a thin dusting of snow lying over it. Strifbjorn had sharpened my knife that morning. "Of all the creatures in the world, you would ask me to aid him? Muire was kind to refuse this errand. You must tell her to leave Heythe's hall. The war is about to begin."

She hissed through her teeth and spread her hands, helplessly. "I understand him, Bright one. And the . . . It is partly my doing that he is unwell."

"My doing as well." Yrenbend took the short step needed to set himself between the mortal girl and Strifbjorn. Strifbjorn wondered if he looked as if he might do her harm.

He turned away from them and from Herfjotur, who

stood at his shoulder and did not speak. "Did you poison his ale? Pity you didn't use more."

"I gave him a talisman." Rannveig ducked behind her fringe. "A ward of clear vision. I thought he might see what he has become. I did not know . . ."

Strifbjorn's eyes came back to her. When she would not look up he turned to Yrenbend. "Did not know what?"

He blanched. "Heythe must have laid some sorcery on him. It does not remove culpability, or wash the blood from his hands. But since Rannveig broke it, he sits staring; he is sick or mad. . . ." His voice trailed off. He looked Strifbjorn in the eye, and said nothing.

"He saved my life," Rannveig said quietly. "I destroyed his. I had to—"

Herfjotur's hand had somehow fallen on Strifbjorn's shoulder. He stared. The girl stammered to a halt.

"There are seen hands and unseen hands," Yrenbend finished, glancing down. "I am einherjar. We do not believe in coincidences."

Strifbjorn's hand fell to my hilt. "We are not *for* forgiveness, my brother."

Herfjotur's milk-white hand pressed harder. "I told Yrenbend you had said you would kill the Wolf yourself."

Rannveig looked up. "No," the mortal girl said softly. "Not death. He must not die."

"He took your whole village from you, girl."

"And my family. But." Her hands fluttered, helpless. "We deserved it."

No words would come until at last, into the silence of three who would not meet his eyes, Strifbjorn said, "I came to kill him. You can go, all of you. I will not ask your sanction. You do not have to wait for me."

They shifted, avoiding each other's attention. Herfjotur turned Strifbjorn to face her.

"I am a widow, too," Herfjotur said. "I will await you."

Strifbjorn unlaced the diadem from his belt. "I had counted on Muire to enchant the circlet. Without her, I cannot promise I'll be back."

She still would not look at him, but Rannveig reached into the pocket of her jacket and drew out a carved wooden flute, while Yrenbend brought forth his metal one.

The mead-hall bustled. Heythe, too, was calling her troops to war. Strifbjorn entered through the front doors, a half step behind Yrenbend and preceding Rannveig, hidden by their magic and protected from accidental contact by their bodies. Inside the doorway, they drifted apart, leaving Strifbjorn to find his own way to the Wolf.

He laid his hand on Alvitr again, and thought of how he would kill him.

Yrenbend had told Strifbjorn that Bergdis had found Mingan crouched in the snow unmoving two nights since. He had not spoken.

And Yrenbend had also told Strifbjorn where to find him.

He did not turn as Strifbjorn slipped into the niche he had been led to. Strifbjorn had seen him even as he walked up: there was a bench, but he was not sitting on it. Rather, he had slung himself up onto the ledge of the high window and lounged there, staring out at the sea, above the height of the partitions. He did not turn, but Strifbjorn could imagine his ears twitching at the tapestry's rustle. The earring that pierced his left earlobe glittered in the sunlight with the slow rhythm of his breathing. The flesh was red and swollen around it. He had not troubled to heal the small wound.

He did not move as Strifbjorn crossed the space. Strifbjorn took a breath and spoke his name: "Mingan."

A shiver ran his length; his arm tightened around the drawn-up knee.

"I know you can hear me. Rannveig told me what the earring is for."

He took a breath. His voice sounded more harsh and disused than ever when he spoke. "You should go. Do not risk yourself for me."

"Don't make me climb up there."

He turned slowly, his eyes like ash-covered coals. His hand uncoiled from around the knee, came up, touched the earring. Poised as he was on the ledge, he was visible to anyone who happened to look up.

But he pitched his voice low enough that Strifbjorn strained to hear. "I am beyond saving."

Strifbjorn drew his knife out of its sheath. He thought of Alvitr, but flinched from her hilt. What blade he used today he would not touch again.

"I'm not here to save you."

He stared, and then he smiled, and then he nodded and slid from the ledge in a fluid arc. He landed in a crouch before Strifbjorn, and when he stood he lifted his chin and looked him in the eye. "I was hoping you would come."

Strifbjorn drew a breath, full of the scent of him. "There's going to be a war."

"You cannot permit me to fight against you."

"I know." Strifbjorn set the dagger against Mingan's breast. He did nothing to prevent it. "Mingan, tell me you'll walk away from this, and you can live."

Strifbjorn wished he would lie, anything, give him the excuse to set the knife aside. He leaned forward, on his toes, so the knife pierced his shirt and blood welled around it. He pressed his dry mouth to Strifbjorn's mouth.

Strifbjorn wondered if he could taste all those deaths on it.

His voice was cool when he leaned back. Strifbjorn listened to the rusty rise and fall, and tried to memorize the sound even as he wished he had already forgotten it. "I sent the Imogen away."

"I cannot risk it."

"I understand." Mingan placed his hand so-gently over Strifbjorn's. Strifbjorn could not tell which hand trembled more as Mingan moved the point a half inch up, so that it rested between his staring ribs, below his collarbone. The knife would slip effortlessly between the bones, sever the big vein over the heart. Strifbjorn already felt the heat of his blood across his hands.

"I will not throw myself on the blade," he said. "So you see, I have not loved thee as I ought."

Strifbjorn moved to put his weight behind the blade.

He could no more have pressed it through stone. The knife would not move. His arm would not move it. His hand shook palsied on the hilt, and a second thin, dark circle surrounded the tip of the blade.

Strifbjorn heard a footstep on the boughs beyond the curtain. "Hurry!" Mingan said.

He stepped back against the bench. "I cannot."

The hanging slid aside. Sigrdrifa entered, her crystal blade naked and dark in her hand.

13

Hard-hurt the heart hewn past healing:
Despairing die even the bold!
—The Life and Death of Cormac the Skald

The Wolf

Sigrdrifa lets the curtain fall shut behind her and comes forward. Her blade rises, leveled at my throat. As if he does not exist, she never glances at Strifbjorn, who stands an arm's breadth away, though she stares about this way and that, as if seeking who I speak to.

I gulp air I never thought to taste, the scrapes Strifbjorn left on my chest stinging, a throb in my roughly pierced ear. That breath is sweeter than it has any right.

Snake-swift, hawk-cunning, my sister. Svanvitr hangs beneath my cloak, unreachable. One death is as good as another. I am grateful that Strifbjorn will not have to strike the blow.

I smile at Sigrdrifa. Her eyebrow rises, but she does not hesitate. Her sword darts forward like the beak of a heron. I don't expect to feel a thing.

I'm shocked when pain like molten wax spills down my chest. Her sword plunges through skin and flesh, grates on bone, pokes from my back below the right shoulder blade. A cry wants to fill my mouth, but what comes instead is blood and froth.

I fall to my knees, topple backwards.

The sword stays lodged in my breast, knocked from Sigr-drifa's hand by Strifbjorn's lunge. She crashes down, and he falls with her. Then I cannot see them; I am on my back, my legs folded under me, the swordpoint lodged in the rammed-earth floor. Two feet of her hilt and the forte of the blade stand out of my chest.

Strifbjorn hit her, and Sigrdrifa missed my heart.

Wood and cloth rend as the combatants strike the partition, pulling it down around them. My own blood fills my mouth, hot to steaming. Strifbjorn grunts, a sound of pain coupled with the sound of metal meeting flesh. I moan and tug the blade—

Cloth tears once more. They roll on the floor, Sigrdrifa's pained shout following the sound of fist or elbow thumping against her head.

Strifbjorn. I reach up with both hands, the right one a twist of agony, and splay my palms on the flat of the sword. Outcries and running footsteps in the mead-hall, the hanging pulled back as more wood cracks and Strifbjorn cries out.

I press my palms together, straighten my elbows and slide the blade from my breast.

Crystal grates on bone, the edges of the blade slashing my palms. I risk a breath: it comes with more frothed scalding blood on my tongue, a sensation like ground glass filling up my lung.

Enough. I make myself whole and healed.

Relief of pain comes with a hundred-mile-runner tiredness.

I put my elbows down, shove. The world tunnels dark, as if Heythe strangled me.

I am the Suneater.

I will stand. Now.

I *will* stand.

Sigrdrifa's blade is in my hand, dark as midnight water. I reverse it, catching the hilt in my left hand. My right darts to Svanvitr's hilt, draws her across my body.

A circle of observers has halted outside the doorway of the alcove. I suppose they can see Strifbjorn now. I hear their noises as he hauls himself up beside me, his knife left wedged in Sigr-drifa's eye.

She will not be standing again.

"Walk away," Strifbjorn mutters.

Swaying in exhaustion, I shake my head. "I swore to serve her, brother. Wouldst have me oath-broken, too? Kill me now, as thou camest to."

He takes a breath and turns away.

The children of the Light fall back as Strifbjorn advances, stiff-legged as an old wolf walking out to a fight he thinks he can't win.

Bergdis comes forward, frowning, reaching out as if to lay her hand on his sleeve. He doesn't glance at her, but her motion is arrested and her hand drifts back to her side. I know the look on her face, on all of their faces. It is the recognition of domi-nance.

I almost think they will let him leave the hall. Until Heythe steps in front, a pair of sdadown snarling and hackling at her heels.

"Stand and speak with me," she says, in a clear voice that carries. I sway, two swords in my hands. My healing came dear.

But I will stand.

He gives her nothing but a scornful glance, until she bars his path with an outreached arm. "Why are you here?"

He glances down and brushes Sigrdrifa's blood. "I came to talk to my friend. I am done now."

Dizzy exhaustion blurs my vision and weakens my knees. I set Sigrdrifa's sword against the floor and lean on it.

"You have entered my hall uninvited. Will you swear fealty to me, then?"

"I will not," he answers.

"Then I will challenge you."

"Not so quickly, my Lady." The voice rises from the crowd, and Yrenbend thrusts through the crowd. "I demand an explanation."

She inclines her head, gracious and imperious.

He pushes Strifbjorn aside as he advances. Small hands reach out and draw my love into the crowd. I see his platinum head among the golden momentarily, but I cannot follow. The most I can do for him is to pretend that I saw nothing.

"Aye, Lady," Yrenbend says. "Your plans are senseless, and there is still no sign of the war you prophesied. Make me understand."

She gestures dramatically to the Banner behind her chair. "There is my proof."

But the Raven on the Banner is draggle-tailed, stoop-headed in defeat. Faintly, over it, lies the flicker of an illusion. *That* Raven, the false one, is spread wide-winged in victory.

A glance shows me no one else has noticed the change. A heavy weight swings in my ear—no more pain; it healed with my lung—and I realize there has been no change. Now, I but see a hidden truth.

Another lie. Another lie, in the belly of all this horror. Heythe—

But that is unfair. I have visited horror upon myself.

Yrenbend has let a long, jag-edged silence hang. Now he tosses his plait over his shoulder and lays one hand on his blade. "I'll not fight for you, Lady. You claim you wish to strengthen the children, but your practice sets us at one another's throats, crushing our strength."

He draws a breath and his sword. Starlight flares in his eyes, licks the length of the blade. He turns and gestures with that sword at where I lean against Sigrdrifa's dark blade.

Against the weariness and the numb tingling in my limbs, I straighten my spine and return the salute with two swords. My blade and Sigrdrifa's flare not.

I lower hers to the floor, arm trembling, and stumble toward Yrenbend as Heythe advances from the other side. The blade carves furrows behind me. My eyes are drawn to the Lady's face, bright and lovely in the light slanting through the high window.

"I will not have my orders questioned," she says, in a voice soft as death. My brethren withdraw, a circle forming around Yrenbend, Heythe and myself. Sdadown growl behind her, a sound more like a hissing of adders than the voices of wolves.

"What I do I do for the future of the world, and old jealousies will not be permitted to destroy it."

"Whatever you want," Yrenbend says, "it is not our future."

Her eyes skip past him, meeting mine. "Master Wolf, hold your hand." I stagger to a halt, although I did not intend to strike down Yrenbend. I am not sure, in fact, what I had intended, but when her eyes meet mine my collar tightens as if she twisted it. She is lying.

Lying.

The Suneater knows. He is the end of the world, that beast—Ragnarok, Apocalypse, born for devouring. He is pure and ruinous as the wildfire, as the ice storm; he has no pack, and all sanity has been choked and chained and tortured from him, and the man who held him in check has been shattered and warped just like the chain that held him before.

There also used to be another wolf inside me, besides the Suneater, a clean devoted wild thing. That wolf is dead with his pack, resurrected as a gaunt abhorrent yellow-eyed monster. The sdadown are more than a weapon. They are a lesson. She has bound my skinned body in her shadows, too, and like them I must love her for it.

The world is ruined. Let the sun go dark.

It has the feeling of an old thought, long hoarded and long recalled. Feral strength wracks me, the exhaustion falling aside as I walk past Yrenbend, leaving Sigrdrifa's dark sword lying among the dry-needled boughs littering the floor. Among the faces in the crowd, I see Rannveig's and I see Muire's, but Strifbjorn is gone. *Gone, or cloaked under his pass-unseen again?* It does not matter. The bonds are shattered, though the collar still twists at my throat. I know my master. I have sworn my service. I know my task.

In bondage now bides the Wolf, 'til world's end. Old words. Old worlds. Still true.

I take my place at my Lady's side with my brothers, all in shadow wrapped.

A sane wolf growls before it kills. Hackles rise, and teeth are bared. I make no display. With my left hand, I open the clasp of my cloak. It slides from my shoulders, puddling at my feet like a shed skin. Yrenbend meets my eyes and nods, his sword in his hand like a stinger, dripping Light.

"I say you are corrupt, Lady." His voice is clear and level. It carries, and the children mutter.

I step forward. Behind me, the sdadown tense. They smell of old meat frozen in a cache.

"I said stay your hand, Master Wolf," Heythe murmurs. "Give me your blade."

Svanvitr stays dark. I reverse her, and give her hilt-first to Heythe, never taking my eyes from Yrenbend's face as it registers his shock. I am permitting another to wield my sword—the symbol of my covenant.

Strifbjorn never should have given me this blade. I am more tarnished than any, and never was anything but a shadow set up to reflect their Light. Under my skin of darkness, a dead wolf squirms in pain that will not end. But the Suneater smiles.

Heythe takes the blade. At her touch, it flares instantly, hurtingly into light. "Corrupted?"

But I can see through the light, see a grayness in the shadows it casts. Rannveig's earring swings warm in my ear. Another illusion. Destruction follows this one, and I follow destruction.

"Will you recant?" Heythe again. "I need you, bold Yrenbend. I need you all. All my children." The nonexistent light casts flickering shadows across her face, making her seem taller.

"Am I meant to be impressed?"

Heythe shakes her head sadly and steps forward, with one last warning glance to me. *Do not intervene.*

I have no such intention. The Suneater does not care if she dies or if Yrenbend does, so long as there is blood. A white star hangs in my breast. I wonder if Heythe knows what she has unleashed. I am certain Rannveig does not.

I am the Grey Wolf. My bindings are not lightly parted.

Crystal blades flash and sing and clash upon each other. I hear myself laughing like a stranger in a darkened room. And then little Muire steps into the fight, singing a war-chant, her sword blazing blue and white in her right hand. The wood-cutter's daughter is a few steps behind her, stooping to pick up Sigrdrifa's fallen blade. She swings it like a wood-axe, clumsily, charging Heythe from the flank.

Faced by an einherjar and a waelcyrge, Heythe does not even bother to toy with the girl. Her sword—my sword—flickers sideways and severs Rannveig's hand at the elbow. The girl goes to her knees as Muire shouts and lunges.

Heythe sidesteps Muire's blow, parries Yrenbend's thrust and minces sideways to flank him, prowling like a cat. He pivots, keeping her before him, as Muire spares a glance for the bleeding girl but comes up beside him. I step away from the silently watching sdadown and kneel beside the girl.

They have practiced together, Muire and Yrenbend, and they press Heythe as a pair. She gives no ground, my sword dancing in her hand with a skill I have never seen equaled—not by Skeold, Strifbjorn, even Menglad. I dismiss Muire and Yrenbend from my thoughts and turn to the girl. Already, I can see that they will die.

The woodcutter's daughter is also dying. So much crimson

hides deeper wounds than the cut to her arm. The blade continued down. Blood pulses from a razor-edged wound on her thigh, flooding from the stump of her arm. It covers my hands and body as I gather her. "Foolish candle-flicker."

"Master Wolf." Her lips shape a whisper. "There is no pain."

"Only what I gave thee."

Her lips shape a curious smile. "Take it back." Her left hand comes up as if to rest in my hair, falling away before it more than half-lifts. My hands brush her flesh. *Kiss me again.*

The Suneater laughs at the thought, revealing his red, mocking maw. *We create suffering. We are not for the easing of it.*

The silence between the pain and me is all I have. I am sure that to shatter it would mean my destruction.

Then let me be destroyed. Blade clashes on crystal blade. I do not raise my head. I bend and press my lips over the girl's.

Too late.

Hers lie slack and still beneath my mouth, and no breath trickles from them. She is gone. All my grief and love goes down into darkness with her, leaving the shadowy memory of emotion.

Muire cries out, and the noise drags my head up. She sags to her knees, the sword tumbling from her fingers. Heythe has half-severed her right arm. She clutches the wound, blood dripping between the fingers of her left hand.

Yrenbend steps between the two women before Heythe can finish the waelcyrge, deflecting her blade with a grunt. He cannot give ground, not and protect the waelcyrge struggling to rise behind him. Muire staggers to her feet, that song bubbling from her lips again, her sword dragging from her left hand.

Somehow she lifts it, stepping up beside Yrenbend. He side-steps to give her room, and she lunges toward Heythe, who parries the blow contemptuously.

It is the best the wounded waelcyrge can do. She slides to one knee again, her right foot going out from under her, and drops her sword, dragging the edges of her wound together with her left hand. Yrenbend stands over her, taking up the song, Light sparkling and arcing between his blade and Heythe's when they ring on one another. The tones are fragile and clean, like flicked crystal, but these blades do not break.

Heythe gives a step, suddenly, something she has not done before, and I see the realization of his mistake on Yrenbend's face the instant he moves to take advantage of it. Heythe's feint is toward the woman on the ground, her eyes hooded in concentration as she seals the rent in her upper arm. Yrenbend moves to parry, his chest unguarded for a moment as Heythe reverses her cut, smooth as a twisting cat, and thrusts Svanvitr through his heart.

He falls across Muire, dying without a whimper.

Her eyes flick open and she shouts. Yrenbend's body lies in her lap, his eyes open and dark. She bends over him, her own blood spilling across his face as she tries futilely to wipe it away. A moment and she snarls and shoves him aside, face tight in concentration, the wound in her arm sealing over.

She fumbles her sword up and begins to lever herself to her feet. Something about her expression, the weary determination in her eyes, brings me to my feet as well. Rannveig tumbles from my lap.

Heythe steps forward, my blade still shining falsely in her

hand. She raises Svanvitr to guard while little Muire brings her blade up with blood-slick fingers, her arm shivering with exhaustion. Heythe smiles and draws her hand back for a blow that will brush Muire's wavering guard aside like an axe through a willow wand.

Unthinking, I step over Rannveig's body and catch Heythe's wrist in my hand. "Enough."

She turns to me mildly as Muire falls back on one knee, still struggling to stand. "We'll only have to kill her later, if I do not now."

A historian and a poet, not a swordswoman. Born for something different than the rest of us. I tell myself it is her blind courage that stirs my heart, drives the Suneater to silence for a moment. "Strifbjorn has already made his escape." I know it's true, and that Yrenbend and Muire chose to give their lives so that the rebel prince might flee. "There is no glory in killing an enemy too wounded to stand."

Knowing Strifbjorn, he believed them when they promised a diversion, and that they would meet him on the mountain after. He would never have left them to this.

Heythe examines my face, turns and regards the dead. Last of all her eyes fasten on the poet, who has gained her feet and leans heavily on her sword. Heythe smiles then, nods and stands on her toes to kiss my forehead. Her fingers brush mine as she gives me back my sword. "So glad I am to have you by my side again, my love, I can deny you nothing."

She glides away, her sdadown following at her heels.

I nudge Yrenbend's sword with my boot. "Take it for his wife."

Muire spits at my feet. "Don't think this will buy you for-giveness."

My own laughter, cold as the pealing of a bell. The Suneater howls with it. "I think I'm beyond that, sister." I step away, bend to collect my cloak from the floor and follow behind my Lady.

The Historian

Strifbjorn's face paled as I toiled uphill to him, blessing the crust over the snow. My skis and my fiddle were left behind in the mead-hall, and I had no intention of going back. "Yren-bend?" he asked, when I came close to speak without shouting. "Rannveig?"

My tunic was rent. Blood soaked my tunic and trousers. I reached over my shoulder and drew Yrenbend's sword from where I had thrust her under my cloak. Silently, I handed her to Strifbjorn, and kept walking past him, over the shoulder of the mountain, away from where Herfjotur waited.

"Muire?"

"You go on ahead," I called over my shoulder, not turning. The hollow place between my breastbone and my spine hurt too much, and if I looked at him once, I would sink down in the snow and I would never stop crying. "I'll walk."

It was five days by foot from our hall to Arngeir's in good weather, with a clear road. I estimated I could make it in nine, over snow, walking without rest—or in four on skis, once I talked a tree into sharing some with me. I wanted the cold and the silence. I wanted the bitter wind in my hair, and I wanted to be alone. I thought of turning south and skiing until I ran out of snow, away from the winter and the war.

It was only half a temptation, though. I was not all that eager to live to see the coming world, and I didn't want to be alone that much, or for that long.

On the second day, I knew that I was followed.

I glimpsed my stalker from the corner of my eye, pacing me through the dark boles of the trees on the north side of the road. Whatever it was, its footfalls bore it lightly, barely disturbing the snow. Through the night and into morning it drifted alongside, just out of easy line of sight.

As the third night approached, I realized that it was waiting for me to sleep, so I made myself comfortable in the lee of a white oak, back to the broad trunk, and obliged it. It wouldn't do to leave things like that out to trouble travelers less resourceful than I. Besides, if it was one of Heythe's creatures, I wanted the chance to test it.

The snow reflected what little moonlight there was, and the light of the bright close winter stars as well. I leaned back in a drift and laid my sword across my knees, waiting. Half an hour later, more or less, I saw it picking its way through a pale patch of light between the barren trees.

The fell thing looked to have been a lynx or a young lion once, all angular shoulders and lashing tail. Its eyes shimmered green in the darkness, a slack mouth shining wet as it prowled across the drifts in a dreamlike silence. When it was only a few feet away it sniffed the air deeply, one foot raised like the hunt-ing cat it must once have been.

I rolled to my feet and dove forward, Nathr extended be-fore me, even as it sprang. Starlight flickered the length of her blade, lighting the snow-swept scene in shadow and brilliance. The foul thing wrenched aside, snowshoe feet scattering pow-dery crystals left and right. It whirled, and I turned, keeping my back to the tree on the chance that these creatures hunted like wolves, one the distraction and the others creeping around to flank the prey. It crouched, tail lashing, just out of sword reach. I jeered at it, shuffling through the drift, unwilling to give up the shelter of the oak.

The thing lowered its head and *hissed* at me. I shouted and it sprang, a foolish frontal attack. I plunged Nathr through its throat, expecting to have to scurry back a step through the snow to dodge the dying beast's claws.

But its lunge didn't end with feeble twitching and the spurt of blood from a severed artery. Instead it pressed itself the length of the blade, and would have fastened its teeth in my shoulder if I hadn't thrown myself down in the snow and rolled clear, levering it over my head with the fulcrum of the sword and a kick in its underbelly, which was not soft but hard as oak.

It smacked into the trunk of the tree, tumbling snow onto our heads from the branches. I rolled to my feet while the thing shook its head, and brought Nathr down between its ears.

The skull split top to bottom, shedding tatters of darkness, and still the thing came on, reaching for me with flopping jaws. Swallowing bile, I scrambled to the side, bringing my blade around for another cut, meaty resistance and then the scrape of crystal on bone as I lopped the thing's mutilated head off.

Horribly, it scrabbled randomly through the snow even when I had dismembered the body.

I was glad indeed that I rejoined my brethren at Arngeir's hall without meeting another one.

The Wolf

Heythe waits three days past Yrenbend's death while her partisans return to the hall. There are fewer than she had planned to see, and I expect anger, but she seems curiously satisfied with the tally, and curiously pleased with my behavior. She keeps me as close by her side as if tethered, feeds me tidbits I neither need nor desire from her fingers. The nights are spent by her side as well, staring into the high darkness of the banner-hung rafters while she breathes peacefully, head cradled on my shoulder like a child's on the flank of a trusted hound.

As if she could trust me. As if she ever would.

Even when I bathe, her scent never leaves my skin. It is just another chain, and I am grown accustomed. And the Suneater will get what he wants soon enough.

Blood, and plenty of it.

Before sunrise on that third night, I slip out of bed when she turns in her sleep, sighing. I rise and dress in the dim red light that angles under the hanging. The sdadown beside the bench watch with unblinking yellow eyes as I stuff feet into boots and make my way into the hall.

The children . . . the *tarnished*—Muire's name, a truer

name, good Historian—are scattered about the hall. I move among them silently, and they fall away like surf running back from a rock. Yrenbend is dead, and none of the others will meet my eyes.

The chiming of blades comes faintly from outside, and I follow it. Two einherjar fence in the starlight before the doors, moving through the trampled snow. A ring of our brethren surround them. Several of them turn at the spill of faded fire-light when I open the door, and turn away as quickly. I watch for a moment and then walk past.

The stairs down the cliff to the ice-clotted beach are slick and jumbled with trodden snow. The ocean is a dark tumble far below, moving like coils of hair tossed on a pillow. It is not a pleasant place, in night, in winter.

I make my way down to the sea.

The moon was a barest sliver, and already it has set. I cannot summon the world-Serpent, the Bearer of Burdens, the Dweller Within—and I would not want to. Still I walk down to where the combers touch my boots, and after a long silence I find my voice, somehow. I draw a salt-prickling breath and speak to the sea.

"I understand now what you could not tell me, Brother. Yrenbend understood it, too, I think, by the end." The numbness in my chest makes it difficult to continue. I close my eyes and let my neck go slack, the collar tightening when I permit my head to roll forward, chin to my chest, my cloak furling back from my shoulders in the wind off the water.

"I wish I could tell you I was sorry, Bearer. But this is . . . what I want. What I have always wanted, for the second chance you gave me was nothing but another sort of bondage. And I am weary of my chains, Brother." I stand for a moment, watching the sea come and go. Ceaseless, immortal, life-giving.

There is no heart in me but for the hating. Hunger gnaws my breast, a hunger that will not be assuaged until all the world is consumed in flame and ice. "I am weary of love, and expectation and family. The Lady has not come to conquer. She has come seeking vengeance. She thinks she's bound me to *her* sort of destruction, but she doesn't understand the leash she slipped. And she doesn't know the Suneater. But you, Brother . . . blood of my blood, and flesh of my flesh. You knew what I was. And still you gave me a place. For that—I am sorry for what happens next, and if I were other than I am, I might even sacrifice myself to buy your intervention."

The indifferent sea licks at my feet. I draw Svanvitr into my hands and hold her out before me. The light of the so-distant stars shines along the ink-dark crystal of her blade, but no answering light flares within. Even when I try to call it into her, the sword is a darkness I could lose myself in. "You see how close to my true self I have drifted, Brother."

I speak into silence, and silence answers.

"She means to kill you. It's plain before me—she'll wield the children one on another like stone on stone until all are shattered, and then she will turn her attention to you. So I give you the warning.

"But I warn you also—when that battle comes, I will stand by her side. And should she defeat you . . . Well." A low, soft chuckle rises up my throat like a growl. "Destruction is what I am for, and we have proven, I think, that the only protection from something like me is to keep it eternally chained. I will still be at her back when she is weakened by battle. And what good are gods to me, save the dining on?"

Half-hopeful, half-hateful, I wait for an answer I do not expect to hear.

I wait, and then I say, "When I have devoured her, Brother. You must be ready, after."

Nothing comes, and at dawnlight I summon the Imogen, and feed her the unsatisfying leavings of my grief and my sorrow. She whines for more, and I have nothing more to give her—but a cold immortal hate and a hunger almost the equal of hers.

And those things are *mine*.

The Warrior

Herfjotur asked only two questions when Strifbjorn rejoined her beside the frozen waterfall, her eye skipping off the gaudy spots of blood to fasten on the sword in his hand. It wasn't Strifbjorn's, or Mingan's, and she paled.

The first thing she said was, "Mingan?"

"I failed."

Her tongue clicked against the roof of her mouth. "And the others?"

"Muire will meet us at the hall."

She didn't speak again. Strifbjorn was grateful for the silence of the flight.

Arngeir's hall, with its angled roof of blue slates and glass-paned windows, caught a glare like ice off the afternoon sun. It sat in the midst of a little village, not so isolated as Strifbjorn's own hall had been. Herfjotur and he rode her steed in a tightening gyre into the courtyard, which was also paved with slates and shoveled clean of snow. His hooves belled on the pavement, and Strifbjorn took a long, slow look around and then glanced down at Yrenbend's blade in his white-knuckled hand.

Sigrdrifa's blood stained his sleeves and the front of his trousers. The small sheath in his belt hung empty as the ache in his belly, innocent of the knife he had left in her eye.

Herfjotur dismounted. Strifbjorn slid down behind her, boots clattering on the cold stones.

He had never killed one of his brethren before.

When he looked up, Arngeir and Brynhilde were hurrying across the court. Cold recognition flickered in Brynhilde's eyes as they glanced off the sword in Strifbjorn's hand and up to his own. Herfjotur stepped out of her way and Arngeir stopped in his tracks, but Yrenbend's wife came forward steadily, never dropping her gaze. Three feet away, she paused, looking up into Strifbjorn's face, and then quietly reached across the distance.

He gave her husband's sword into her hand.

Her fingers tightened on it, convulsively, her jaw clenching as if in pain. Strifbjorn saw the ring that Muire had made for her catch the light, and then fall into darkness as she turned her hand over, weighing the sword. She nodded once, curtly, and turned away, walking down a gentle slope to the beach. She crossed the boards to the pier, which in summer would have hosted snake-prowed warships and fishing vessels. Those were all now hauled safely to rest under shed-roofs until the threat of storms passed with the spring.

Strifbjorn followed the widow only with his eyes, Herfjotur and Arngeir turning as well to watch her walk the length of the dock. The pommel of her own sword caught sunlight at her hip; Yrenbend's unsheathed blade shone darkly in her hand. She reached the end of the pier and stopped.

She drew back her arm, raising the sword high. Strifbjorn did not look at Herfjotur, but he heard her suck back a sob of memory. Brynhilde stood for a long moment, and then Strifbjorn saw her weight shift. She leaned back, looked up—and slung the sword on a glittering arc out over the sea.

When she climbed back up the slope, her eyes were dry. "Do we wait for them to come to us, or do we take the war to them?"

Muire returned at midafternoon four days later with tidings of Heythe's shadow creatures. She had encountered one on the road and bested it—but not with ease.

The next morning Strifbjorn and his army moved out through the snow, four hundred and thirty-four children and seventeen valraven strong, with the wind at their backs and blue and silver banners snapping overhead. Brynhilde and her steed reported that Heythe's larger force was arcing cross-country to meet them: all the remaining children, a few steeds and a foul sea of sdadown. Not to mention Heythe herself, and—of course—Mingan.

Arngeir's hold and hall were too close to cities for Strifbjorn's liking. He wanted the sea at their back, and no humans nearby whose protection they would have to consider, or who could become weapons for the tarnished.

The army of the children of the Light fell back to the

edge of the glacier, where the snow gave way to a windswept tundra and moraine, and beat east.

Heythe caught them before they caught the sea.

(M)idafternoon glazed the ragged ice overhead. The children made a broad column at the foot of the glacier, the valraven and their riders flying scout. Herfjotur herself brought Strifbjorn the report, sitting astride her heads-tossing stallion. She leaned down to speak to him, her legs concealed under the covert feathers and the bend of wings.

"Five hundred and more, war-leader. Moving north and east: they have cut in between us and the sea."

"All the rest of us, then." This from Menglad, walking beside Strifbjorn.

Herfjotur frowned. "The rest of them. Yes."

"How far?"

She shook her head. "Half a day. They'll be on us at morning."

Strifbjorn nodded. Unfamiliar terrain for all of them, and he would have waited for sunrise, too. That would put the light at their backs—as if he needed another disadvantage.

He stared up at the glacier. "Here, then. Better to have the tundra before us and the ice at our backs than try to cut south through the taiga with fell beasts nipping our heels."

Menglad rocked back on her heels and stretched into a crouch, levering her sword out of the way with a hand on the pommel. "We won't win this. Strifbjorn. . . . I told Arngeir, I would break away. Give myself to the Bearer."

Strifbjorn spun on her. "I forbid it! Not—"

She interrupted. "They have sdadown, Heythe, Mingan . . . the Imogen. It cannot be wrong to buy an intervention."

"They are our brothers," was all Strifbjorn could say, and she shook her head. Herfjotur fell so silent he could clearly hear the twinned breathing of her stallion. "We all serve the Light. I will not . . . countenance . . ."

Menglad stood and turned away. "I'll see to sentries. We may as well get comfortable, then." She looked up. "Herfjotur, have you seen Brynhilde?"

She shook her head, and a distant expression crossed her face. "I have not. And my steed says that he does not know where she and her valraven are, either."

They waited while sunset ran blood down the white slab of the ice and night stained the sky. Strifbjown stood near the edge of camp, straining his eyes into darkness. When small, bright baubles scattered the dome overhead, Muire came to him.

She stood beside him for a little, waiting for his acknowledgment silently as any old friend. He glanced down at her, noticing her tight-pressed lips and the dark bruises surrounding her eyes.

"I brought you a cup of brandy." She held out a little carved ivory bowl. He caught the scent of it on her breath, as well, very lightly. She passed it with infinite care, so her fingers did not brush his.

"Thank you." It tasted of cinnamon and summertime, exotic and sharp, the opposite of what hung over them and what lay before. He breathed in, drawing the scent.

They stood in companionable silence a few moments longer, and then she turned to him and took a breath. "Strifbjorn."

"Yes?"

"Let me stand with you tomorrow." An earnest expression marked her face, a line drawn between her clear gray eyes.

Strifbjorn wondered, in a different world, what might have been. *Mingan loved me enough to give me away to this woman.* Another day he might have pushed the thought away quickly.

This was not any other day.

She continued. "Herfjotur will be with her steed, and Yrenbend. . . ." Her voice trailed off. She had often fought beside him, while his wife reined her ice-white drake overhead. "And you won't have Mingan to watch your back, Strifbjorn."

There was generosity in the offer, and in the level regard of her eyes. She'd set him free—or her hopes for him, whatever they might have been—and now here she was, telling him he didn't have to die alone if he didn't want to.

And he knew he would rather die a thousand miles from everything he loved than watch this brave little sparrow torn by hawks. "Muire. Thank you, and I mean that as deeply as I can. But no."

Her regard was unsurprised, her voice low and sympathetic. "Oh, Strifbjorn. Faithful to him, even now, even in this . . . insignificant thing?"

He took a breath and turned away. "You will fight in the second rank. Behind me."

Strifbjorn heard her draw a matching breath, and before she could answer, a pale shadow descended before them. It was Brynhilde's valraven, the coiling wyvern, looming with widespread wings. He lowered his head and spoke on the low hiss of an outforced breath, tongue flickering.

"Einherjar, waelcyrge."

"Bright one," Strifbjorn said, as Muire curtseyed to the valraven.

"I bring tidings of my mistress' death."

Strifbjorn stepped back. "What happened?"

The valraven hissed. "She has given herself to the Serpent, war-leader. You will have your help, an you reach the sea."

14

You will hear the wolves wailing
Over your husband.
—"The Second Lay of Gudrun"

The Wolf

I imagine the eyes of my enemies glimmering like campfires in the darkness. As many lie behind me as before. The eyes of my enemies, the eyes of my brothers. The eyes of my lovers.

I slip past the perimeter, and the sentries never see me. Sdadown flit through the darkness, insensible of me as they are the moonlight. A moon like a metal-filing hangs overhead, its dim light silvering a bank of clouds on the eastern horizon.

My lovers. I have no lovers. I am alone, as I was meant to be. The one, I have broken with. The other . . . I chuckle, dark and cold. I remember her touch, her strength, the moist silk of her skin. *That's not loving.*

The Suneater laughs in his hunger, tasting the salt of her flesh. *Love having served us so well.*

I have no answer for him, but I walk into the night nevertheless.

Once, I would have known where Strifbjorn stood, almost the edge of what he thought. I would have read his presence in the patterns of the night. But he has changed, and I have changed, and darkness has taken us both.

Knowing the inconsistency of my own actions, ignoring the howl of the Suneater under my skin, I step into the shadows. I follow his scent on the wind that blows between worlds. And when I pass out of the dead world he turns toward me, hand on the hilt of his sword, and raises his eyebrow. "Well, my love," he murmurs. "If you wish, we can settle this now."

"Strifbjorn." It is too near, too dark. Too much to bear. "I have not come to fight you."

"I have come to fight you," he answers. "With the dawn one of us dies."

The finality in his voice brooks no argument. "Aye."

His hand slips from Alvitr's hilt. "Mingan. Why?"

I shake my head. "Because the end of the world is sweet, and it calls me. It is what I was born to."

He sighs. "Didst ever love me?"

"Until I die." My voice chokes off. " 'Tis not enough," I continue at last. "Love is not enough, in a callous world. It is"—a breath—"it cannot live."

He smiles and comes a step, two, three, closer. His breath is cool on my face, and tastes of roses. "Nothing will survive this, Mingan," he says. "Except the memory of love."

"I know," I answer, but I do not move away. *How can love be so true, and yet so piteous?*

"Thou dost choose her over me?"

"She will die." The conviction in my voice is a revelation. "I swear it."

"Then *why?*"

Oh. Strifbjorn. I look into his eyes, and he is as he was: true, and shining and untouched by what gnaws my soul.

He cannot understand. "Ruin," I answer, and turn away.

But his hand falls on my shoulder. "Mingan."

I shiver. My name is a caress upon his tongue. "What?"

"We'll be killing each other tomorrow."

"We shall."

"Then kiss me."

I turn back to him. He stands in the shadows of an unkempt moon, of the windwracked stars. His eyes gleam silver in the darkness, and I know mine are dark. "What dost wish of me?"

"Just . . ." His voice breaks. "Thy kiss."

Oh. Love is a thing like a whip, like a briar that entangles and strips skin from flesh. *Thy kiss.*

Who was it loved the wild thing? Kept faith in darkness and secrecy? Burned in my heart like a star? I breathe. "No."

"Kiss me. I have things to share that you will not trust."

My love. "Tomorrow is a war."

A snarl tautens his mouth. "I will kill you if I can."

"I have loved thee," I answer, and lean into the offered embrace.

His arms encircle me; my fingers tangle in his hair. Hopeless, storm-torn, my heart soars. His lips brush mine as I take a breath, preparing. I blow my soul into his waiting mouth, and a moment later he returns the kiss—and the comprehension.

Love. I am filled with warmth, a bittersweetness and a vertiginous brilliance. A sorrow bottomless as the night.

Mingan, my love. She has deceived you. His fingertips outline my face, hardly more than a trace of a touch. I spin on the rush of it, the forsaken taste of his love, his soul . . . unbridled giving.

Heythe? She has deceived us all.

She has no intention of winning this war. Only of destroying us all. Destroying you as well, Wolf.

I am already destroyed.

Nay.

I am destruction itself. Deny it not.

I deny—his breath flowing back into me, bearing the trace of his life, his love, his soul—*that you are only what Heythe shapes you to be. My love, you have been controlled. Deceived.*

Strifbjorn, I know.

You know nothing. And he shows me the village, the wolfhunt. He shows me the lovely woman with the glittering necklace, leading the hunt. He shows me the death of my pack, as he has imagined it.

My eyes burn.

Do not blame poor humans for a goddess' work, Mingan.

You saw this?

I deduce it. So who is deserving of your destruction? The taste of his breath entangling mine, the sorrow and the wrath and fear that snarl us both. I do not know my soul from his own, or the darkness from the day. He abandons himself to me: total trust, revocation of self, of dignity; a total gift of his soul—no remorse, no thing held back. He is einherjar: he cannot lie.

I can only lie to myself.

I thrust him back. He seethes in me, the kiss like a flame held to my skin.

"I will destroy what I can," I answer.

I am turning away as I hear him whisper. "Recollect your-self, my love."

I answer with silence, that silence chill under my skin. I will not see Strifbjorn again.

I do not return to Heythe's side.

The Historian

Swordplay might not be my strength, but history was, and the history of the world is the history of war. We had a host of problems—not the least of which being that the towering ice protecting our left flank could become as easily a boulder for the enemy to dash us against. By sunrise, snow was falling. A minor gift: low-lying clouds concealed the heights of the gla-cial escarpment, gentled a dawn sky which otherwise would have had us fighting into the glare of sunlight on snow. The blizzard had come across the ocean, and I wondered if there was a guiding hand behind it. But the storm was a hindrance as well as a help, limiting the effectiveness of the valraven for aer-ial support, and I thought it would make it easier for the sdad-own to slip around our flanks.

At least the enemy would suffer from the footing as much as we.

We took up spears and shields and formed the wall. The valraven and their riders—and Brynhilde's steed flying alone, for he had not yet chosen another—covered the right flank. At the center rear of the line paced Herfjotur's steed, his rider bracing our silver-embroidered indigo banner at her boot, snow caught in the carved detail of her helm.

The first line was the shield wall, and they were armed with their crystal blades. As Strifbjorn had promised, I was in the second line, behind and to the left of him. Nathr stayed sheathed across my back, a plumed spear ready in my hands.

Across the snow-blanketed moraine, through the blizzard, I glimpsed our enemy drawing their lines. My stomach shuddered in anticipation. Heythe was unhelmed, but clad in a chain hauberk worked in some metal that seemed almost as white as the ice above us. Her green fur-trimmed cloak was unmistakable as she walked the line, even through the feather-thick snow, but I strained my eyes in vain for a lean gray shadow following her like a cur at heel.

I leaned forward and murmured in Strifbjorn's ear, apprehension a bright line down my back. "Mingan's not with them."

His voice was dry, assured, but I caught the gleam of unspoken misery in his eye when he half-turned to speak over his shoulder. "I'm sure he'll be along presently."

Then he drew his sword and raised her overhead, commanding silence and attention. The length of the line in both directions, other swords went up—Arngeir and Menglad side by side to Strifbjorn's right, Herewys and Njal to the left, the line stretching in both directions like reflections in facing mirrors, disappearing into the storm.

Strifbjorn began to beat the flat of his blade against the rim of his shield, a chiming rhythm soon taken up by the rest of the line. It echoed across what was soon to be a battlefield, but the blue-white light that flashed about the blades and piled into the storming sky flared on our side only. Menglad raised her voice in song and I joined her, other voices following.

"Forward!" Strifbjorn's voice rang above the song and the

rhythm of swords on shields. Singing, wreathed in Light, we advanced across the slick rocks in the shadow of the glacier.

The snow fell.

And the enemy came on. Five hundred yards, three hundred. I could see their faces under their helms, the Raven Banner wind-rippled behind, the sdadown like a poisoned black tide before. I breathed deeply, quietly, peering around Strifbjorn's broad back and the edge of his shield.

I heard him murmur, "Mingan, where are you?" The spear-wielding einherjar on my right glanced upward nervously. I didn't bother. If the Imogen came on us, a third of us would be dead before we knew.

We'd never see her, under cover of the storm.

Two hundred and fifty yards, and then the sound of thunder.

I felt the magic writhing under my skin even as it took effect. The Grey Wolf's hand lay on the weft of the world, on the reins of the ice, and I knew the runes he must have drawn there, although I never could have touched such power. *Hagalaz, Isa, Dagaz.* Storm, ice, rousing.

He could only have done it from the face of the glacier itself, in the seconds before it tumbled away beneath his feet.

A shattering rumble danced the stones under my boots. I fell. Majestic, languorous, moving with deceptive speed, jumbled blocks of ice and rock somersaulted out of the obscuring storm, wreathed in coils of mist like rising steam. I screamed, and Strifbjorn called a retreat that would have done us no good at all—if the falling ice had been aimed for our line, instead of before it. I dragged myself to my feet and ran.

We fled the tumbling ice, falling back, hearing eerie animal cries cut off as the avalanche plowed through the line of sdadown. I staggered again, and Arngeir caught my shoulder, pulled me up. "Strifbjorn says south and across the tundra. We flank them while they are in disarray and head for the sea. He says we will have help if we make it so far as that."

"Aye," I answered.

"Get everyone moving!"

He turned back and was swallowed up in the crowd and the storm.

The Wolf

I've bought you the ocean, brother.

The cliff face tumbles beneath me, and for a moment I fall, wrapped in the wings of the storm. It might be a peaceful ending, but darker wings take me and bear me into the mist and clouds, and then through them to the sunlight above. The Imogen cradles me in her arms and bears me away.

And now I am oath-broken, too.

The air is thin, torn from my lungs by a rush of wind. And yet I laugh. The remnants of Strifbjorn's kiss warm my belly like the memory of a night of love, and old pain awakens anew at the touch of it. I laugh because the Suneater is in me, too, and he hates that kiss, and he hates my heart, and he hates the fire that burns under my skin. He tastes blood—his own, and the blood of others—and he craves the hot lick of it down his throat. *More. More.* Like a starving man's hunger, that taste of death. He revels in the tumble and rush of the ice beneath his feet . . . and I laugh because of his strength, and because he is no stronger than I am and because what Strifbjorn gave me back on his kiss was myself as much as it was of him. The Suneater is not other. He is a part of what I am and what I have become.

New worlds rise out of the foam. Saplings from the wrack of ruined trees. Ashes from the scars of fire.

Someone has to break things.

And somebody has to dine on gods.

The Imogen sets her bloodred lips against my ear. "Whither, my Lord?"

I take a breath. "To the meadow by the waterfall," I answer, and she bears me onward, above the storm.

I am a weapon, and she is moreso. And it is time for laying weapons down.

She lands me lightly at the base of the high cliff, turns as if to vanish into the blowing snow. "Imogen, with me."

I lead her to where the waterfall whispers still, delicately under its pall. I lay my hand against the ice. It melts under the flat of my palm, and with the trickle of water come the trickling memories.

I had brought him here on a midsummer's day. He followed me through the forest, nearly keeping up, strange and golden in the light through the leaves, and laughed in delight when we broke out of the birches and into the clear. His voice echoed the sound of water chattering on the rocks, and the air was sweet with meadowflowers. We were a pair of wild things then, a cub and a colt, perhaps—painfully young, and falling into the spiral of a friendship that seemed almost . . . foreordained.

I didn't know about the cave. I'd never ventured under the waterfall. Strifbjorn found it by plunging his head under the water to soak his hair.

When the rest of him followed, I went to see what he had found. He stood just inside the fall, wringing out his shirt, standing on a sandy floor. "It goes back," he said. He laughed and stepped away when I shook the water off.

Wet leather clung to my legs. I wrinkled my nose at it. "Explore?"

He nodded and hung the damp shirt on a jag of rock. The watery light made his hair seem white. "At least until the light runs out."

"We can use starlight, after."

It did indeed go back a long way, forking and twisting, formed of huge slabs of rock leaned up against one another. Somewhere in the darkness, brightened by the light of our eyes, I reached to help him up a slope. My ungloved hand clasped the bare skin of his arm and I hauled . . . and then we stopped.

Unmoving, as if frozen face-to-face in the darkness. His skin was cool and moist, the muscles cabled hard in his forearm—a swordsman's arm. His eyes flared brighter silver, and I tasted the shift in his scent when I did not release him. "What?"

I let my hand slip off his wrist as if scalded. "You were . . . just thinking."

He might have taken a step away if the incline had not been just behind him. "You . . . know what I was thinking?" I could almost smell the blush creeping up his face.

I nodded, knowing it was visible in the Light spilling from his eyes. "When I touch. Sometimes I can tell."

"Oh." He looked down, avoiding my gaze. "Mingan, you're my friend, and I hope how I have been feeling won't . . . ruin that. I never would have said anything."

There had been no way to answer in words. I had smelled him breathing in the silence that stretched between us, and then I had taken the half step forward and kissed him hard on the lips, using his braid to drag his mouth down to mine.

I blink in the memory, ice water coursing over my hand. Something else he'd given me in the darkness of the night before. Our first kiss. And our last one.

"Kenaz. Kenaz. Kenaz." I call on fire, the torch, the rune of passion. My wet fingers sketch a chevron on the ice-locked waterfall. A moment and the ice cracks, falling away, revealing a thin trickle of frigid water drizzling across the mouth of the cave. *A time for laying weapons down.*

Snow flecks scatter the Imogen's wings and face like stars in a midnight sky. I lead her down into darkness and the belly of the earth.

"Brother?"

"Hush, love."

The deepest cave is a small chamber, the floor deep with earth that has filtered through the cracks in the living granite. "Stand against the wall, please, Imogen." She does as she is commanded.

I draw Svanvitr into my hand and I begin to sing.

Power stirs under the mountain, the deep throbbing heart of the earth pulsing around me. Starlight flares in my eyes, tainted pewter and stained like ink, but no Light comes to my blade.

No Light at all. I said it myself. *I am beyond forgiving.* The darkness still sears me . . . sears the self-that-was, the self that Strifbjorn has given back to me.

The Suneater chuckles. *I told you so.*

It doesn't matter. We were used before, my sister and myself. I will see neither of us used again.

What grows from the floor is a stone box the size of a bedstead, the dark surface etched with deep lines of runes. The top lies open. I sweep my cloak from my shoulders, and fold it into the bottom of the box.

"Come, Imogen. I have made a bed for you."

"Brother?" But she comes to me, as bound as any of us, and she lies down quietly while I sing her tomb closed over her head.

She does not struggle. She cannot struggle.

She is made only to obey, docile as a sword in the hand that kills, and as blameless.

The stone is thick.

I almost cannot hear her screaming, cannot hear the rasp of her talons on the inside of the lid when I sheathe my mud-black sword, turn and walk away.

The Warrior

Strifbjorn and the children fled under cover of the storm and the enemy's confusion, and turned at bay on the narrowest part of a long spit of land. Some miles north of the Ulfenfell, it reached between a pair of inlets where the north sea tossed against the rocks far below. The spur widened again behind them, but the place Strifbjorn chose to make their stand in was narrow.

Ranks stretched across it in a thick double line, they waited.

The terrain was worse here, and Heythe would have to come to the children. Strifbjorn was content with the small advantage, and happy to have the sea at their backs. The storm was less of a blessing now, but it had served its purpose. He was grateful.

Muire, at his back again, took up a sorrowful song, and other voices joined her, Light flickering about them, drawing their enemies down like a moth into flame. Like the ache of a missing limb, Strifbjorn wished Mingan were beside him.

Strifbjorn knew Mingan wasn't coming. He hoped the Serpent was.

A mourning cry drifted to them on the breeze, and the voices faltered. Strifbjorn raised his shield on his left hand, settling it firmly into place. "Form."

Shield-edge rattled on shield-edge as the wall took shape. Behind him, spears readied and another rank of warriors prepared to step into the place of any that should fall. A valraven snorted, hooves chipping ice.

Through the snow, Strifbjorn glimpsed the Raven Banner, broad wings snapping on a stiff sea breeze. Before it, the tall striding figure of Heythe, a dark blade in her hand.

It had belonged to Sigrdrifa.

That more than anything crystallized his rage into something brittle and throat-cutting. Around him, Strifbjorn heard the shouts and taunts of his brethren: Menglad's wild ululating shriek rising by his side, Muire behind him singing high and sweet. He bellowed—and the children set themselves to meet their brothers' charge.

No sign of the Serpent.

The mass of the sdadown hit them first, unkillable, driving themselves up the spears of the second rank and, even when beheaded, scrabbling forward. Strifbjorn kicked one back, breaking the neck of a second with the rim of his shield. A moment later, shield wall collided with shield wall, the weight of running warriors behind it.

It is a sound anyone who had heard it carries forever, the impact as of a barn door slammed back by a bull, repeated three hundred times.

The sdadown made the difference. Strifbjorn's line held against the charge, striving shoulder to shoulder, leaning into the shock. But the vile wolves came *under* the shields, and then the weight of the enemy drove the shield wall back against the second rank as they were abandoning their beast-weighted spears and rising from the crouch, swinging swords like axes. The tarnished struck what remained of the shield wall like the ocean striking a cliff, a staggering force, a blow and a sound like a metal-clad ram striking the hull of a ship.

Strifbjorn's line shattered. He staggered back under the weight of the tarnished, unsure of how he found himself back-to-back with Arngeir, and then with Herewys a moment later.

Gore smoked on the snow, boots slipping on icy blood-wet stones. Strifbjorn staggered, striking downward with the edge of his shield at motion half-glimpsed. The back of another sdada cracked under the metal-shod rim, a rank meaty smell clotting Strifbjorn's nostrils. He gagged and brought his sword back into line.

Alvitr danced in his hand, flaring blue-white, moving like a scythe through the sdadown and then ringing on the shadowy blades of his brothers, his enemies. Teeth met in his thigh. He saw Muire fighting beside Menglad Brightwing as he turned and struck the head off the sdada. Blood stained the length of his leg.

Shouting, he parried a blade away from Arngeir, then stepped into a gap and took Ulfgar through his throat. The bodiless thing still gnawed at Strifbjorn's leg until he knocked it away.

A moment later he stood face-to-face with Skeold. She howled, her eyes dark in a determined face. Blades crossed and Strifbjorn pressed his shield on hers, trying to overbear—and then they were swept apart.

Something pale hurtled overhead, casting Strifbjorn momentarily in shadow. Herfjotur and her white-winged steed, diving into the center of the fray. Strifbjorn traced the line of his flight and saw Heythe, killing everything that came before her, blood spattering her silver chain mail. Someone shouted a warning. She whirled to face the valraven's silent, furious charge.

Strifbjorn turned into the tide of battle. Arngeir and Menglad flanked him, Muire at their backs. A break in the combat, like an eddy in a current, opened before them, and they ran toward Heythe and Herfjotur.

The goddess dropped her borrowed blade, stepped to the side, ducked Herfjotur's sword as if the movement were a dance and reached out with her bare hands. Strifbjorn could not see how it happened, but the steed tumbled and fell, throwing Herfjotur, and a pack of sdadown were on her before she could arise. The valraven staggered to her rescue, wings dragging, one head dangling, and the beasts turned on him as well.

Heythe raised her hand to her throat, and shimmering light sparked around her. Strifbjorn and the others shouted aloud, four voices as one, and redoubled their charge, slipping over rocks and ice. To no avail.

A wave of sdadown and tarnished was on them before they came within fifty yards of Heythe. Strifbjorn cared nothing for them—they were an obstacle to be surmounted. But before they could break through the line, Heythe stepped onto her rainbow and rose into the storm. The snow and the stones were red all around. Bergdis ran, shouting, and Strifbjorn saw Arngeir miss a parry and take a wound high on his shield arm. He started to shake the shield off. As Strifbjorn turned to interpose his blade he felt a tug, a tearing. Something wet and heavy slipped down his thigh. He struck out by reflex; a sdadown fell in halves. He reeled, saw another of the tarnished knock Menglad's blade off-line when she turned to help her husband, went to his knees in sudden weakness that he did not understand.

The sword fell from his hand.

The Serpent was not coming.

Arngeir fell, and Bergdis, weeping beside Ulfgar's body, raised a black-bladed sword and struck off his head. All around the battlefield, the Light flickered out in patches, the bodies of the tarnished and the children scattered everywhere. Strifbjorn pushed himself up on one knee and gutted Bergdis, smoking intestines spilling over his arms and hands. He lost Alvitr in her body, his hand too weak, and as he fell he realized what the hot wetness that covered his belly and thighs must be.

It doesn't hurt at all.

Muire was hacking her way through the sdadown toward Strifbjorn while another tarnished caught the disarmed Menglad by the throat. He drew her toward him and yanked her mouth open with his other hand, and Strifbjorn lost sight of them as a valraven descended between them, blood spattering from immense rent wings.

The last thing he remembered was Muire's eyes across the tar-black wave of sdadown.

The Historian

I had no recollection of how I made it off the battlefield alive. I remembered Strifbjorn falling, Arngeir, everyone around me taken at once—and the sdadown like a river of teeth, and the mad wild thought that if I could get to the war-leader, somehow, I could save him.

And then the pack rolled over him, and there was nothing left worth fighting for. I remembered turning, and the scrape of teeth scoring my thigh and not quite taking the tendon or the artery, and I remembered the pain in my knees and the ache in my lungs when finally, somehow, I stopped running and fell into the snow. Somewhere, I had lost my helm, and Nathr was dark in my hand.

It was cold. I was alone.

When I looked up again, crusted snow shifted on my hair

and broke, sliding down my back. I blinked flakes from my eyelashes and reached out to the light. Nothing answered but the cold and the dark between the stars. *Why am I alive?*

If I lived, maybe someone else survived. A bitter thought. I did not want to go back and face my disgrace, and so I argued with myself. I fled. I fled a field of battle. I should have died first.

Maybe someone else is alive.

And they would spit on me if they saw me.

Maybe someone is wounded and needs help.

And so I wiped the gore from Nathr, sheathed her over my shoulder, stood and trudged back through the snow.

The silence lodged in my heart. It was a strangely peaceful scene. Snow quilted over the bodies scattering the battlefield, the scraps of hacked sdadown twitching as they froze. The falling snow had drifted over the blood, but my boots broke through the top layer to lay a red-inked trail behind me. I walked back to the place where I had broken.

I knelt down in the snow and dug with my bare hands.

I found Arngeir first, Bergdis lying half over him, as if they embraced. Wrapped in ice, though, not in flames. Menglad lay cold not five feet away, her hand cast over her mouth.

Strifbjorn. He had died badly. The body was too cold by the time I got there even to close his eyes, and I couldn't bear to look too long anyway.

If I were mortal, I would lie down in the snow and freeze beside them.

Night fell behind the storm. Again, I called on the Light, and this time, a pale, shredded flickering shone from my eyes and covered my hands. It tattered when I moved. The Light gleamed around me for a moment. The power built and slid within me—and then like a great, faltering heartbeat fell away. I called on the strength, the Soul of the world. . . .

And the world did not answer.

But something else did. Further on, from behind a tumble of snow-covered rocks, rose a thin, exhausted neigh. I pushed myself to my feet, frozen blood clinging to my boots and trousers, and scrambled through ice and over rock, using Nathr's scab-barded blade as a crutch until I saw what cried.

Herfjotur's stallion was gnawed and bloody, but he was not dead. Snow still fell between us, gentling the contours of the battlefield, but I saw him sprawled in the gathering drifts among the gaunt bodies of a half-dozen sdadown. A final sdada still panted, wheezing, nearby. Its jaws snapped, but its spine was severed. It had not the strength to drag itself.

The stallion was crippled, his wings bent horribly and jagged with splintered bone. His eyes were white-rimmed and wide with fear beneath the horns, and his other head, the antlered one, flopped on a broken neck. His lungs heaved; the blood that foamed in his nostrils was bright.

I am ashamed to say I hesitated.

Oh, Muire, I thought, *for pity's sake.* So I went to him. I reached out an uncertain hand for his porcelain muzzle, and I let what Light remained shine out of my eyes, feeling as if it faded already. "Bright one," I said, and had to clutch his horn to keep from falling.

He grew quiet at my touch, and I almost wept at the terrible extent of his wounds. He sighed and pushed his face against me, as a horse might with a friend. That act, somehow, struck me with more pity and horror than any other thing that I had seen on all that cruel day. And then he said—inside me, as I had never heard a valraven speak—**Alive? Alive how?**

I snatched back my hand. "Cowardice," I said. "I ran."

The Light?

"No more." I leaned on the sword. For now, it held me. My leg almost would. "Bright one, I cannot heal you."

I could not even heal myself.

But I could give him mercy. I shifted my weight and slipped Nathr from her sheath, far enough that he could see the blade. I could give him mercy.

Live.

"We *can't*." I finished drawing my sword and thrust her scabbard through the baldric. Ridiculous to keep it, but I would carry her away from here. The echo of a howl reached me. It prickled the hair on my neck. I had nothing to give the stallion but a promise. "I will be quicker than they."

He surged out of the snow, broken wings flopping. Uncontrolled, one knocked me down. I sprawled under the weight of my mail.

Live. An order. A command. He extended his head, so I could haul myself hand over hand up his mane. **Live.** One last time, a wistful murmur.

I stroked his forelock from his eyes. The sdada howled again. I could have left him. I could have fled again.

But then the stallion would be alone.

"As well here with you as later, otherwise," I said. I picked up my blade and whipped ice from it. He shrugged his broken wings wide, to cover my flank. I winced to think how it must hurt him.

It would serve.

The sdadown howled to hunt, but when they struck it was in perfect silence. That suited me also; there were only four, and it had taken more to murder Strifbjorn; but then, I was not Strifbjorn.

The monsters circled, flanked us, and two struck for the valraven's quarters. I dove over his wing and skidded down before them, blade-first. The valraven kicked one tumbling, and Nathr found the throat of the other—I know not how.

Of course it did not die, but dragged itself back, snarling.

Oh, we fought. What does it matter? By sheer luck I killed one, a chop through its heart that silenced the damned thing where all my hacking couldn't, and the stallion crushed another. The third closed teeth in my arm and bore me back, against his shoulder. I hammered its face with Nathr's pommel. Teeth shattered; I knocked it free.

It struggled on in silence.

No more, I thought. No more. If I must die, I would die like a waelcyrge.

Singing.

Let it call down every vile-wolf left prowling the battlefield. Let them come. Let them *come*.

I waded through drifts and tripped over corpses. I drove the sdada before me; it circled and snarled. Perhaps a bit late, but I was dying now as I should have died before. There was some satisfaction to be had in it.

Unlooked for, Light flared from the blade, and I stared at it so hard I almost dropped her. The sdada, not so foolish, leaped; I cut it from the air. Behind me, a great snap and rattle. The stallion shook the last one like a dog killing a rat. Remembering the trick with the heart, I ran it through while he held it down.

The stallion nudged me with his bloody muzzle and tumbled into the snow. And the pale light died from my sword.

Wait with me, he asked.

And of course I could do not other.

I tore the ruined harness from him, working with stiff fingers. I unbuckled saddle and blanket, and let them slide into the snow. I sat down in the snow beside him and leaned my blade over my knees.

Sometime in the night, he pressed his cheek to mine.

He was still alive in the morning.

I did not lift my head or open my eyes when redness behind their lids told me the short winter day was beginning. Cold ached in the joints of my hands. I had never felt the like.

The stallion breathed into my hair.

Kasimir, he said.

My thigh hurt less, but it had not healed as it should have. I scrambled up, limping, turning, seeking the danger as Nathr, uplifted, flared blue-white.

There was nothing but the snow, white as a waelcyrge's gown, and the sky, enamel-blue as Heythe's eyes. In the night, the storm had passed over.

Kasimir, the stallion said patiently.

Only a valraven's rider may hear his name.

I let my blade fall. "I am not worthy," I said. "But I will still wait with you."

Live.

"I cannot—"

But the sword in my hand seared, and did not flicker. "Maybe I can."

The Dweller Within never came to our aid, the stallion said, tossing his mane. **The Serpent lies dying. That is why there is no Light for you to call on. No Light but your own.**

"Oh." There *was* something I could do. Although the answer might be terrible. "I could ask for a miracle. I don't even know if it will work, if the Serpent is dying. But I could ask."

Ask, he said.

I̶t was not as it had been. No presence surrounded me. Rather, what I called came from within, a pale frail thing entirely.

I could not heal him. But perhaps I could change him.

The earth quivered and ruptured, throwing me from my feet. The snow at the crevice melted instantly, the torn brown soil laid bare. Bone shredding his hide, the valraven fought for his feet. He did not shy. He did not cringe.

But as red metal crawled from the ground, he screamed, and would not stop screaming.

I had been a smith. I had been waelcyrge. But the forge-heat drove me back, made me flinch as the stallion would not do. I smelled scorching meat, heard it sizzle. He shrieked, but he did not struggle, and I know not how, but he stood.

Over the awful crying I heard the nauseating crack of twisted bones healing, of bent limbs straightening. The white-hot metal burned through him, reworked him inside and out, made him more than alive, something alien, something *other*. . . . And yet he endured. He lived on.

I looked down at my hands. The Light had left them.

Conscious, impassive now, he straightened slowly. Both heads on their long necks turned to regard me, white rings already fading around living brown eyes in sculptured faces. He fanned glittering wings pinioned with razors, and blade rasped on blade. Steam hissed under pressure as he stepped forward. His breath came forth like a whistle.

He shook out his mane, and it rattled like wire.

The snow sublimated under his hooves. He nuzzled me. My clothes smoked. Where I touched his cheek, my hand seared and stung.

I heard my own voice as the voice of another. "What *are* you?"

Kasimir, he answered, as if in my ear. **Metal and meat. Sorcery and steel.**

"What are you?" I asked again.

I am War.

"No," I said, and couldn't find the words to ask. Everything had changed, and he had changed with it, and I was afraid to know what it meant. "What have you become?" I reached for him, but his heat defeated me, and I scrubbed my hand against my thigh. "You are the future."

The gaze he turned on me was solemn as a lion's. **I am the world, what the world will need and what the world will be.**

I looked away. "Why did you tell me your name?" I knew the answer. "I am not worthy of you."

I would not choose one unworthy.

"I fled. I fled the sdadown, and the tarnished, and I hid while our brethren died. I am a coward. I will bring you pain."

What pain could equal the pain of creation? The antlered head ducked down. He made himself small and shy, nudging the snow about his hooves with his muzzle so it hissed and vanished into steam.

"Kasimir." Surely, I could forgive myself for saying it, just once. "You said it yourself. The Dweller Within is no more. The Light has failed."

The Dweller Within still lingers. We are the Light that remains, he replied.

"No," I said. "Oh, no. . . ." With the last of my strength, I stepped away.

Behind me I heard the hiss of steam, the clatter of steel feathers. **You will come back to me. I am Kasimir. I am the new Age of the World.**

When you name me, I shall come.

I did not turn to watch him leap into the sky. His feathers did not brush me as he passed.

They would have cut me to the bone.

I stood on that battlefield a long time before I came back to myself. The snow returned. It fell all that night and into the morning, and the next dawn was recognizable chiefly by a lightening of the gloom. The cold and wind hurt. I hoped they might kill me. But in the end, the simple passage of time returned me to my senses.

I had no way to bury the bodies in the frozen ground and no fuel to raise a pyre. I labored in silence, piling up course upon course of stones there at the edge of the cliff over the ocean where we had turned at bay. When I could not reach the top

I packed snow into a ramp, up which I toiled until I had built a wall eight feet tall and a bowshot long. The wound in my arm healed, a white scar. I learned cold, then. I learned hunger. I had already known—and quailed at—fear.

When I fell into a snowdrift and could not lift myself, I rested. I chewed snow from the battlefield for water—for thirst began to haunt me—and sometimes that snow was frozen solid with blood.

When the wall was built I stacked the bodies in its lee, course upon course. I thought I might die of these new pains: cold, weariness, famine. There was nothing to eat. *I am becoming mortal*, I thought. *Perhaps there's a death in it for me yet.*

But the suffering did not kill me.

I found ways to move the bodies of the valraven to lie among those of their masters, though I will not speak of what I did. I buried the tarnished as well as the waelcyrge and the einherjar: we were brothers again, in death.

I left the sdadown where they fell. Their swords I returned to the sea. From whence they came.

It snowed and I was thankful for the snow, because I did not wish to look up and see the stars. I did not find the Grey Wolf. And no trace of his Lady.

I walled the bodies around, stone upon stone, and then I levered up the slabs for the barrow's roof and laid them over. As day piled upon day like stone upon stone, I grew thin. My first strength waned and then began to grow again, although I was not so hale as I had been.

In the end it was complete, and the snow stopped falling, and the clouds broke, and I stood over the grave and watched the sunrise paint the gray granite boulders with lichens of blood and time. I hoisted Nathr to my shoulder. I had thought of leaving her there, to mark the barrow, but . . .

Instead, I plunged a tattered standard of midnight-blue into a crevice, and the torn Raven Banner beside it, wings draggled in defeat.

The sun flamed, breathtaking, crimson and incarnadine and vermilion and hellebore and scarlet. I gasped as it rose over the sea. I breathed the light and air with all my strength, coughing when the cold air struck my lungs.

It was new, all new, and I hated every shiver and chilblain and cracked lip and droplet of snot.

I could step into that sunrise from the top of the barrow. I pictured my fall, tumbling, and the wreck of my body on the boulders below. I imagined the brief sensation of flight, and I closed my eyes.

I spread my arms wide, the bitter sea breeze tugging at me, almost lifting me up, and I took a deep and singing breath. This time, I did not choke on it.

I stepped forward.

Live.

I'm no good to anyone and no one will grieve for me and Strifbjorn is dead anyway and who cares, who cares, who cares?

Silence. Long, still, empty silence. And then his voice, or the memory of his voice: I was too far gone in hunger and grief and exhaustion to know which.

Live, it said. And the moment passed.

I opened my eyes. The sunrise was over: splinters of gold danced on the dark water far out to sea, and that was all. It looked like a path.

I turned around and headed south.

15

✳

May ravens tear   thy wretched heart.
—"The Second Lay of Gudrun"

The Wolf

The mead-hall stands empty of even the thralls.

I know where their strength went, and who dined on it. I do not find their bodies, but I do not search. *Kenaz. Kenaz. Kenaz.*

The old pine logs that make up the walls are massive and dry.

It burns like a funeral barge, and even the weight of snow on the sod roof does not damp the flames. Somewhere north of the Ulfenfell, I imagine, my brethren are dying, and a new, darker world will follow on their loss. In a little while, I will go and try to kill a goddess, and perish in the attempt.

For now, I stand and watch flames leap while the snow settles on my shoulders and my hair.

I stand at the edge of the cliff and draw Svanvitr, weighing the black crystal blade in my hand. Not a trace of Light gleams within her. I cannot even fool myself with the glimmer of reflections.

I raise my eyes at last to the sea. "I renounce her," I whisper. Silence and darkness greet me.

Under my skin, the Suneater laughs. *It is not because of her you are condemned. It is because of what you alone have done, and will continue to do.*

And I answer, *I know.*

The sword is dark, but I raise her over my head like a beacon. Nothing shines in her, as nothing shines in me. *What faith have you kept? You have betrayed Strifbjorn. You have betrayed Heythe. You have betrayed the Imogen, and the pack. And last and most truly, you have betrayed the Light. And worst, you have changed nothing in so doing.*

It is true; it is true; it is true.

It is not the snow that stings my eyes and blinds me.

The sword makes a long, slow, glittering arc through the falling snow into the sea. I turn away before it strikes the waves, and leave its sheath lying in the drifts near the burning building.

You should have fallen on that blade.

My footsteps lead me down by the waterside, along the border of the sea.

If I did not love Strifbjorn enough for that, I tell the Suneater, *how then shall I love you?*

I shall never be bound again, be it by love, vows or duty.

No more chains.

It is almost sunset. Strifbjorn must be dead by now.

Still the snow hisses into the ocean. Still the waves hiss on the sand.

The town of Northerholm lies empty as well, deserted as a stage when the actors have gone home. They, too, fed Heythe's army, the hunger she trained us to until her coaxing sorceries darkened every blade that served her. *Kenaz. Kenaz.* The town burns behind the pier, and the pier burns to the waterline. *Kenaz.* I leave a path of pyres.

South I walk, aimlessly now. Soon the coast will curve west, and then northwest, and the inner curve of the peninsula will bring me to what was Arngeir's hall.

I will burn that, too, when I get there.

I do not expect, and then I do not know why I did not expect, to watch her rainbows coil down the sky and then see Heythe ride her good red mare onto the beach, still clad in blood-streaked armor. She kicks the mare lightly and canters toward me, stopping twice my height away.

"Mingan." Her voice is musical and light.

My hand drops to the hilt of the sword that is not on my hip. "Have you come to kill me?"

She laughs. "Come back to me."

I close the distance, catch the mare's reins. "I planned killing you."

That laughter again, musical, as if I have said the wittiest thing in the world. "I know. But I'd rather have you. You don't have to be alone."

I taste that for a moment. "What if I *wish* to be alone?"

She reaches out and lets long fingers trail down the angle of my cheek. "You forget, Master Wolf. I've got a little splinter of your soul in me, too. From Strifbjorn, even though you and I have never kissed that way."

I tilt my head to feel the caress against my face. "Are they all dead?"

"The children and tarnished? Yes. All. They would not flee, and so they fell."

"And the Bearer of Burdens?"

She makes a little dismissive gesture with her hand, raising it from my face to float in the wind as if shaping the snow. "It will take some centuries, but I played a clever trick on it. And with you by my side, I can wait. Watch."

She turns and gestures to the sea. I stand at her stirrup and watch an image take shape—an image rendered hollow by the heavy silver dangling from my ear, but otherwise convincing.

I see Brynhilde.

Her valraven watching, straining against her command as I have seen the Imogen strain against mine, Brynhilde wanders down to the sea. She spreads her arms, beseeching . . . and then draws a knife from her belt and opens the veins along the lengths of her arms slowly, with methodical care. The illusory blood spills into the sea. I smell its taint on the wind.

"The sacrifice works when the intervention is bought of the supplicant's free will. But not if the supplicant is compelled." Heythe's hand strokes my shoulder.

I want to taste her blood.

"Compelled?"

"Muire gave her a little charm, a talisman to protect her. I hung a little do-my-bidding on it as well, is all."

For once, the Suneater and the Grey Wolf are unified in their desires. And Mingan the man—he has long ago decided. What there is left of him.

"You tricked the Serpent into a false intervention."

"Clever Wolf." She strokes my neck like she might stroke the neck of her red mare. "There was no willing sacrifice to summon it, so when it came . . . Shall I show you that scene as well, Wolf?" She raises her hand, and bits of light sparkle about it.

I step away. "No!"

"I was waiting for it. Once it made itself vulnerable, I got it a mortal blow."

I cover my ears with my hands like a child.

The Wyrm, my brother.

She talks on. "It will probably take it a few thousand years to die. Gods are slow about these things."

"Oh." I stare out at the sea, which tosses gray and unknowing. The touch of her hand is the heaviest thing I have ever felt. The Light is dead. Not just the children. But the thing itself.

Doubling fist into fist, I strike her across the face.

And she laughs out loud, rocking back with the blow, blood spattering from her mouth as she brays her mirth. The hand on my shoulder clutches, pulling me hard against the side of her mare. She leans across the horse's withers, dropping the reins, and the red mare sidesteps, dragging me.

Contemptuous, Heythe shreds my shirt and thrusts her hand under my collar, lifting me into the air. She leans back in the saddle, and holds me up to her face. I claw her wrist with both hands, fight to ease the choking pressure. The red mare spooks as my feet bang her side, but Heythe must calm her, for she dances but does not bolt.

Black edges my vision as the goddess draws my face close. "Wolfling, wolfling." She smiles and leans so close I can taste her breath. "Remember the last time we wrestled?"

She throws me down upon the sand. I roll into the water.

Blood smears my hand when I pull it from my throat, and my breath sounds like the rasp of a saw.

"I remember."

And then she's all tenderness again, sliding down the shoulder of her horse, crouching in the spray beside me, taking my head in her hands. Her lips brush mine. She nuzzles the torn skin of my neck and rocks her head in a little, burrowing motion I have reason to know oh, too well.

"You're right," she whispers against my skin, while the waves soak my tattered shirt. "You should kill me. But you can't. So come with me, Suneater, Fenris-Wolf, darkness incarnate. We can keep each other company until God is dead, and then we can rule."

She wanted them all dead. All the children, all the survivors scavenged from the world before. She wanted to tear down whatever the Aesir built that outlasted her prophecy. Gullveig, her name was Gullveig, and they roasted her on spears for her words of ruin, but she could not die.

She will destroy everything the conquerors, the enslavers of my father's folk, built. And yet she doesn't want to be alone. How strange. I taste her offer like an exotic wine, a heady savor under my tongue, the aroma of power filling my head.

She draws me to my feet and I stand before her, eye to eye, cold seawater dripping down my back and filling my boots. She is flawless, lovely, with the snow caught in her golden hair and her blue eyes gleaming with excitement.

"I will be everything you ever wanted in a lover, Wolf. Every goddess you ever imagined."

The breath of the sea runs in and out of my lungs while I let her offer hang. I lean toward her. I smile. Almost, almost, I kiss her mouth. Sparkles of light spill from my collar and dapple both of us, like sunlight reflecting from rippled water. In time, by her side, I could even learn the power to kill her.

She does not want to be alone.

Well, there is one revenge I can hang on her.

"The prettiest collar you can think of is still a collar, my Lady."

Her laughter peals as I walk away. She calls after me. "Mingan! Then I'm going on ahead, without you. It will be brief for me . . . traveling my roads. But what say I look for you in a few thousand years?"

I am not inclined to answer, walking down the long and empty shore, although I do turn back when her rainbow descends, and watch her ride out of sight.

Someone waits for me several days south, where the cliff finally staggers down to the beach, ending in a black jumble of rocks smoothed by the tide. His cloven hooves give purchase like a goat's on the sea-cleaned stones, and he bends his neck to regard me. Moonlight crystallizes along the spiral of his horn.

I stop, and turn to look him in the eye. "Silken-swift. If you bring a message from your master, take one back. He was a fool, and he earned his death. And his dying."

He does not speak into my ear, neither name nor acknowledgment. A moment taut as a silken rope stretches us.

I take a step forward; he minces a step back. The wind flips his mane over his eyes, flaps the tatters of my shirt. "Well," I whisper. "If you can find a heart in me, then put your horn through it. Last chance to slay the Wolf, before the end of the world."

He lowers his horn and sights along it. I turn my head and

close my eyes, waiting. *Oh, it hurts; it hurts; it hurts; it hurts. And it cannot hurt enough.*

The pain does not end.

When I open my eyes, the unicorn is gone. I stand alone on the salt-stained shore.

The direct sequel to Bear's highly
acclaimed *All the Windwracked Stars*

The Sea Thy Mistress

Elizabeth Bear

Beautiful Cathoair, now an immortal
warrior angel, has been called back to
the city of Eiledon to raise his son—
Muire's son as well—cast up on shore as
an infant. It is seemingly a quiet life. But deadly
danger approaches: The evil goddess Heythe has
traveled forward in time on her rainbow steed.
She came expecting to gloat over a dead world,
the proof of her revenge, but instead she finds a
rekindled land, renewed by Muire's sacrifice. She
will have her revenge by forcing this new Bearer
of Burdens to violate her oaths and break her
bonds and thus bring about the true and final
end of Valdyrgard.

★ "Bear's ability to create breathtaking variations on
   ancient themes and make them new and brilliant is,
   perhaps, unparalleled in the genre."
   —*Library Journal*, on *All the Windwracked Stars*
   (starred review)

tor-forge.com
978-0-7653-1884-8
TOR® In hardcover January 2011